# Cover Girl
## Confidential

### Beverly Bartlett

NEW YORK   BOSTON

Copyright © 2007 by Beverly Bartlett
All rights reserved. Except as permitted under the U.S. Copyright Act of 1976, no part of this publication may be reproduced, distributed, or transmitted in any form or by any means, or stored in a database or retrieval system, without the prior written permission of the publisher.

5 Spot
Hachette Book Group USA
1271 Avenue of the Americas
New York, NY 10020

Visit our Web site at www.5-spot.com.

5 Spot is an imprint of Warner Books. The 5 Spot name and logo are trademarks of Warner Books.

Printed in the United States of America

First Edition: March 2007
10 9 8 7 6 5 4 3 2 1

Library of Congress Cataloging-in-Publication Data
Bartlett, Beverly.
    Cover girl confidential / Beverly Bartlett.—1st ed.
      p. cm.
    Summary: "Addison McGhee hosts a hit morning TV talk show, but a strange series of events causes her luck to start to run out"—Provided by publisher.
   ISBN-13: 978-0-446-69558-9
   ISBN-10: 0-446-69558-0
   1. Women in television broadcasting—Fiction. I. Title.
   PS3602.A8394C68 2007
   813'.6—dc22                           2006026950

To my parents, my husband, and my sons

# Acknowledgments

I'll never forget the first time I encountered a refugee family, newly arrived in the United States. Exhausted from a long flight, far from home, with only a few words of the language, they arrived with only what they could carry and piled on top of one another in a single donated bed, trying to find the rest they would need to build a new life. I never viewed the concept of *starting over* quite the same way again.

Thanks to Kentucky Refugee Ministries and Catholic Charities, many such families and individuals have found and made a home for themselves in Louisville, and the city has become more interesting and diverse because of it. The refugees I've met here share the spunk, determination, and on occasion the style of the main character of this book, Addison McGhee. But however superficial Addison may be, I hope her family's story sheds a little light on what it's like for new Americans.

In addition to my husband and parents and friends—all of whom helped make this book possible—I want to thank the refugees in Louisville who have enriched my life, the refugee agencies that are truly welcoming strangers to a strange land, and Kris Herwig and Steffani Powell, who both took time from their important work to discuss immigration law with me.

# Author's Note

While the events of this book are entirely made-up (and often ludicrous), I have taken literary license and used real names and places in order to make the fictional world I've created more vivid and familiar. I have completely invented all of the personal quirks, foibles, actions, or comments attributed to some characters who bear the names of real celebrities. Those inventions do not reflect reality and are, in any case, only supposed to represent the subjective report and imperfect memory of one exacting fictional character, rather than any sort of objective truth. George Clooney's ab muscles, for example, may be disappointing to Addison McGhee, but I have no reason to believe they are not impressive by normal standards. If necessary, I'm sure I could scrounge up some volunteers to check.

# Cover Girl
## Confidential

# Prologue

$\mathcal{I}$ licked my lips slowly, provocatively.

George Clooney clipped his pen to the chart he was holding and looked at me curiously.

"Is something wrong?" he asked, his head cocked in that devilish way he cocks it.

"Nothing that you couldn't cure, Doc," I replied. I popped my tongue against my teeth on the word *Doc,* as if I'd practiced it a lot.

I had.

I reached down to snap open the top button of my blouse. As I did so, I imagined my mother, four states away and still wearing the veil, gasping in horror and disgust. Then I unbuttoned another.

George did his best to look intrigued. But since I'd done this a thousand times that very day, I think he was just bored.

"You appear to be healthy enough," he said. He winked.

"No, no," I said, "I demand a physical." This time I winked. I released another button.

I grabbed his tie, used it to pull him close to me. I could smell on his breath the garlic from the salad dressing at lunch. *Men!* I thought. *They can actually eat dressing on their salad.* I'd had vinegar. No calories. No fat. No carbs.

"Aren't you dating Dr. Carter?" George asked. "And that new male nurse in radiology? And the hernia patient?"

"Not right now," I whispered into his ear as I loosened his tie with one hand and ran my hand through his hair with the other. "Not at this very moment."

He nuzzled his rough skin against my cheek until his lips found mine. He pushed me down on the hospital bed. He was heavy against me. I moved my hands along his waist. His stomach was softer than I expected. *Maybe he should drop the salad dressing,* I thought.

I was supposed to groan with pleasure, but the garlic and the soft stomach and the constant retakes were spoiling the mood. I tried to think of something pleasing. I imagined the headline my publicist expected in the next *Entertainment Weekly:* NEWCOMER ADDISON MCGHEE AND RETURNING GEORGE CLOONEY REVIVE *ER*!

I yowled.

The director called "Cut," then sighed heavily.

"Addison, Addison, Addison," he said, shaking his head dramatically. "This isn't HBO."

Days later, I ran into George. He had the uncomfortable look of a man who can't place a name.

"Madison, isn't it?" he said.

I started to correct him. Then thought the better of it. It was one of those parties after the Oscars. To get me in, my agent had to call in several favors—*and* create life-size posters of my new *Sports Illustrated* cover to mail to the party organizers. He'd had no favors left to get me a date.

"So you're doing all right for yourself," George continued. "*Sports Illustrated* cover, eh? Gauze bikini?"

I nodded, and he sighed with relief at having gotten it right.

He turned to his date, an auburn-haired woman who

looked brainy in the most willowy sense of the word. "Didn't you say you saw it on the newsstand?" he asked her.

"No," she said.

"Well then," he said, awkwardly.

I gave a self-deprecating wave, as if to say that she hadn't missed much. "I don't think it's out yet, anyway."

He repeated himself. "Well then."

"Who are you here with?" his date asked, smiling in what I imagine she thought was a *we-girls-like-to-chat-about-our-guys* kind of way. Of course, if my guy were George Clooney, I might like to chat about him, too. Garlic, stomach, ill-advised return to *ER,* and all.

I smiled gamely, raised my drink: "Just me and Jack Daniel's," I said.

I wasn't serious about the Jack Daniel's. Are you kidding? My parents would die. Plus, that's 150 calories right there. I was drinking Diet Coke, which I thought I could pass off as Jack Daniel's and Coke, if pressed. I had read that men now think it's very cool for women to drink manly drinks like that, even if heavily diluted with a noncaloric soft drink.

George had apparently not read that article. He looked a little shocked. His date looked more shocked. Surely this reaction wasn't about the Jack Daniel's? Maybe the part about being dateless?

I nervously tugged at one of the dangling ringlets I had left around my face; the rest of my hair was pulled up in what I thought was a casually sophisticated way. I had spent virtually all my remembered life in America, but I never knew, at moments like this, if I had made some cultural faux pas or was just naturally awkward and socially ill at ease in any culture.

Then Tom Hanks walked up, his newest Oscar slung casually across his hip and Rita looking bored on his arm. I was spared any further awkwardness, for suddenly I wasn't even there.

*Well, that won't last long,* I thought. *Someday, even Tom and Rita will know who I am. Someday.*

# Chapter 1

*T*hat was three long years ago.

I'm pretty sure that Tom and Rita know who I am now. My face (and body) have graced a thousand magazine covers, a huge moving billboard in Times Square, and some pretty seedy Web sites—those without my authorization, of course. I've been fawned over by presidents. (Well, I guess technically by *one* president.) Threatened by first ladies. (Well, again, *one*.) I've attended all the best premieres, adorning the arms of all the nation's most eligible bachelors. (Mostly arranged by my publicist, but still.) I launched a morning television show that was dubbed by leading academic journals as the most scandalous blurring of entertainment and news since—well, since the last time they were scandalized. They're so sensitive sometimes.

I was celebrated in talk shows and women's magazines for being an inspiration to young women of color the world over. And then, when things went bad, I was hounded by some of the same people for having a quick temper and bad judgment about men.

I suppose they were right about my judgment. Though, in my defense, I do not have a lot of experience. I've been photographed on red carpets with more men than I can count, but actual dates are few and far between. I spent a lot of lonely nights in pricey hotels before becoming the bride in one of the most spectacularly controversial and short marriages of our times. And the nights after that were lonelier still.

In a roundabout way, I guess, that's how I ended up here, in prison, serving time on a trumped-up felony charge and awaiting a deportation hearing. My agent is thrilled. "You've never *been* more famous," he said in his last letter. (That's the great thing about prison. It encourages the long-lost art of letter writing.) But my father is terrified that his little girl will be sent back to the country he fled all those years ago. I guess I'm a little scared, too.

Last night, my lawyer—an old high school friend—visited. I will confess with some shame that I hadn't thought much about her during my heady rise to fame. I assumed she was still living it up in unincorporated Slater County, Nebraska, riding in the back of pickups and getting chased out of the parking lot by Wal-Mart security. I never dreamed she would have gone to law school and moved to Albany, New York. This oversight on my part was not personal, I hasten to add. I failed to think about her not due to any fault of hers—nor, for that matter, any particular disinterest in Slater County. Cassie was, and I guess still is, the best friend I ever had. And those were good times in Slater County. It's just that when you're trying to project an air of sophisticated beauty, stylish grace, and informed commentary, the last image you want bouncing around in your head is any memory at all from high school—with the baby fat and the pimples and the really sad crushes on impossibly glamorous older men. (In my case, the PE instructor, Mr. Stinnett.) Kate Hudson tells me that everyone feels that way, but I think it was worse for me. There weren't many immigrant families in Slater County, and my early attempts at assimilation had only patchy success.

Cassidy Von Maur was one of the people who accepted me,

however. And though I'd rarely thought of her or high school in the intervening years, I recognized her right away when she showed up in the prison visiting room a few months ago.

"Cassie?" I said, not quite believing my eyes. Then, more confidently, I squealed with glee, "Cassie, my lassie!" (This was my oh-so-cool greeting for her in high school. You can see why I prefer not to think about those years.) I continued with another high school classic: "Get out of here!"

She smiled, said that she preferred *Cassidy* now, and explained that she had heard I needed a good immigration lawyer. "Lucky for you," she said, "I am one."

Once you're famous, you know, that's how things happen. Whenever you need something, it shows up at your door. Cassie was exactly what I needed. It felt so good to have someone to giggle with again.

But during last night's visit, she ignored my efforts to reminisce. She lectured me, sternly. She narrowed her eyes and looked exceedingly cross. She said that she didn't think I was taking this whole thing seriously enough. She pointed out that if I got deported to my father's homeland—the only other country I had legal standing in—I would be in a hopeless, helpless situation. "You don't speak the language," she said. "And you don't have a lot of—" She hesitated, then spit out the ugly truth. "—skills."

I cringed. Making small talk on television for hours at a time is a lot harder than people think. But I said nothing.

"Furthermore," she continued, "you're famous the world over for being photographed in shameful costumes."

I started to protest. The world over? I seriously doubt that. I'm not Madonna, after all. I'm quite sure there are a few remote Siberian villages or an odd South Pacific island or two where people are completely unfamiliar with my work—or at least my "costumes." But my vanity got the best of me. I didn't want to talk about the places where I'm not famous. So instead I just said: "I don't know about *shameful* . . ."

"Cotton balls?" Cassie said incredulously.

"Oh," I said.

I don't know how I'd forgotten about the award-winning *Vanity Fair* cover in which I am clothed only in cotton balls—and not very many of them, I might add. That cover was the talk of the nation for a while. My own show hyped it tirelessly. Baxter Bailey, the rumpled weatherman, would constantly find smudges that needed rubbing off his map. "Got a swab, Addison?" he'd say, with a mischievous grin. And Hughes Sinclair, my dapper and dashing co-host, would chuckle and warn Baxter not to borrow too many, as I appeared to be running quite low.

Cassie smirked. "I think it's a safe bet they would consider cotton balls shameful," she said. "And in case you're unaware, this is not a culture that takes shaming lightly."

She said my only hope of surviving in my father's homeland, really, would be for me to marry as soon as I arrived. But because I'm twice the age of the average child bride there—*"easily, twice the age,"* Cassie emphasized, somewhat meanly—I'd be considered too old and, given my well-publicized past, too previously married for any decent man there to be interested.

I waved my hand gamely to show that I did not care. "I'm done with marriage," I said. "So that's no loss."

Cassie sighed. "This isn't a joke, Addison. You'll be surviving on your wits in an economy that doesn't value wit. You won't last three months."

I looked at my fingers, noticed that I needed a manicure, and then thought, for the first time, about my chances of finding a good manicurist if I got deported. My paternal grandmother has terrible nails. So do all my aunts. The evidence suggests that theirs is not a culture that highly values cuticle health. I gulped. (Discreetly, I hope.)

"Couldn't they just deport me to London or something?" I asked.

Cassie snorted. "London?" she said. "Oh yeah, London is just begging the United States to send over any spare convicted felons we have on hand! Begging!"

She sighed and started over in a more even voice. "That's just not the way it works, Addison. When people get deported, they get deported to their home country. You don't get to pick and choose."

I nodded.

"ICE is serious about this one," Cassie said. "This isn't going to go away."

"Ice?" I said.

"Immigration and Customs Enforcement. We call them ICE because they're coldhearted when it comes to this stuff."

She muttered that last part, and I wasn't sure if I was supposed to have heard it. So I just said, "Oh."

"All these terms are explained in the material I gave you to read," she added sharply. "You really need to read it."

But then she patted my hand in a conciliatory way. She said that if she was going to save me, she needed to know everything. So she gave me an assignment.

That is why I'm writing this, you see. She told me to record every single thing that happened to me from the moment I was photographed splayed across the lap of the sitting (and obviously seated) US president, through all the conspiracy theories about my incredibly short marriage, and right up to the exact moment I—in her words—"nearly killed" my ex-husband on live television.

"And if you could write a coherent explanation of why you, the Little Miss All-American Girl-Next-Door Movie Star, never bothered to become a US citizen," she continued, letting the sarcasm back into her voice, "and why you pled guilty to a felony we're now claiming actually wasn't, that would be nice, too."

I bristled, but nodded.

"I'm doing my best, Addison," she said. "But you have to help."

I nodded again. As she left, I made a great show of gathering up the paper and marker (no sharp points allowed here). But once she was gone, I decided I would not confine myself to the topics she had specified. If I'm going to write it down, then I'm going to write it *all* down. Because my life, despite her snotty aside, really is *the* American story. Cute little immigrant girl with a dream come true? Well, that's just dying to be told, isn't it?

All I ever wanted was to exceed my parents' modest ambitions for me and to become an American icon, a symbol of the sort of good fortune that follows those who apply themselves. Sort of like Donald Trump, only with better hair.

And abs.

And taste.

Sure, I've had a bit of a bad run lately. But that only makes the story better, doesn't it? It will only make my comeback more impressive!

And I will come back. You mark my words.

So that's what I'll do. I'll start at the beginning. I'm sure Cassie will understand. Besides, it's all pertinent, isn't it? Everything I am today, including this current unpleasantness, is a product of everything I've ever done. That's the American way of looking at it, I'm certain of that.

I did not attain all that I've attained by being lackadaisical or halfhearted. I've thrown myself into every task with unquestioning dedication—whether making out with George

Clooney, launching a quirky morning talk show, or embracing the ten-thousand-steps fitness craze. (I read about it on a marvelous Web site. You wear a pedometer constantly and shoot for ten thousand steps a day. But I set my goal at twice that and was delighted to find that it really worked. If diligent, I could, once or twice a month, have an entire handful of M&M's with no noticeable ill effects—although I did need to be especially stringent with the astringent the next day or my forehead would positively glisten.)

So I will apply myself to this writing task with equal ardor. It all began for me, let's see, when I was six and I got my name. Yes, I suppose that's right. Or, arguably, six years earlier than that—you know, when I was born.

# Chapter 2

*I* have noticed that most Americans do not think much about the circumstances of their birth, much less their genealogy. My high school boyfriend once told me that his ancestors were "European or something." And none of my friends could name their great-grandparents, much less recite their lineage back through seven generations as children are taught to do in my parents' cultures. They had no idea who was the first in their family to be a US citizen, and they did not appear to have given any thought to how significant that designation is.

But while Americans aren't particularly interested in their own genealogy, they are often quite interested in mine. People look at my dark olive skin, my thick, deep black hair, my angular features, and they wonder: *Filipino? Native American? Greek? Egyptian? Angelina Jolie with a tan?* (And better eye makeup, obviously.) My agent has always said my uncertain ethnicity, what he calls my "exotic" appearance, is my secret weapon, my key to stardom. I represent, according to him, a "glorious blending" of the human race, a composite sketch, of sorts, of all humanity. My skintone embodies the beautiful Amber Glow shade of foundation in CoverGirl's Queen Collection. Latifah said so herself! All of this interesting "women of color" loveliness is only enhanced, according to my agent, by my inappropriate Irish name. He says it gives me an air of mystery.

I guess he's right. People often do seem mystified. Just the other day, while working out during exercise time, I caught other inmates discussing me. I was doing my usual chin-ups in the prison yard, located on the rooftop of the eight-floor prison, when I overheard a convicted embezzler giving a new girl the lowdown.

"That one over there," said the embezzler, "is Addison McGhee. You know, that funny-looking black nurse on *ER*."

I glanced their way just in time to see the new inmate squint at me and wrinkle her nose. I could see the Statue of Liberty behind her. It was very picturesque.

"Addison McGhee?" the new inmate repeated with surprise. "I always thought she was Hispanic. And didn't she play a doctor?"

The embezzler shrugged and said, "Whatever."

See? Mystery.

The story of my unusual birth and my odd name is simple enough, really.

I was born Ada Sinmic Ghee in a squalid, semi-permanent refugee camp in Turkey, a place where people fleeing a variety of war-torn Mediterranean, Arabic, and African nations huddled together, occasionally intermarrying and producing exceptionally beautiful children. My mother had come from the east, seeking refuge from war and famine. My father had come from the southwest, up through Egypt, seeking refuge from famine and war. They had, you see, a lot in common. And to hear them tell it, it was love at first sight. Although they do not use the word *love*.

"I could tell she was a good worker," my father says. "In his eyes," my mother explains, "I could see that he was not a drinker."

It was a match made in heaven, or at least Turkey.

They quickly produced my brother and me, who were, as the children of a refugee camp, denied Turkish citizenship. So my birth records, such as they are, list me as a citizen of my father's homeland, an arbitrary geographic region that is home to several warring and nomadic tribes. It is also, by law, home to me, though I have never even seen it. (It looks like that might change soon.)

The Turkish camp was safe at first, but soon it became overrun and outgrown. It developed into a festering hotbed of disease, crime, and celebrity photo ops. The pope got involved. So did the "We Are the World" singers. The Bee Gees toured our camp and handed me a small doll—giving me, during one ten-minute visit, my first toy and my first glimpse at the world of celebrity. Robin sported splendid, sparkly platform boots, and Barry had a way of shooing off the photographers that seemed, to my untrained eye, the epitome of cool. (*Cool* was a concept I could not have articulated at the time. Still, I knew it when I saw it.)

With that kind of pressure—the Bee Gees were still big in those days, at least relatively—Turkey eventually accepted the US offer to take us in. Jolly good of Turkey, wasn't it? I still remember the soldier who circled my obviously mixed-race family as we stood with downcast eyes in the hot sun, waiting in a long, winding line to be processed for emigration. "Mutts," said the soldier as he poked my brother with the point of his rifle. "Worse than mutts."

I thought for a moment he would kill us, or at the very least take our small jug of water. He thumped my father in the chest and tried to pull back my mother's veil. He was loud, leering, and drunk—whether on alcohol or power, I cannot say.

I remembered that moment years later when cornered by Robert Downey Jr. at a surprise birthday banquet that Brad threw for Jennifer. They were so cute together back then. Brad introduced Bob and me, but then got called away to referee a dispute between the elephant trainers and fireworks handlers. Bob gave me a long, slow look. I thought I saw the same brazen intoxication of that soldier all those years ago. Bob took a sip of whatever he was drinking—not Diet Coke, I'm guessing—and said, "You're, like, Asian, right?"

I shrugged. *Oh, why not?*

"And African, too?"

I nodded, uncertainly. I wasn't sure where this was going.

"Co-ol," he said and swayed toward me, though I could not tell if it was an advance or just, you know, a stagger. He casually put his hand on my shoulder and smiled wide enough to create furrows across his forehead. "Like, wa-ay co-ol."

That had not, obviously, been the opinion of the soldier, but when he reached for my mother's veil, another soldier stopped him. "They're not worth your time," he said. "If America wants them, let it have them."

The intervening soldier is like an angel to my family. We often say a prayer for him, though to this day we do not know if he was motivated by kindness or if he truly thought we were beneath his contempt. Either way, his actions allowed us to continue in the emigration line. Eventually, one by one, we entered a tent where a federal bureaucrat processed our papers and, as it turned out, gave me a new identity.

"Name?" the bureaucrat barked at me, his huge hammy hands shuffling through my family's papers.

"Ada Sinmac Ghee," I whispered back, nervously.

He divided the syllables wrong and used creative spelling to come up with Addison McGhee. And with the stroke of a pen, he took my most obvious tie to my family heritage. But then he stamped the appropriate boxes, initialed the appropriate pages, and sent me on my way. Quick as that, he gave me something as well—a ticket to America.

Soon enough, I was sitting in a Nebraska elementary school, confounding classmates who tried to reconcile my sad ragtag dresses and my racially unclear features with my cheerful and chicly androgynous Irish name.

More than one American has invited me to be outraged, offended, or at least a little disappointed by the involuntary name change. The eager-to-be-angry set always grilled me about the guy's motivation—was he too small-minded to understand? Or too lazy to care?

"Was it American *ignorance*?" asked Susan Sarandon, never one to back away from a national failing. (She had pulled me aside at a premiere for some awful David Schwimmer movie.) "Or was it American *arrogance*?"

I wanted to ask the same question about her presence at a David Schwimmer premiere. But I said nothing. After all, I was at the party, too. One of the first rules of Hollywood: Never admit that you're scraping bottom. Or partying with David Schwimmer. Lisa Kudrow told me that once, and I think she's quite right. Dave is a dear soul, no doubt about it. But so is my great-aunt and I wouldn't have much hope for a movie she made, either.

"I don't know, Sue," I said, using my standard quip. "I always thought the guy was Irish."

What I really thought was that I had been extraordinarily lucky. In my family's experience, if you escape an encounter with an authority figure having lost nothing but your name— you've done well. And if you gain, at the same time, a ride out of a refugee camp, you've done even better.

My parents adjusted to life in Slater County with all the typical immigrant pluck. My mother took a job as a Wal-Mart greeter. My father mopped the bloody floor of a pig-slaughtering house, a job abhorrent to most Americans even without the added burden of a cultural and religious taboo about pork. But my father had what many Americans did not: a deeply held cultural belief that nothing was below him, a well-rooted sense of desperation, a long- and hard-learned lack of expectation. He was sort of like an aging Hollywood actress in that sense, only more so. I'm telling you, if my father and Sharon Stone ever got together, they could talk for *hours*.

I appreciate my parents now. But in high school, they only embarrassed and mortified me. I was ashamed at what I considered their lack of ambition and their inability to fit in. By contrast, I studied American culture with an intensity that I, sadly, never devoted to my academic work. I read everything I could find that gave me a window into America—*People* magazine, miracle-diet-drug ads, and most importantly a slim volume on immigrant etiquette filed in our dated high school library between books by Emily Post and Miss Manners. I thought it was a delightful volume: *Miss Liberty's Guide to Impeccable Assimilation*. It spelled out in careful and practical detail things that no one else bothered to explain. What is Thanksgiving? What is the difference between Flag Day and the Fourth of July? Why did Cassie's mom give me two forks when I visited for dinner? And did it matter which one I used? (Yes, yes, very much so.)

Miss Liberty told me not to wear white shoes before Easter, no matter what my religion, and never to serve "native" food in my home to American citizens.

The book had been written in 1910, and I could tell that some of the information was out of date. Did I really need to call the landlord's eight-year-old son "Master Scotty"? I sensed not. I observed that the chapter on "covered ankles" was no longer in effect. Still, I found the sections on such items fascinating. It helped me, in some way that is difficult to explain, make sense of the fashion rules that did prevail. Why could cheerleaders wear skimpy uniforms to school, in clear violation of the dress code? I didn't know and I suppose I still don't, but if reading Miss Liberty taught me anything, it taught me that sometimes the rules simply are the rules and as a little immigrant girl, it was not my place to change them.

The glamorous PE teacher found the book in my locker during one of our regular drug searches. He picked it up, flipped through it, and whistled in disbelief. "Oh great," he said. "How to throw off the shackles of your true heritage in eight easy chapters." He pushed it back into my locker and slammed the door.

I flinched. I didn't remember Miss Liberty saying anything about "shackles."

As an adult, I can see where he was coming from. I can admit that it was not the most enlightened publication. But as a child that book helped me tremendously. And looking back, perhaps I would have been better off if I'd kept a copy handy.

I tried to get my parents to read Miss Liberty, but they did not have the time, the inclination, or the vocabulary to do so. They did not like her insistence that I needed actual, engraved invitations to my high school graduation. And they did not understand why she thought we should drink hot liquids only out of real china, when church workers had given us a collection of perfectly serviceable and nicely sized mugs. So what if they advertised defunct tire shops, distant public radio stations, and more than one failed congressional candidate?

My belief in Miss Liberty was just one of the differences between me and my parents. They arrived in this country with such modest ambitions for me. They wanted me to learn the language and to find a good man who would marry me. Perhaps I could find a job and make a living wage. When we first arrived in Slater County, my mother marveled as she watched a veiled woman drive a school bus.

"Look," she said to me. "Maybe you can do that."

By any American standard, I have exceeded those expectations. But they have not judged me by an American standard. They could not have imagined how quickly we would become foreign to each other. They had not allowed for television, had not anticipated its hypnotic hold on my brother and me. Television taught us English, which pleased my parents. It also taught us sarcasm and irony and teen fashion rules, which they were not so happy about. Television introduced us to jobs we could not have previously imagined—espionage, news producing, even ranching. Agent 99, Mary Richards, and Victoria Barkley were my role models! Bus driving? Please.

With every passing commercial break, I was less the child of my parents and more a child of America.

I watched everything, even the news. I especially liked Peter Jennings, who in those days was ABC's foreign anchor and covered, among other things, the daily ins and outs of the Iranian hostage crisis. It was, in large part, those stories that ultimately convinced me I would never wear my mother's veil. All those angry women, without makeup, shouting in the streets, burning effigies of Jimmy Carter. Are you kidding? I wanted to be one of Charlie's Angels. Or at least, you know, the Bionic Woman.

(As a footnote, I think it bears mentioning that I did, in fact, *almost* became one of Charlie's Angels, being narrowly beat out for a part in the movie remake by Lucy Liu. My brother expected me to be terribly disappointed about losing the part, but it was a childhood dream I had outgrown. I was, really, rather relieved. Honestly, I wouldn't have been able to stand all the blow-drying.)

If there was one moment in my high school years that

crystallizes the two cultures I was caught between, it was the summer when Cassie attempted to convince me to enter the Pork Queen competition, an annual event put on by the local hog farmers' association. The winner received a month's supply of pork and the opportunity to compete in the state competition for a modest scholarship.

My family did not eat pork. And my parents could not imagine anything more vulgar and profane than competing for a generous allotment of unclean meat by parading around in a swimsuit on the back of a flatbed trailer, especially one festooned by bunting on the town square.

But my own reluctance to compete in the Pork Queen competition had nothing to do with my family's dietary practices or decency standards. My concern was more pragmatic. I suspected Cassie and I would both lose.

I had a skin problem, which my mother blamed on American food. And unruly hair, which she blamed on her mother-in-law. And crooked teeth. (She didn't blame this on anyone because she did not see it as a problem. Everyone in her home village had crooked teeth.)

I'm not just engaging in false modesty the way many celebrities do, with their homey little stories about their difficult teen years. (I warn you: Don't get Uma started.) I really did look, in those days, simply awful. Cassie was worse off still. If I had a skin problem and unruly hair, she had a hair problem and unruly skin. She also slouched.

Still, as Cassie correctly pointed out, the Pork Queen competition, looks-wise, wasn't that stiff. The really good-looking girls couldn't bear the thought of having the word *pork* anywhere on their body, much less on a banner across their chest. If this was just about appearance, we maybe had a shot. At least, I did. I had recently discovered the magical substance known as concealer in the CoverGirl section of the local drugstore and so, when properly made up, I looked quite nice—as long as I didn't show my teeth or hair.

But I always trusted my gut feelings, and my gut told me this would be a mistake. I was pretty sure that I couldn't cover my hair with a ball cap during the competition. And the judges would expect me to smile. And then, there was the problematic talent element. (Because what, really, would a Queen of Pork be without talent?) I didn't play an instrument. Or sing. I didn't twirl baton and I most certainly did not dance. My family never had money for lessons. And anyway, we weren't so inclined. It never occurred to my parents that as good American children, we should be creating a portfolio of expensive hobbies.

I also was completely lacking in any of the athletic arts, not that they generally lend themselves to talent competitions anyway. A neighbor boy, Kevin Ford, would sometimes invite me to shoot basketballs in his driveway, but always ended up laughing at me. "Are you looking at the basket *at all*?" he'd ask. My performance on the archery test in PE became legendary. The class scattered. I guess it would be fair to say that I did not have true aim.

Cassie had been given more talent-developing opportunities. But she had not used them to any advantage, having constantly changed instruments and sports until she had a similar level of mediocrity in all of them.

If we were to participate in the Pork Queen talent contest, it was going to have to involve prose reading, the lamest of talents, or—in Cassie's case—hog calling. (A talent that might win her more points with pork producers than with most judges, but still.) Rumor had it that Desiree Johnson was going to belly dance in a red bikini. We did not have a chance, and I told Cassie as much.

I said: "Look, Cassie. Let's just hit the movies and then

cruise the square." But she stood up unusually straight and said, "Well, you can give up, Addison McGhee, but I'm just going to believe in myself."

She came in third.

There were, exactly, three contestants. And while she never publicly wavered from her oft-repeated statement that just being in the competition was a privilege and a joy, I think she came to see my point. Perhaps it takes self-confidence to make it in the world, but that is not, actually, all it takes.

(Ask Simon Cowell. This is a pet topic for him. He trots out numerous examples from that little show of his. He would go on and on about it.)

It occurred to me, as I watched Cassie accepting her third-place banner, that there are at least two competing standards of womanhood. There is the standard of my parents, who value humility, fertility, and the ability to do backbreaking work without complaint. And there was the standard of Slater County, Nebraska, which valued elegance (as measured by the ability to gracefully climb onto a flatbed in heels and a swimsuit), talent (as measured by the likes of baton twirling), and toothy smiles.

It appeared to me that I did not measure well by either gauge.

That night, in a moment common to American girls, I cried in front of the mirror and told my mother that I feared I was ugly, fat, and lacking in talent.

"Oh please," my mother replied, in an answer that reflected a lifetime of perspective. "Take a look around. You're not much worse than most."

At least that's what I think she said. The sad truth is that we do not communicate well. We didn't then and we still don't.

Here in prison, I watch the other inmates sometimes, easily chatting with their mothers during their collect calls, *arguing* with them even. I'm stunned and envious. There is no repartee or banter with my family. I am no longer fluent in Arabic, the language that my blended family had used in the camp. And my parents did not, truthfully, learn English well. Oh, they can order a hamburger pizza by phone. They can rent an apartment or apply for a job. My mother can argue with the butcher if she thinks the cut of the meat is not right.

But we have trouble communicating the more mucky sentiments common to family relations—unruly mixes of pride and disappointment, hope and fear, sorrow and rejoicing, that familiar guilty feeling of glee about each new season of a reality dating show. (My mother *loves* those, for they remind her of the awkward matchmaking efforts that prevailed in her homeland. "That Trista," my mother said more than once, "would look better in a scarf.")

They are not bad people, my parents. My mother is inspirational, really. And my father is the best man in my life, not that there is much competition. But they were just ultimately unprepared for me. My parents, with their modest ambitions, could not have imagined in those early days, as we first gathered around the television, what awaited their little girl.

If someone had told them then that I would someday be paid more than a bus driver's yearly wage to unbutton my blouse in front of George Clooney and a large camera crew, that I'd be the primary factor in the revival of—tight—parachute pants, that I'd be famously photographed on the lap of a US president . . . well, it would have filled them with wonder and awe.

It would have sickened them and broken their hearts.

But it would have filled them with wonder and awe.

By contrast, the part that American parents would consider truly shameful, my arrest and imprisonment, has not shamed my parents at all. They are worried and fearful but not ashamed. Where they come from, all the best people are arrested eventually.

My mother was, in fact, awfully disappointed the first time she visited me here in prison. She looked at all the other inmates—who were generally, shall we say, rough around the edges. She was expecting, I think, a more refined bunch of dissidents and agitators, not bank thieves and check kiters.

But she didn't say so. She just put her head in her hands and looked at me with pity. "Ada, honey," she asked. "How did you get yourself into this mess?"

# Chapter 3

How did I get myself into this mess?

I thought about that again a little while ago. The Monday-morning visiting hours began and the guard surprised me by saying I had a guest. "It's that guy," the guard said. "The grumpy one?"

She was not the type to utter sentences as if they were questions, so I was a little puzzled. Was she uncertain about the visitor's mood?

"You know," she added, still sounding unsure. "And the bow tie."

"Baxter," I said.

I squealed with glee. His visits had become the highlight of my time here in prison. I practically danced all the way to the visiting room. "Baxter," I whispered excitedly. "Baxter. Baxter. Baxter."

I checked my hair in the one-way mirror and cursed—not for the first time—the dreadful orange of our prison uniforms. (It did not favor my Amber Glow complexion and, judging by the looks of my cellmates, it didn't flatter any other complexion either.) I sat very straight in one of the stiff chairs and tapped my toes as I waited for the guard to bring Baxter in. I imagined what was about to happen. I pictured him running his hand through his shaggy hair, stuffing his bow tie into his pocket, and greeting me with the usual, "Hey, Ada." He's the only one other than my family who calls me that.

But when I heard the door open, I nearly fainted. It wasn't Baxter at all! Hughes Sinclair stood before me, wearing a cheap, shiny wig and a terrible pink bow tie with green stripes. The scar that ran down his left temple was barely noticeable.

"Hi, Addison," he said gently as he pulled up a chair. "You're looking good."

My shock dissipated into a surge of anger. What gave him the right to sneak in here under false pretenses? He knew perfectly well that I would never have agreed to see him if he'd been honest with the guards. At least, I might not have. Besides, he's got some nerve to leave me in a cell for six months—no calls, no cards, no visits—and then show up and say I'm looking good. I crossed my arms in a defensive posture.

But then he grinned at me. His eyes got that crinkly look I love and that made him look so boyish. (It's so unfair. Eye lines make women seem positively ancient, but on men they can actually look youthful—as well as impossibly sexy. I've always been a sucker for smile lines on men. I guess it was all that *Magnum, P.I.* viewing in childhood.)

Hughes's grin succeeded in softening my anger. It always did. I tried, however, not to indicate that. I started off sarcastically.

"You're looking your usual dapper and dashing self as well," I said, gesturing to the bad wig and the tie. (People always described Hughes as "dapper and dashing." It had come to annoy me. What was I? Dowdy and—I don't even know what the opposite of dashing would be—dawdling? So I knew it must pain him to dress like Baxter, with the bow-tied look that screamed *tenured professor of economics.* I'd have been remiss not to rib him a little.)

"I wasn't sure if they'd let you see me," he whispered, glancing back at the guard. "So I thought I'd try to pass myself off as Baxter. Picked his work ID off his desk and used it to sign in."

"A bad wig and a bow tie, that's all it took?" I asked skeptically. I refused to whisper, and he cringed and looked around to see if anyone was listening. There were visits going on all around the big room, but the other prisoners were too busy crying over their kids or arguing with their husbands to be concerned about Hughes and me. The guard was engrossed in a magazine, the latest issue of *Celebrity Gourmet*. (It had the cast of *Charmed* on the cover. Do they still count as celebrities? Hasn't that show been canceled?)

Hughes adjusted the tie and the wig. He cast his eyes down at his "Baxter clothes," then glanced back up at me with another crinkly grin. "It's humbling," he said.

*Especially for Baxter,* I thought. I felt another surge of anger at Hughes. If he was going to pass himself off as Baxter, couldn't he at least invest in a decent wig? I mean, really. That hair was practically plastic. It didn't look at all like Baxter. Sure, Baxter had, as often as not, a bit of a rumpled look. *Recently loved* is the way one of the women on the online discussion boards had put it. But his hair was lush and soft looking, not AstroTurf-y. I started to say something, but then I just rolled my eyes and changed the subject. "How's things on the show?"

"Oh," he sighed. "You know."

"Actually," I said, "I don't. Haven't the faintest." Baxter and I never talked about it during his visits. And all the televisions in prison are permanently parked on the Lifetime channel. "I don't get to watch these days," I said.

"Oh," he said. "Well, Mia's okay. I guess it's working out."

"Mia?" I felt my eyes narrow.

He looked at his feet.

"Uh, Mia Hamm," he said. "I thought you knew."

My heart clutched. No wonder Baxter never talked about it. I was replaced by Mia Hamm? So Hughes really did have a thing for her. He'd always said he did, but I had thought it was an act.

He shrugged. "It's not the same anymore," he said. There was a long pause. "The ratings are down."

I found that hard to believe. With Mia Hamm? Her Q Score—the index that measures both your recognizability and your likability—had to be through the roof. She's so all-American. In fact, I'm sure they did that on purpose, after this whole thing with me and the deportation and all. I can just hear network executive Cal Gupton blasting around the studio, saying: "Get me someone all-American!"

"Besides," Hughes continued, "it's kind of boring."

I glanced around the gray visiting room and simply repeated that word. "Boring."

He leaned toward me. I imagined I could feel his breath on my face, but surely he wasn't really that close.

"I think about you every day," he said.

It was silent, except for the sound of each of us breathing.

"Why didn't you come sooner?" I said in a weak whisper. "Why didn't you do something . . ."

He put two fingers to my mouth to silence me. My lips tingled at his touch.

"I never thought it would go this far," he said. He pulled his fingers back, used them to pinch the top of his nose, as if fighting off a migraine. He looked so tired. I suddenly remembered how it felt to be doing the show each morning, getting to the studio at 4 AM every day, which meant waking up at 3. Katie had warned me during one of her "Farewell *Today!*" parties that you never get used to the schedule, and she was right.

You never do. At least I never did, and I could tell by looking at Hughes that he still hadn't. He sighed.

"I don't see what I can do about it anyway," he said.

And then, quick as that, he left.

It took me hours to settle down enough to write this account of Hughes's visit. Getting a visitor always throws me off. It's so strange to be reminded that my old friends are still out there in the world as if nothing had happened—getting up early, going to work, having migraines, flirting with Mia Hamm. Meanwhile, I sit here in a cell, alone.

I paced around my cell probably a thousand times after Hughes left. I wished I had my pedometer. All those steps, not even counted.

At first, as I paced, I just thought about Hughes and Mia. But eventually I settled into the question of how on earth I went from sitting at the top of the world—or at least the top of the celebrity B list—to where I am now. I guess I should begin with the story of how I got into acting.

My parents greeted my decision to move to Hollywood with the same stoic resignation that they brought to all of life's trials. A ten-year civil war and famine? A long stint in a quickly deteriorating Turkish refugee camp? A daughter in television? Is there a difference, really?

They sighed dramatically and clucked their tongues and muttered, but they did not try to stop me. I eventually convinced myself that my parents understood; even, in some limited way, approved. They had, after all, each disappointed their own parents by marrying outside their culture, and my father mopped up pig blood for a living. We had lived here only three years when my mother gave up her objection to shaking hands with men. "I still think it's disgusting," she said to me, after I saw her exchange the greeting with a used-car salesman. "But these American men *insist*."

So my parents understood the world of compromise and disillusionment. Surely they did not think that I would survive in America without giving up some of the old ways, without—on occasion—letting them down.

I was not rash about the move. I graduated from high school and even took some drama classes at Omaha Community College. My instructor there was quite encouraging and, when she learned I was moving to LA, she arranged for me to stay with her cousin, a cranky, vain, delusional guy who was himself pursuing a rap-star dream. He was in a group called Pharm Boyz. (They considered themselves the first great rural rap act, but they never really caught on.)

Pharm Boy and his friends let me use their sofa for what I considered an astonishingly high three hundred bucks a month. That sum did not even get me exclusive rights to the sofa. Pharm Boy would, after Thursday nights on the town, insist on sitting up, watching *ER* on videotape until the wee hours of the morning, interrupting the commercials to slur through an assurance that if I wanted to go on to sleep, I could just stretch my legs out right over him. He would not mind at all.

I declined.

And I feigned interest in *ER* to politely explain my rejection, though I was not so much a fan of those early episodes. I thought it unnecessarily gory and found Dr. Carter increasingly insufferable. Still, I would point to the screen during a finely acted moment and say: "I'm going to be on that show someday."

And I was.

The story of my casting on *ER* is the very stuff of Hollywood dreams. I struggled along, spent loads of money sleeping on that nonexclusive sofa, paying for it by waiting tables at a cruddy, touristy establishment called Sports Illustrated: The

Restaurant. All the waitresses wore swimsuits. (No, I did not mention that detail to my parents. Why do you ask?)

I dragged myself into one miserable audition after another, being rejected in innumerable ways—including the humbling day in which I was turned down twice by the same studio for being "too ethnic" and, alternatively, "not ethnic enough." When the tips were good, I took acting classes and got my teeth straightened. When the tips were bad, I dropped out of class or skipped orthodontist appointments.

Then one day at SI, I saw a bored-looking young man vainly trying to corral a gaggle of giggling characters at one of my tables. It's a scene all too familiar at theme restaurants. The young man clearly lived in LA; the giggling characters were visiting Midwestern relatives. Vacationing family from out of state is the only thing that can drag a true LA resident into a place like SI.

The relatives had made all the usual special requests and substitutions when the young man's niece looked at me and asked—well—if "they" were "real."

I gave my practiced smile. (They were and are, but I did not really feel the need to explain that to her.) The young man clamped his hand over his niece's mouth and smiled wearily back at me. "Forgive them," he said. "They're visiting from Oklahoma."

I leaned down to place the drink in front of him and whispered, "No problem. My family is from Nebraska. I know the drill."

(This was not strictly true, as my parents never visited me in LA and would not have insisted on going to any place remotely like SI: The Restaurant even if they had. Furthermore, I found those sorts of dismissive remarks about the heartland baffling at best and tiresome at worst—as if the middle part of the country somehow had more than its share of boorish louts! Still, I did "know the drill," simply from having observed it so many times while waitressing. I also knew that mentioning Nebraska was good for tips. *Poor plucky Cornhusker trying to make good in the city,* the tipper thinks. *Let's round* up, *shall we?*)

You've heard all these "being discovered" stories before, so you know what happened next. Later that week, I showed up at an audition for a small part on *ER,* the role of Dr. Benton-Vance, a nymphomaniac neurologist who also happened to be Dr. Benton's long-lost third cousin. I walked into the audition room and saw the Oklahoma guy flipping through the script in a distracted way. He glanced up and our eyes met. He laughed. And the next thing you know, George Clooney and I were making out on a gurney.

Sports Illustrated tried to enforce a fine-print clause in my employment contract, which I had signed stupidly without reading. *It's a waitressing contract,* I had thought. *What could it possibly say?* Quite a lot, as it turned out. Among other things, it gave the magazine/restaurant a substantial portion of any proceeds from acting or modeling work generated from contacts made while taking orders. The *ER* attorneys successfully got the contract voided, but only by offering a compromise that required me to pose—for free!—on that year's cover of *Sports Illustrated*'s swimsuit edition. I wore that utterly ridiculous and much-too-quickly-put-together bikini made of surgical gauze, a nod to my new *ER* fame.

It made quite the splash at the time. (In the world of pop culture, I mean. There was no way you could *swim* in it.) But the whole thing was an unpleasant ordeal. The gauze was itchy and the sun was hot and the photographer kept smiling at me in a manner that I can only describe as being the perfect advertisement for teeth whitener.

The day the magazine hit the stands, Cowell called. Soon

we were being photographed at all the best resorts and parties. I snagged the lead role in that over-the-top movie starring Jim Carrey (terrible kisser) and got some critical acclaim for my smaller role in an art film directed by Quentin Tarantino. (I played a cave woman sucked through a time warp to become a trained assassin.) I had nine lines in Tom Cruise's submarine flick—not much, but since I was the only woman in the movie it did, at least, get me on the poster and billed as a "star." (It also got me invited to Katie's baby shower, which was just as creepy as you'd expect.) I played a sassy and very mysterious barmaid on a much-hyped episode of *Will & Grace*. I portrayed Sawyer's girlfriend in a flashback scene of *Lost*. I had a minor role as a visiting grand duchess of "vaguely East Indian origin"—the casting director's words—in one of the *Princess Diary* sequels. I drew a royal flush on *Celebrity Poker Showdown*.

*People* magazine called me the "new it girl" and the "international Nicole Kidman," which I hear burns Nic up to this day. "*I'm* the international Nicole Kidman," she purportedly says.

President Samson Briarwood, a former Kansas governor, apparently thought I represented the Midwest well. He sent me a congratulatory letter about the *Sports Illustrated* cover, noting that I "put the heart in the heartland." I wasn't sure what that meant, really. But my agent thought it was quite impressive. He said that I was on the "cusp of real stardom."

"You're about to take off, baby," he said.

But I didn't.

Not then. Things sort of sputtered. My stint on *ER* did last several episodes longer than it was supposed to—the better part of two seasons, ultimately. But Dr. Benton-Vance was always considered a secondary character and never appeared in the show's opening credits. Then I was killed by a terrorist who had been brought to the hospital with food poisoning. (A bad batch of hummus—horrible stereotype, got all kinds of great ratings and bad press coverage.) Meanwhile, neither the Jim Carrey nor the Quentin Tarantino movie opened as well as the buzz had projected.

Cowell started ignoring me at parties to talk to the likes of Judge Judy and then stopped returning my calls altogether.

And before I could say "flash in the pan," my publicist actually relayed a date request from the staff of Steve Burns, whom you may know (but probably don't) as the original lead actor, indeed the only original nonanimated character, on the television show *Blue's Clues*.

I confess I was not entirely displeased with this date request. I was honestly flattered. Steve does have a disarming boyish cuteness. I noticed this when babysitting Alex Kingston's daughter on the *ER* set. (And yes, in retrospect, being assigned to babysit another star's child during a shoot should have been a sign my stock was falling on the show.)

But Hollywood dates are not about "disarming boyish cuteness." They're about press. My agent was the one who taught me that. He had been very put out with me once for agreeing too quickly to date one of the producers of Coldplay's new album. "You're not going to get anywhere by dating producers," he had said.

My publicist let the Steve Burns matter drop, but he did not seem pleased. Didn't he want me to play hard-to-get on these arranged dates? Had the rules changed?

About that time, I taped my second episode of *Celebrity Poker*, which had been filmed on location in a dive bar in a seedier neighborhood of LA. Fans stood on the sidewalk outside, waiting for the celebrities to be escorted out.

I hate those sorts of situations. People hand me napkins, maps, backs of candy wrappers to sign. Most of those items are not really suited for writing. I scratch and retrace because most pens are unable to penetrate the wax lining. Alternatively, I tear right through the cheap (and often damp) napkins. And the maps? Don't get me started. It's almost impossible, without a Sharpie, to write darkly enough to be read over the printed jumble of highway numbers, river names, and tourist attractions. Needless to say, fans never have a Sharpie. It's more likely a fragment of eyeliner pencil or a broken crayon, dusty from the bottom of some mother's purse.

I spent a lot of time apologizing during that encounter, and others like it. I was sincere in my apology. At moments like that, I always felt that if I were a better celebrity, if I were deserving of my fame, I would have stashed in my elegantly minuscule purse a stack of glossy eight-by-tens and a suitable writing instrument with which to personalize them. That's what Sandra Bullock does. She is grace personified.

On my best days, I go through this routine of scratching and apologizing with charm and panache and a seemingly endless supply of patience. This is my public, after all. And I love each and every one of them. I owe them everything, really. Almost everything at least.

That *was* one of my better days, so I patiently eked out messages of good cheer and glad tidings to everyone with a stub of something to write with and a scrap of something to write on.

And then it happened. A young man read my signature aloud to his girlfriend as they walked away.

"Addison McGhee," he said.

And his girlfriend clapped her hands together. "Oh, that's right," she said. "I think she used to be somebody."

And the guy said, "Yeah, I think she did."

I gasped. I had been off *ER* for less than six months. Could it be over so quickly?

I had breakfast with my agent the next day, and he said we

needed to "ramp it up." We were supposed to "brainstorm," but mostly I sat in stunned silence listening to a storm of bad ideas come from his brain. This was the man who, mere months earlier, had urged me not to go shopping with Jessica Simpson. He said she wasn't good enough for me. Now he wanted me to go to a David Schwimmer premiere? "No way," I said finally. "I still have some standards. I will not compete in *The New Celebrity Mole*. I'm not dating Matt Damon. He's married. Keep up!"

I clapped my hands impatiently at that point. My agent cringed, but didn't speak.

"And I'm certainly not farming myself out as an 'ethnicity expert' for a *Biography* piece on Michael Jackson."

I crossed my arms dramatically and was sure I sounded quite authoritative. My agent had always urged me to be more fierce in defending my status as a star. Perhaps this was just a test to see how well I could do. I was shaking inside, but I decided to go for a big finish.

"I don't want to hear the words *Hollywood Squares* again," I said. My brother had made fun of the celebrities on *Hollywood Squares* ever since we were children. "Who is this Jack Cassidy?" he would say. "And how does he represent Hollywood?" It's one thing to be considered a has-been by random *Celebrity Poker* fans. I couldn't bear for my own brother to see me that way.

My agent glanced at his watch and sighed dramatically. I wasn't sure if he had even heard what I said about *Hollywood Squares*. It occurred to me that this might be the best example yet of my knack for always behaving in exactly the wrong way. Earlier in my career, I had acted humbly when I should have been snooty. Now I was being snooty when it was time to be humble.

"So," he said, finally. "Back to Loveland?"

I looked at him suspiciously. Was he making some sort

of point? I had, in fact, recently purchased a showy-from-the-outside, one-bedroom log cabin condo in Loveland, Colorado. I felt it to be a prudent move, financially. LA real estate was expensive, and I had, rather foolishly, used some of my *ER* windfall to start a scholarship for refugee children. When money started getting tighter, I thought selling my place in LA and buying what I could describe as a "Rockies ranch" was a clever way to stretch my resources, and my accountant had agreed—rather too enthusiastically, I'd thought at the time.

"Yes," I said, bristling a little. "I'm headed back to the Rockies. My ranch needs checking on. Besides, I feel like Victoria Barkley out there."

"Ah," my agent said, raising his coffee cup in a toast of sorts. "Well, you'd better get driving."

I fumed about that comment for one long interstate mile after another. What had he been getting at, exactly? It's not as if I couldn't afford a plane ticket. I just needed my car, you know, on the ranch. How would it look if I hadn't driven? He always told me I needed to be concerned with how things look. "Not just your clothes," he used to say. "But everything."

People don't want their celebrities to appear too ordinary. They say they do. But they don't. People want us to live exotic private lives on expanses of expensive real estate. I *could* fly. But I was trying to project the image of a shrewd and sophisticated steward of the valuable American landscape, someone who was spending her money and her celebrity promoting a vanishing part of American life.

Besides, a nice long drive can be relaxing. It's like yoga or, well, hypnosis. I had thought this all out, in case I was ever asked about it by some enterprising entertainment reporter. *Nothing beats a day on the highway to detox your mind and uplift your spirit,* I planned to say if asked. But entertainment reporters were not, at that particular point in my career, calling much.

When I got to Loveland, it was dark and snowing. The lock on the door of my log cabin condo had frozen shut. I called the manager and stood around in ankle-deep snow in slinky sandals, shivering, until he finally let me in.

I thanked him, popped a Lean Cuisine into the microwave, and logged onto my somewhat out-of-date computer. By the time the "Asian-style" chicken was ready, I was poking around television discussion boards, trolling, I suppose, for a compliment. I went to an *ER* forum, saw that there were discussions of plot lines, writers, episodes, and characters. I clicked on "Characters."

I then had a choice of "Current Cast" or "Former Cast."

Sigh. I clicked on "Former."

I then had a choice of "Moved to Another Hospital" or "Died."

"Died."

Then, "Natural Causes" or "Violent Death."

And there in "Violent Death," between Lucy and Dr. Gant, two spaces up from Doug Ross's father and with only a quarter of the traffic of the ancient Dr. Romano discussion, there was a thread about my character—Dr. Benton-Vance.

Only two posts had been added in the past ninety days. Someone calling himself ERfanatic wrote: "Man, did Madison McGhee suck as an actress or what?"

And someone called Ilovedocs had responded: "I thought her name was Allison."

I chewed my chicken and stared at those two posts.

I was, by that time, ready for a nice hot bath, so I took some scripts—well, okay, one script—into my cramped bathroom so that I could read over it while I soaked. But when I dipped my foot into the water, I was so shocked that I dropped the script into the icy bath, ruining it. The water heater was out, again.

The next morning I called Home Depot and priced water heaters. The next afternoon, I called my agent. He chuckled with satisfaction.

"Circle," he said with a laugh. "Circle gets the square."

# Chapter 4

$\mathcal{I}$t was probably my imagination, but I thought Whoopi gave me a sad and knowing look when I showed up for the taping. Maybe it was my brother's bias about the show affecting my judgment, but I thought I read in her eyes a certain ruined longing, a miscarried hope. *So,* I imagined her saying, *you've come to this, too.*

My up-by-my-bootstraps, hardscrabble story of immigrant suffering had made me the darling of the liberal Hollywood establishment during those heady *ER* days. I'm sure that Whoopi had expected better from me.

Violating the *never-admit-you're-scraping-bottom* rule, I decided I might as well address the issue directly. Why beat around the bush? All of us in the greenroom were in the same situation, after all. May as well admit it.

"Is this where you get on the *Love Boat*?" I quipped. I thought I'd get a nervous laugh, or at least an awkward smile. But the other "stars" cringed, looked away from me. Nancy Kerrigan sipped a diet soda and didn't meet my eyes. Liza was doing some sort of stretching exercise. Carrot Top was balancing his checkbook. I wondered if that was as tough for him as it was for me. Well, he did make those phone company commercials. That probably helped.

In a chair in the corner, Kermit and Miss Piggy sat in a crumpled and tangled mess. *That's so sad,* I thought. *And they don't even get their own squares.*

"You know Emilio Estevez was with us a few years back," said a woman with red hair. She raised her chin and looked at me defiantly. She said it again, emphasizing each syllable: "E-mi-li-o Es-te-vez."

I could imagine my brother saying: *Yes, exactly.* But I made a pleased look and said something vaguely nice about *The Mighty Ducks.*

"And last season, we got some of the latest castaways from *Survivor,*" she added.

"Really?" I said, genuinely surprised. "That cute guy who won?"

"Well, no," the redheaded woman said.

"Oh."

"But we got the woman who caught the shingles and quit," she offered up slowly.

"Oh," I said, giving what I considered an encouraging smile. I lowered my voice and tried to sound like Jeff Probst. "The shingles have spoken." I switched back to my own voice and added: "That was a good episode."

"Yes," the redhead said, then nodded.

I touched up my makeup and, while looking in the mirror, discreetly stared at the redheaded woman. I didn't know who she was and wondered if I should. I thought about asking, but I could see on her folder that she was designated for the top center square. I was in the bottom left, meaning that she outshined my star power, at least in the eyes of the show's producers. I was afraid that asking who she was would seem catty, under the circumstances.

So I just smiled, picked a banana out of the fruit basket,

and took a (small) bite. She smiled at me, and I asked if she had any pointers. "You know," I said, "for the show."

"Depends," she said. "Do you want to look good or make friends?"

*Is that a serious question?* I wondered. *I'm a former "new it girl" forced into making an appearance on* Hollywood Squares *by a bum water heater. Obviously, I want to look good.* I looked at her intently, searching for a clue that she was joking. No hint. I decided to play it safe.

"Some of both, I guess," I said, giving her my most sincere smile.

"Miss questions on purpose," she whispered.

This was perhaps the most obvious advice you could give a celebrity guest on *Hollywood Squares,* a game tragically flawed not only by its lack of real stars but by its very rules. The host asks a question, the celebrity gives an answer, and the contestant agrees or disagrees.

No one wants a smart celebrity in this situation. If the question is "Who was the first US president born in the presence of a doctor?" a smart celebrity might say Lincoln or Taft or Coolidge or Kennedy. Who knows?

But a dumb celebrity will say Jed Bartlet—you know, from *The West Wing.* That's easy! Disagree!

(That is, unbelievably, the answer Emilio Estevez—of all people—actually gave to that question. I know, because the *Hollywood Squares* regulars are still talking about it. Did he think his father really lived in the West Wing? Did he not understand that it was, you know, a role?)

Telling a celebrity to miss questions on purpose in this game is like telling people to try not to run out of money in Monopoly.

I looked at my not-quite-recognizable redheaded adviser and thought: *No duh.*

I said: "I'll try."

About then, a fan burst into the dressing room—not tight security on this set—and handed the redhead a book with a homey-looking general store on the cover. He asked her to sign it and said she was like a cross between Fannie Flagg and Charo.

I had once had the displeasure of witnessing Jennifer Lopez being compared to Charo. Tears! There were so many tears! So I was quite sure the redhead would be upset. I grabbed a tissue and tried to hand it to her, but she was beaming! She said "Thank you" again and again as she signed several of the fan's books.

"I don't know how you have the time to combine your career on the regional theater circuit with your writing," the fan said. "You know *Match Game* never would have been the same without Fannie."

"And *Love Boat*," she said, "never would have been the same without Charo."

Just then, the fan turned and looked at me in what seemed to be a sheepish, embarrassed way. I thought, for a moment, that he was about to identify himself as a fan of mine as well, that he was about to admit—as men had done very recently—that he entertained wild fantasies or at least embarrassing dreams about me. I thought he was probably going to ask for my autograph.

And then he said: "Are you someone, too?"

I was spared the indignity of answering by a page, who at that moment popped his head in the door and yelled—with no identifiable irony—"Stars, take your squares!"

Liza rolled her eyes. Carrot Top scooped up Kermit and Miss Piggy and handed them to the page. Whoopi led us onto the set, and we each climbed into our square, silent, but filled, I think, with a kind of vain hope, an optimistic conviction that while this was not a dream come true, it could at least be a redemptive moment. Maybe none of us was the most sparkling star in Hollywood, but on that day we could be the most sparkling star on *Hollywood Squares*.

I, myself, was sure I would be witty and wise and a favorite of the contestants. I would be like Richard Dawson—only without the unfortunate smoking habit. That is what I told myself as we taped the show's opening. The announcer called my name and I waved awkwardly and winked in a campy way. I looked sly! I looked smart! I occupied the (occasionally) critical bottom left square. I would rule this show! I would dominate the game!

I only got called on once during that first episode. "Phyllis from Philadelphia" even mispronounced my name when she did so. "Addison McPhee to win," she said. (Luckily, the show was taped and they let her do it over.) But though she might not have known my name, she was glad she called on me, because my incorrect answer was fortuitous for both of us.

"Though hopes are raised virtually every year," Tom Bergeron read, "this crowning event hasn't occurred in more than a quarter of a century, which is too bad because the sport could use a new stud."

"So it's been that long since Prince William was born?" I said with a yawn. I didn't *mean* to yawn. It wasn't a calculated move to feign boredom with the breeding practices of the British royal family. I was just a little sleepy. It's a long drive from Colorado.

"Yeah, yeah," I said, drumming the table for effect. "Diana's boy has to be twenty-five." I made a breezy motion with my hand. "You know, more or less.

"That's it," I said finally. "That's my answer. The 'crowning event' is the birth of a future king of England."

If this answer made sense, it did so only barely. After all, I don't think royal reproduction really counts as "sport." But that didn't matter. What mattered was that at the very moment I gave this answer—or at least at the very moment that the taped version was aired in LA—Cal Gupton was sitting in a swank hotel room, smacking the remote control against his bedside table, wondering how on earth a four-figure-a-night hotel could offer its guests a dead remote. (And further wondering the odds of the battery expiring just as he clicked on something as awful as *Hollywood Squares*.)

But then—he told me all this later—he saw me yawn sensually. He noticed the ease with which I recalled, "more or less," pertinent facts of the British royal family, a long-standing interest of his. And he saw the smug, satisfied way I leaned back in my square and crossed my shapely legs. Cal saw me gracefully and elegantly pick up my classy Missoni Bianconero teacup, which featured a sophisticated black-and-white "graphic" wave pattern.

"After all," I continued, after taking a sip and giving Phyllis from Philadelphia a bemused look, "what could the word *stud* mean other than Prince Wills?"

Then I winked.

I was basically begging her to "disagree"—the real answer was horse racing's Triple Crown. Even I knew that. At least, I knew it had nothing to do with Prince William. I was pretty sure, anyway.

Phyllis did disagree, winning the game for herself and much applause for me.

"For those eight seconds," Cal told me later, "you were the coolest thing on earth." He paused, then added, "Or at least, you know, the coolest thing on syndicated television."

If my career were one of the redhead's plays, then this would be the end of the first act. Cal Gupton, the founder of the upstart GUP network, put down the remote, reached for a pen, and made a note on his left arm. "Addison McGhee," he said to himself. "Hmmmm. Addison McGhee."

# Chapter 5

A few weeks later, Cal had his people call my people. And when I say he called "my people" I mean that he called my agent, the one who'd considered *Hollywood Squares* a viable career move in the first place. So you can imagine how thrilled he was to learn that Cal had an idea that he'd been describing as "modestly brilliant" and that he wanted me to be a part of.

When Cal had ideas, even those of only modest brilliance, people listened. His network had first made a name for itself with a "family" of overacted, sexed-up teen soaps—the stars of which were forever making guest appearances on one another's shows and getting into tabloidesque trouble.

Cal had been branching out, adding to the lineup some moderately sophisticated comedies, a few gory police dramas, and, most famously, the National Football League season. He had shocked the older, more established networks by making a spectacularly high bid for broadcast rights to the NFL games, and he shocked them again by putting together an unlikely cadre of commentators to call the games, including several who seemed more likely to appeal to women than to the NFL's core audience of young men.

The most controversial of the bunch was the "dapper and dashing Hughes Sinclair"—the witty, poised, smart, and elegant son of a former Supreme Court justice and his famous ballerina wife. Hughes was universally loved by bright women and almost always tolerated by enlightened men. He was, however, generally despised by the NFL's most hard-core fans, who suspected he did not truly love their sport. (For example, he waxed on a bit too long about missing a family dinner during one of the Thanksgiving Day games that year. "I can practically smell Mom's apple-cider–braised pork loin and oven-dried pears from here," he said.) Fans were further appalled by his decision to wear a lavender tie on Super Bowl Sunday.

A columnist from Detroit—not Mitch, he was on a book tour at the time—rather famously took Hughes to task, saying: "It's the Super Bowl, Hughes. Do you even know what that means? It's the annual ode to manliness. Have some respect! Wear red or blue or, at the very least, a good deep Minnesota Vikings shade of purple—anything but lavender!"

Cal can be counted among the enlightened men who appreciated Hughes's dry wit and biting commentary, but he knew after the Super Bowl that the man's days as a football commentator were numbered—especially after Hughes unwisely prolonged and enhanced the controversy by protesting to Larry King that the tie wasn't, technically, lavender, but "a true periwinkle if ever there were one."

Larry gave him a long, quizzical look. "So," he said finally. "You're one of these metrosexuals, are you?" (That term was just coming into vogue for sharply dressed and accessory-savvy heterosexual men.)

Hughes beamed and said: "But of course!"

Cal immediately began looking for a new venue for Hughes. He was also looking for something else.

Cal had enjoyed, by that point, more success than most people could dream of, but he still had one unrealized dream. He wanted a news empire to rival CNN or Fox. So he had, for a while, been looking for an easy, pop-culture–laden, relatively short-lived news event during which he could experiment with "journalism."

When he saw a *People* magazine article about an unlikely confluence of important weddings—three European royal ceremonies had been scheduled for the same week as the much-hyped nuptials of the sitting US president to the junior senator from Ohio—Cal was so excited that he took notes all over his left hand.

Cal had a clear vision. He would bring together two witty, smart, and good-looking people for an early-morning show that, thanks to the time change, would run during primo wedding time in Europe. Hughes quickly became the obvious choice for a male anchor, and after Cal saw me making flip comments about the British royal family, he thought I was the obvious choice for the female spot, at least the obvious choice among the women who would consider it. (Scarlett Johansson, I heard later, had not returned his calls.)

"You even played a princess in that *Diary* movie," he said excitedly during my only interview for the job.

I nodded enthusiastically, even while feeling obligated to contradict him. "Grand duchess," I said. (But I continued to nod.)

He looked at me with a slight air of defensiveness. "What's the difference?"

I started to say: "Well, a grand duchess is, I suppose, like a *really great* kind of duchess and a princess is, well . . ." But then I realized the futility of going down this road. I leaned toward him, smiling widely enough to show off my left dimple to best effect, and whispered, "There is none."

He patted me on the knee and said I was hired.

Cal's show would be called *Wedding Week,* and it was to last no longer than the name suggested. A successful run would not, could not really, extend the show's duration, but would add fuel to Cal's plan to eventually launch a daily "news" operation.

So Hughes and I sat on a cheap sofa in front of a flimsy-looking map of Europe. We sipped coffee and tea and pretended to nibble on fat-free scones while chitchatting about the weddings as the live feeds came in. (The scones were inedible, but you know what I always say: Inedible food is the best kind!)

I had spent several months preparing for the big week, including reading every journalism book I could find at the Tattered Cover Book Store in downtown Denver and watching dozens of *A Wedding Story*–type treatments of various celebrity ceremonies the world over.

My agent laughed at me when I told him this. "You know, you're not becoming Diane Sawyer," he said. "It's more like you're playing her."

But I had a dream myself. My dream was of a full-time, respectable job. A steady gig. A regular employer. Maybe I could be the first person in my family with group health insurance and, not incidentally, world renown.

I had a secret hope—more than a hope, really, a gut feeling—that *Wedding Week* would somehow work its way into something permanent, and I was thus determined to approach my role in it with professionalism and pride. Diane Sawyer nothing. I was going to be Peter Jennings.

So I showed up for my first day of *Wedding Week* with several folders full of clipped newspaper articles, all of them alphabetized and cross-referenced. I came with a framed JOURNALISM CODE OF ETHICS to lean on my desk. I had splurged on five Tiffany teacups and saucers, each with a floral pattern chosen to match the color scheme of that particular day's wedding. (My favorite was the Audubon pattern, which I liked enough to reuse many times over the years. It was immortalized eventually in the Times Square billboard.)

No other actress, I am sure, would have come to this job with any more enthusiasm and dedication. I was never going to suffer with a bum water heater again, and if a talky news show (or a newsy talk show) would prevent that, then I was going to be pretty good at talking about news. (To the extent that the marriages of distant heirs to minor and largely symbolic thrones count as news anyway.)

I confess I had a bumpy start. I knew nothing about appearing on live television, and it couldn't have been more different than the scripted television of my past. No second takes, no scripts to study. During the first day, especially, I struggled to casually work into conversations the information I had compiled in my long detailed notes. This led to a stilted delivery and unnatural transitions.

"I'm glad you mentioned the bride's veil," I said, after Hughes had raved about the intricate needlework worn by a distant cousin of the king of Liechtenstein. "Because I've been meaning to talk about her college degree."

There was also, that first morning, an embarrassing incident in which the producer confused me by twirling his finger just before a commercial break. Twirling your finger is the universal television signal to "wrap things up quickly," but I didn't know that. To me, it looked like a signal to "keep going." I babbled and babbled and babbled. He twirled his finger faster and faster. I babbled more and more. Finally, in desperation, the producers just faded to commercial. Viewers, not that there were many that first morning, saw the lights dim and heard the sound fade as I uttered the memorable line, "There's nothing like a wedding to get you thinking about, um, marriage . . ."

Cal was not happy. He yelled a bit and threw a scone. (It bounced against the wall. Hard.) He screamed at a totally innocent cameraman, sacked the producer who had not prepped me on the hand signals, cursed a page, and threatened to fire me, too. All this during the three-minute commercial break!

The commercial break ended and Hughes, with unflappable professionalism, introduced a taped story about royal bridesmaids in history. While the tape ran, Cal finished his speech. Luckily, he had softened a bit by then.

"Don't worry," he said. "I've got an idea of extraordinary brilliance. We'll add a weatherman."

"A meteorologist?" Hughes asked, incredulously. "How on earth will that help?"

It seemed like a good question to me—unless the weatherman was going to teach me the hand signals. But Cal ignored Hughes. "Yes, that's it," Cal said. "A forecaster! But not one of those fat, friendly guys like everyone else has."

"No," I said, eager to pipe in with something. "I certainly don't think he should be like anyone else."

" 'Course not," Cal said. He smiled at me, and I appeared to be in his good graces again. "We need to be different. Edgy. Out there. We need someone sullen and mysterious."

"Sullen?" Hughes asked. (He was a big believer in chipper and did not at all appreciate the appeal of brooding.)

"Sullen!" Cal said.

He smiled brightly, then turned to another producer to bark: "And get Addison an earpiece. Clearly the hand signals are too much for her."

The next morning, just before the show, Cal introduced us all to Baxter Bailey, with his slightly shaggy hair, his slightly rumpled suits, and the somewhat outrageous bow ties that never quite matched his shirts. The wardrobe, the hair, and the exasperated frown combined to project an image of a professional contrarian.

Still, Cal insisted on reemphasizing Baxter's mission at the morning staff meeting just minutes before we were to go live with coverage of the wedding of a former *Jeopardy!* contestant to an heir to the now defunct Greek throne.

"Don't smile," Cal said to Baxter. "Don't make jokes or wish people happy birthdays. Don't share diet tips and don't be personable. Why do people think that weathermen should be so damn personable?" Cal looked around at the staff as if expecting an answer. No one offered one.

He gestured toward the window: Charcoal clouds were rolling in over the harbor. "Weather isn't cheerful! It's frightening. Especially at a wedding. A few sprinkles could ruin the whole day!"

He pointed to Baxter. "Your job is to worry. Fret about flooding. Stew over low-pressure systems. Despair about wintry storms. Brood!"

"Flooding?" Hughes asked, incredulously. "Wintry storms? At the wedding? Today?"

"Oh good grief," Cal responded. "Use some imagination, Hughes! Bad weather *anywhere* is important. One natural disaster could cast a pall over the entire proceedings. A flash flood in Crete? An earthquake under Mount Olympus? If enough people die, they might have to postpone the wedding."

"Ah, yes," said Hughes, appearing thoughtful. "A pall."

Baxter raised a finger to interrupt. "Earthquakes aren't really predictable, you know. There's no way for me to say when one is about to happen."

"All the better," Cal said, raising his arms in an expansive way. "It could happen at any time. The wedding party might have to flee to the streets of Athens."

"Ah," said Hughes. "Flee."

There was a moment of silence. I felt that as the co-host, I should add something to the conversation.

"The wedding is actually in London," I said, finally.

Everyone turned to look at me. Hughes started flipping through his notes. "I thought it was the heir to the Greek throne today."

"*An* heir," I said. "Not *the* heir. This guy is like seventh in the line of succession. And it's the *defunct* Greek throne. The Greek royal family is in exile."

Hughes dropped his notes. "Ah, yes," he said.

"Since 1967," I added.

Cal grimaced, but then broke into a smile.

"That's perfect," he said. "In London, there is *always* a chance of showers."

# Chapter 6

*I*t didn't rain.

But the second day of *Wedding Week* did go much better than the first. I had an earpiece, for one thing, so I didn't have to worry about those pesky hand signals. And I demonstrated my impressive understanding of the exile of the Greek royal family, for another.

Baxter offered regular updates on the 18 percent chance of showers in the Notting Hill neighborhood. (The wedding wasn't, strictly speaking, in Notting Hill, but never mind that.) Hughes gamely helped Baxter along with the fretting. "I suppose," Hughes said, "severe weather in Notting Hill could cast a pall on the day's events."

Hughes was, after all, a consummate professional, a seasoned veteran of NFL games. Nothing at a wedding could throw him off—not fumbled vows, not fashion fouls, not even a groom's surprising pause to hug a famously estranged ex–cousin-in-law.

"Astonishing," Hughes would say, in the same tone he had used for an eighty-yard touchdown run. "Simply amazing!"

Soon his confidence rubbed off on me, and my depth of knowledge began to rub off on him. By the end of the third (unfortunately clear) day, when the young possible future queen of Denmark was exchanging vows with a somewhat aged rock star, we had hit our stride.

(She was currently about ninth in line to the throne, but we always called her the "possible future queen of Denmark" because Cal figured there could always be some sort of castle-cafeteria food-poisoning event. Or, you know, some sort of ghastly palace coup. The government of Denmark is generally considered stable, but you never know.)

"I daresay," Hughes ad-libbed during a long lull when the bride's train got caught on the door of the carriage, "the groom hasn't drawn this big a crowd since he had that funky dance hit back in—when was that, Addison?"

"That would have been 'Smog Machine of Love,' " I said, looking perhaps a little too pleased. "The groom's biggest hit spent three weeks at number one in 1978, Hughes, and the video of the song was considered groundbreaking.

"Of course," I continued, "just having a video was considered groundbreaking back then. But I suppose you remember all about that, Hughes."

I playfully patted his arm then and he reacted with mock horror to my reference to his (slight) age advantage over me. (People always assumed he was older, because of his graying temples. But that gray came out of a bottle and was touched up weekly. Gray is considered distinguished on men, don't you know?)

Hughes then turned to Baxter. "Speaking of smog, how's that haze situation?"

"It appears to be clearing," Baxter said, matter-of-factly. Cal glared from offstage, and Baxter's voice turned more grave. "But you never can be sure."

By the time the possible future king and queen of Denmark were tossing bouquets and handling the ceremonial releasing of the oystercatchers (the national bird), I was loose and cool.

"He's beastly, for sure," I said, "but it's beastly in a sexy rock-star sort of way. Don't you think, Hughes?"

Just saying the word *sexy* on air filled me with a secret thrill. My parents were horrified, I was sure.

Even Hughes looked a bit flustered and said he didn't know a thing about "sexy beasts."

"But really," he said, "it's not like you'd expect the possible future queen of Denmark to have her pick of men. Danish fashion has been in a slump for years. They keep making all those unflattering dresses with the billowy cuts."

I looked at him uncomfortably. *Was that right? It didn't sound right.* I felt a surge of panic. I didn't like Hughes knowing more than I do about fashion, even Danish fashion. I made a mental note to read up on that after the show. I said, "Oh please."

It wasn't *all* playful banter. Cal wanted substance, he said. So I did a rather impressive piece on the role of royalty in modern society, and Hughes did a lengthy—some would say way too lengthy—story on the tourism draw of the various royal families. Baxter did an in-depth look at the history of weather patterns at royal nuptials, coming to the surprising conclusion that British royals are the most likely to be blessed by good weather. "They know how to pick wedding days," he said. "Now, if they could just do a better job picking spouses."

My second report, much mocked later, was supposed to be the definitive look at the courtship of American presidents. The current president was the first in more than a century to be elected without a wife, and thus needless to say Samson Briarwood was the first president in at least that long to find a wife while in office.

The fact that Margaret Clemons was a seated senator from the opposing party made it all the more interesting, though President Briarwood laughed off my questions about their political differences in the short interview I was granted. "Do you think you'd be a better match for me?" he said, nudging me a little in what I feared was an inappropriate, flirtatious way. (I left that exchange out of my story.)

The presidential wedding, held on that final Friday of *Wedding Week,* had none of the pomp of the European ceremonies, of course. (It was the second for him and the third for her, so they were trying to make it tastefully understated.) And what little pomp it would have had was ruined by the morning storms. Cal had been thrilled that Baxter finally had some legitimate weather to discuss. But honestly, the storms were terrible for the show. Senator Clemons, fiery dynamo that she is, dashed from the limo to the church so quickly that you could barely see her white Chanel suit or her interesting bouquet of buckeye blooms.

"I wish that were a joke," Hughes said, rather unpopularly. (At least in Ohio.)

The president looked as goofy as ever in one of those double-breasted off-the-rack suits he's famous for. "If you're wondering whether the president met with a tailor for the occasion," Hughes quipped, "the answer is a resounding no. It's appalling, don't you think, Baxter?"

Baxter had not expected to be drawn into this conversation, and his face froze for a moment. Baxter wasn't even wearing a suit, but a blue blazer, red bow tie, and khaki pants. Of course, he wasn't the leader of the free world and wasn't getting married, so the standard was a bit lower for him. But Hughes still seemed mean directing the question at someone with such a clearly stunted sense of style. It's not as if Baxter could help it. He'd gotten his start in radio! No one cares about fashion in radio. I glanced around and saw that everyone on the set had tensed up. This sounded like the beginning of an uncomfortable conversation.

*What is it with fashionable men and tailors anyway?* I thought. Women pride themselves on being a perfect size 6, or 4, or 8, or whatever. Men—those like Hughes, anyway—see no shame in having the waist let out or the legs shortened. Suddenly I saw a way out.

"Oh, Hughes," I interjected. "Classically proportioned men can buy clothes off the rack, you know. You only need a tailor if you've got—I don't know—stubby legs."

Baxter, for the first time that week, chuckled. Hughes cringed.

I flashed a dimple at Baxter, but turned to give Hughes my most seductive smile—the one I had perfected on *ER*—and playfully ran my hand across his chest. "Or, you know, really broad shoulders."

Hughes laughed, too. And the moment was saved.

*Wedding Week* got solid ratings, better than you would expect on the first few days when it was about the distant heirs to defunct thrones and better than you would expect again later in the week, when there was so much competition as the nation built up to the president's wedding.

When we finally had the president married and the first couple off to their Camp David honeymoon, the *Wedding Week* staff went out to celebrate our short but successful run. We ate lunch at a restaurant near the Midtown studio, drinking a bit much for lunch, but then some of us had been up for ten hours by then. Besides, you had to toast the new first lady—a true career gal after all. Some people said she was, by virtue of her seat on the appropriations committee, more powerful than her hubby. And there was no doubt she was smarter and better dressed. "Marginally," Hughes clarified, in a gossipy postproduction whisper.

I saw Baxter scowl at that. "Always with the insults," he said.

But you know, that's just Hughes's thing—being all snarky and negative like that. It's a kind of humor. You shouldn't run for president, and you certainly shouldn't marry one, if you're not tough enough for a little public ridicule. I myself enjoyed laughing at Hughes's little remarks, even though I thought it was neat that the new first lady was such a fireball. When he first took office, the president had been rumored to routinely exchange suggestive e-mails with a series of silly, young, under-educated, and generally inappropriate models. That all ended, reportedly, when Senator Clemons approached him after his second State of the Union address and asked if he was man enough to date a real woman. He had stuttered and stammered—of course, that's not unusual for him—and finally said that he supposed that he *was* man enough. And she then, according to her already published memoir *Courting a President,* leaned close to him and whispered: "Prove it."

That story was positively inspiring. This was a woman who went after what she wanted, even if what she wanted might seem to many of us to be, well, somewhat less than desirable.

"You gotta love Margaret Clemons," I had said that morning on the air, in a clip that was replayed many times later. And I said something very similar that afternoon in our little private lunch. Everyone agreed. Cheers all around!

But I felt a little sad as I left the restaurant. Our show was over. My new moment of glory was gone. The producers were all returning to their teen soaps. Baxter was rushing off to the airport, returning to his regular job at a small radio station in Southern California. "Predicting the weather in San Diego?" Hughes had said as Baxter left. "Sounds challenging!"

Afterward, Hughes offered to walk me the few blocks back to my hotel. He had an umbrella and I didn't.

His umbrella was quite fashionable, ample without being obnoxiously large. It sported an intriguing ridged handle, just nicked up enough to suggest that it was a much-used classic. "Wow," I said, fingering the handle. "This is nice." I had a habit of losing my own umbrellas, so I usually picked up new ones at drugstore counters. There was, I could see now, a difference in quality.

"James Smith and Sons," Hughes said.

I nodded as if that meant something to me. (I later learned it was an English company that practically invented the modern umbrella.)

He tapped the handle himself and said: "Whangee."

I nodded, again as if that meant something to me. But then giggled at my own charade. Plus the word. It's just funny, isn't it? *Whangee?*

Hughes looked at me, and for a moment, I thought I would get one of his withering remarks, but then he just smiled in an indulgent way. Leaned toward me and whispered: "Bamboo. More or less."

"Ah," I said. It strikes me as I remember this that left to my own devices, I probably would have said *Oh*. But around Hughes I tended to say *Ah*. *Ah* seems so much more refined than *Oh*. Doesn't it? If I were writing an updated Miss Liberty book, I would touch on that.

Hughes and I walked quickly, huddled together and whispering. When we got to the hotel, we stopped outside and stood together for a moment, water sheeting down around us. Another few steps and we would be under the hotel canopy, but we stopped, still in the rain, alone under his James Smith & Sons whangee umbrella.

"Well," Hughes said. "It's been a pleasure."

I smiled and agreed.

"We make a good team," Hughes said. "You saved me from looking like a complete jerk about the tailored suits."

I started to protest that he'd not been a *complete* jerk, but I didn't even get a word out before he held up his hand to stop me.

"No," he said. "It's true. I don't know what gets into me sometimes. When I started out in television everyone loved my outrageous cattiness. So I just kept giving people what they wanted. But I went too far today."

He glanced at his feet. "I do that a lot, actually."

He looked back up at me. "So thank you," he said.

And then he startled me by reaching up and pushing a strand of hair behind my ear. I blushed, looked down at my feet.

"I'm sorry," he said. "Was that inappropriate?"

I wanted desperately to be taken seriously at this job, but this job was over. And I was silly-sleepy and easily flirted with. Plus, I was still nursing a bit of a fragile ego after being dumped by Cowell. Besides, I was, I confess, taken with Hughes and his fancy ways. I had never met a man with a nice umbrella before. In LA, of course, no one needs an umbrella, and in Nebraska men just dash from door to car holding a newspaper over their heads or hunching their shoulders, as if that helps.

Besides, the men I dated in Nebraska weren't men at all. They were boys. Fairly immature ones at that. They would never have been able to let the word *whangee* go in and out of a conversation without making some sort of rude remark. All of that went through my mind, as I stood there, with Hughes's finger on a strand of hair behind my ear. And it all flashed through my mind again when he said: "Was that inappropriate?"

I grinned, shrugged. "I don't see why," I said. "Might have been inappropriate this morning, but now . . ."

My voice trailed off, and I looked up and down the mostly empty streets. People had crowded into shops and doorways; only the occasional hurried- and harried-looking person in a raincoat happened by.

"Ah, yes," he said. "We're no longer co-workers, are we?"

I shook my head no.

He reached up, pushed another strand of hair behind my other ear, and then ran his hand down along my cheek to my chin. His fingers lingered there a moment and then he swallowed hard, looking around the street himself. It seemed late, an illusion generated by the dreary, dark day and by the week of early, early mornings.

"So it's back to California for you," he said.

"Colorado," I said. "I have a ranch there."

I hesitated. Did I want to lie to Hughes? I cleared my throat. "Well, you know, a ranch-style place. A condo, actually. And I'm not heading back until Monday. Cal told me I deserved a weekend in the city."

"Ah." Hughes seemed surprised, thrown off a little. Was he appalled that I didn't live in California? Surely it wasn't about the condo. Everyone in New York lives in condos. Right?

He looked at the street sign, as if to get his bearings.

"There's a lovely bookstore around the corner, you know. You should give it a look. If you've got the weekend."

He pointed toward the east, muttered some directions. Looked at his feet, again.

"Thanks," I said. I was thrilled that Hughes mentioned a bookstore. It suggested that my effort to reinvent myself as a journalist had been at least somewhat successful. No one I knew in LA would have mentioned a bookstore to me. They might have pointed the way to a gym or, I don't know, an oxygen bar.

There was a gust of wind, and the umbrella pulled sharply to the right. We each got wet and laughed. I gestured toward the lobby and said I was ready for a nap. Then I blushed. Talking about going to bed in the middle of the afternoon sounds suggestive, doesn't it? Especially when standing this close to a man who has just touched your chin. But as I said, the early-morning schedule had been a killer.

Hughes leaned forward and kissed me on the cheek. It was a gentle move, just ever so slightly slower than a typical social kiss, not that I had ever really moved in the social-kissing crowds anyway. Slater County didn't really have a crowd of social kissers, and in LA people were too worried about their makeup.

Hughes pulled back. "Maybe I could show you that bookstore tomorrow," he said. And I said: "Maybe you could."

I stepped under the hotel's sidewalk canopy and my recently former co-worker disappeared into the rain, his James Smith & Sons umbrella bobbing into the distance. No time was set, no arrangement was made. I don't think either of us was sure if we had a bookstore date or not. I certainly wasn't.

But something had happened, of that much I was sure. Hughes Sinclair was everything that I was not. He was buttoned-up Waspy America, with the best education money could buy and a pedigree of success in the performing and judicial arts. He was the sort of man who could, with great confidence and no shame, discuss the difference between periwinkle and lavender and proudly buy imported umbrellas. (Not from Taiwan.) He was blue-blooded America. And I?

I was the immigrant wave, slightly accented, smelling of exotic spices. He was smooth and confident, while I was awkward and uncomfortable. (In a good way, my fans said.) He was an erudite student of the world, not to mention of Yale, Princeton, and Harvard Universities. I was a dropout of Slater County, Omaha, and Los Angeles community colleges. And Nebraska Cosmetology School, come to that. (What can I say? I flailed a bit in my pursuit of higher education.)

Hughes was a refined and well-bred television professional.

I was a two-bit actress who'd gotten her most recent job by babbling almost incoherently on *Hollywood Squares*.

But as we had stood under that expensive umbrella together—making jokes about the Ivy League–educated producers we had left at lunch, bantering a bit about the nature of our relationship, exchanging a social kiss—something changed. He had pulled me under his umbrella, and in some way that I did not understand, he pulled me into his circle as well. He had treated me as an equal. He had thanked me for saving him. He had suggested, by his sly asides and subtle flirtations, that he and I shared something. (After all, I was the only one he was not making fun of.) I just wasn't sure what we shared. A seat on the national stage? An ironic and detached outlook? Something more?

I'm embarrassed, looking back on this, how quickly and easily I became absolutely besotted with Hughes Sinclair. As I watched him leave, I realized he was everything that I had ever wanted in a man. He was, I thought, sophisticated, articulate, just a tad snarky, and utterly urbane.

I remembered how all the obits about Peter Jennings included the word *urbane*. I had thought it was the perfect word to describe Jennings; it was also what I wanted in a boyfriend. I wanted someone who was urbane.

So I grinned and blushed as I watched Hughes stride away, even though I wasn't sure if we had a date or not. I was confident we had something. I just had a feeling in my gut.

But my confusion about what we had did not matter. We were not former co-workers for long, and we were both busy the next day anyway.

# Chapter 7

Not long after Hughes left me at the hotel, news broke of the kidnapping of the president's niece, who had been vacationing with her boyfriend in France. (It had been something of a scandal—all the leading gossip columnists wondered why, exactly, the president's sister's daughter did not find it necessary to attend the wedding of the American century.)

Cal impulsively decided that the GUP network should launch its permanent news operation while there was big news at hand, an awkward decision given that no staff had been hired. So he made a snap judgment. "Let Hughes and Addison handle it," he said. "They've got that map of Europe."

The network logo artist worked up a new title for the opening sequence, "Parisian Peril," and the production staff used Wite-Out to quickly cover up the cartoonish crowns that had previously marked where the weddings were taking place.

Hughes and I each arrived in the studio at 4 AM, nodded professionally at each other, and started reading over scripts and planning coverage. I insisted on going with a plain white teacup, thinking the floral prints I had been using during *Wedding Week* were too frivolous for the occasion. One of the producers offered me a cup and saucer from Crate & Barrel, the Palazzo line.

I thought it was quite nice, really. I mean, it wasn't Tiffany. But the Tiffany cups averaged eighty dollars apiece and this, the producer told me, she got for twelve bucks. For that money, I was awfully impressed. *I need to start shopping at Crate & Barrel,* I thought.

But Hughes laughed at it. "It's so flimsy," he said, thumping it with his finger.

I cringed.

He patted me on the back in a reassuring way. "Oh, don't worry," he said. "It'll be fine for TV. The viewers won't have to touch it."

When the clock struck 6 AM, we were all back on television, only this time Hughes and I had more serious looks on our faces. (Baxter could not possibly look more serious than he already had.)

Surprisingly, it went just as well.

We talked about the history of kidnapping, the modern scourge of terrorism, and the persistent cloud cover in Paris. Hughes was wondering aloud how someone "holds it together" in a time like this, and I said, "Well, I've known tough times myself. You just have to have faith."

Hughes bit his lip, patted my knee, and nodded gravely. "Ah yes," he said, "the camp in Turkey."

Even Baxter looked touched as he rubbed his chin somberly.

I had actually been talking about the whole experience with the bum water heater, so I was a bit uncomfortable about the knee patting and lip biting—until I watched it later on television and saw how riveting it was. (From the first day, I made a habit of watching the tapes later. If I concentrated on viewing the tapes the way a detached, objective observer would, I could tell what worked and what didn't. That is how

I learned. And one of the first things I learned was that Hughes and I were great TV from the start.)

When the president's niece was eventually released, days later, at the Ritz-Carlton in Paris, I was able to talk in great detail about the layout of the lobby—I had stayed there during the filming of the Jim Carrey movie. I also suggested a nearby café where she could get a good cup of espresso.

"There's a handy tip," Hughes said as Baxter rolled his eyes.

And when it turned out that the kidnapping was not the work of international terrorists, as everyone suspected, but a desperately out-of-hand fraternity prank, Hughes leapt in with surprising gusto, having won awards while working on his college paper for his coverage of fraternity initiation rituals. (Who knew?)

At one point, he threw out an especially interesting statistic or two and quoted from a "famous" research journal on the subject—all off the top of his head. It was the live journalism equivalent of a slam dunk. "What is this," Cal shouted triumphantly (and a bit too loudly) into our earpieces, "freakin' *60 Minutes*?"

Hughes's long dissertation impressively filled what would have otherwise been an excruciatingly long stretch of live coverage of the accused being driven to the courthouse in a white van. (Brian Williams, we later learned, resorted to reading from a world atlas about typical weather patterns in springtime Paris—saying that it would appear from the blooms along the roadway that the season had arrived as scheduled. "See," Cal said. "Brian should have had a weatherman. Where's Roker when they need him?")

When Hughes began his impressive dissertation about fraternities, I had just reached for my teacup. I'd been able, by this point in the week, to upgrade to a simple Wedgwood White, which appeared to be more acceptable to Hughes—

though still affordable. (I got the cup and saucer for less than fifty dollars.) I stopped the cup midair, not yet to my lips, and allowed myself to look somewhat awestruck when Hughes began his insightful run of frat-prank commentary.

*"Well,"* I said, when Hughes had finished and Cal's *60 Minutes* comment had stopped ringing in my ear. "Aren't *you* all that and a bag of chips?"

That was the first time I winked on the GUP network, though it was to Hughes, not the viewer.

So that's how it happened. That cheap European map was not quite three weeks old when the executives at GUP realized they had something special in Hughes and me. Our show got its third name, *It's Morning Now with Addison and Hughes,* and was added to the permanent schedule.

I suppose if I am to be remembered for anything—well, aside from the arrest and the possible deportation—it would probably be for the way I always opened *It's Morning Now.* When I die, they will drag out some grainy video of it, and people of a certain age will say, "Oh yes, I remember all the fuss about that." Although if I get deported and if Cassie is right about how long I'll last in my father's homeland, the video won't be all *that* grainy.

I don't remember how it got started really, whose idea it was, whether I liked it initially; thought it was smart enough. But it is there on the tape of the first show, and it's on every show after that. Every morning they would play the opening music and then the camera would zoom in on me as I sipped tea from a china cup. By the time the camera was close enough that my face filled the entire screen, I'd peer over the rim, wink mischievously, and say: "Wake up, honey. It's morning now!"

Cal said it was my "signature sentence," and it was he who paid for the huge moving billboard, perched at the top of Times Square, which replayed it for the world, over and over again. My big brown eyes—two stories high—peered over a giant cup, cartoonish steam rising from it. In my left palm, a saucer was balanced. My right pinkie was extended in mock elegance. I was winking. Over and over, all day long. No matter where you stood on the streets below, it seemed that winking eye was winking right at you, and my mouth was moving and you could read my lips. "Wake up, honey. It's morning now."

It was spoofed regularly on *Saturday Night Live*. At one point, David Letterman begged me—begged me—to repeat it on *Late Show*. And when I did, he mopped his brow as if he was feeling a little overheated and muttered "Wow."

The president even weighed in during a photo op at a Virginia military post, asking the reveille player (in a jokey way) whether he'd considered just playing a clip of "that TV woman with the sultry voice saying 'Wake up, honey.' "

My mother kept begging me to stop. "Your father," she would say, "your father does not approve at all."

But that's what Cal wanted and that's what Cal got. I constantly feared that my "signature" would become stale. But Cal said it was as fresh on the week I was arrested as it had been on day one. And I suppose the ratings bore him out.

Not that *It's Morning Now* was ever an unqualified hit. It never drew the audience that *Today, Good Morning America,* or even *The Early Show* attracted. But we had "special viewers," the sort of hip, sophisticated, high-spending young people who loved to buy organic coffee blends, nondetergent cleansers, and overpriced and unreliable cars. Our viewers were an advertiser's dream.

Suddenly my old celebrity friends—and a few new ones—were in touch. Denzel sent me a couple of scripts, jotting notes in the margin about how much he would love to work with me. I ran into Paris while shopping for Fabergé teacups at Scully & Scully. She asked for my number and saved it to her cell phone right on the spot. Woody kept inviting me to Soon-Yi's parties, during which he'd follow me around with an embarrassing puppy-dog air. (*Uncomfortable!*) Will and Jada kept leaving messages, saying I must fly over for dinner, but I put them off. I didn't have time to go to LA. (Besides, Tommy Lee hinted to me that they tend to get carried away with the karaoke.) Keanu told Rosie that I was his "dream date." Sarah Jessica and Matt wanted me to babysit.

President Samson Briarwood himself gave our show an impromptu endorsement during an in-depth interview he and the first lady gave to Oprah a few months after his niece was rescued.

"The senator and I were consumed with worry, of course—even after word came that my sister's daughter had been released." (This sentence, historians say, will be forever significant because it is the first time a US president publicly used a title for his wife other than *first lady*.)

"But," President Briarwood continued, as the first lady/senator nodded in agreement, "when I heard that guy on the GUP network speak so elegantly about the history of the sort of violence my niece had endured, and then when I saw Addison speak so movingly about having faith in hard times, well, somehow I knew everything was going to be okay. Really, I couldn't take my eyes off her . . ."

Senator Margaret Clemons-Briarwood stopped nodding and gave a sharp glance toward her husband.

"I mean *it*," the president said. "I couldn't take my eyes off *the coverage,* I'm saying."

He chuckled. "We've been watching that guy and Addison ever since," he said.

"Good grief," Hughes said, when we heard about the president's comment. "Oh please," I added. But the network was delighted. Cal was incredulous. "The *president* watches us? Really?" he kept asking. (We had all assumed the reveille comment had been scripted to make him appear "hip.") "CNN, Fox, all the networks reported on his niece's kidnapping and the president watched a couple of *Hollywood Squares* rejects yammer on like they know something?"

Hughes and I each cringed. First of all, Hughes wasn't even on *Hollywood Squares*. And I was, I hasten to point out, not *rejected* by them. But we couldn't help but laugh when Cal finished up his tirade by yelling: "We're a phenomenon, baby!"

Even Baxter grinned and pumped his fist in the air in a charmingly goofy manner.

We *were* a phenomenon. And I believe we rose to the occasion. Hughes and I really "became" our roles, you know. We reinvented ourselves as journalists. We inhaled news. We lived on information. (Well, I did. Hughes also had salad dressing.)

I took to reading three newspapers a day and two books a week, usually of the ponderous historical sort. With private coaching and careful study of past tapes, I eventually became a disciplined interviewer. Soon I fancied myself an expert on the European Union, the Middle East, and the Far Eastern financial markets.

Hughes was like a mentor to me. He knew the right papers to read, the right books to purchase. Left to my own devices, I would have been getting my news from Salon.com and studying Middle East coverage through serial romances with sheiks on the cover. But my mind positively blossomed under Hughes's tutelage.

Baxter settled into his role as well. He stewed, but in a very affable way, according to all the magazines. They used words like *curmudgeonly*. They found his rumpled hair and wrinkled clothes inexplicably attractive. And mothers, in particular, loved the way he worried and fretted and fussed over the weather. "The only person who cares more than I do about my kids getting wet feet on the way to school," wrote one fan, "is that curmudgeonly Baxter Bailey."

No hip young audience, however, would stand for a steady diet of disciplined interviews on foreign financial markets— much less public agonizing about the possibility of school-children in wet socks. So we interspersed the real news and weather reports with the latest antics of the Olsen twins or yet another "special studio performance" by Clay Aiken.

"Boy howdy, you sure can sing," I'd tell Clay, and I would really mean it. (Larry King had pulled me aside at a party once and told me the trick is to *give the impression* that you really mean it. Also, he said, "It never hurts to throw in a folksy colloquialism.")

We gave viewers the news of the day, but we also gave them tips on cooking crêpes or planting petunias or cutting clutter. And our "sources" for these stories were not experts in any normal sense of the word. Penélope Cruz would explain about petunias. Catherine Zeta-Jones would take us on a tour of her file cabinet. Jennifer Love Hewitt shared her crêpe recipe. (Has she ever actually *eaten* a crêpe? I certainly haven't.)

Real journalists, trained journalists, experienced journalists, were universally appalled. So was Julie Chen. "The final irrevocable blurring of news and entertainment"—that was the conclusion of a solemn *Washington Post* editorial. A lot of people, at least a lot of media critics, seemed to believe that you couldn't care about the Olsen twins and also follow the news about Syria. They thought that if you cared about Clay, you couldn't care about Chad. (The African nation, I mean.) They thought discussion of crêpes and clutter left no room for discussions of corporate ethics or judicial confirmation hearings.

Scholarly journals were soon filled with long-winded articles about how dreadful the whole thing was. Commentators wrung their hands about me at their oh-so-serious broadcast seminars. They threw darts at Hughes and me, I am told, in postseminar cocktail hours.

The only thing that reined in the criticism at all was the "real" journalists' sensitivity toward being perceived as picking on me, a person of color. They did not mind at all suggesting they were too good for Hughes Sinclair, the effete child of a former Supreme Court justice and an accomplished ballerina. But they did not want to suggest they were too good for me, the Nebraska-raised offspring of a pig-blood mopper and his veiled Wal-Mart greeter wife. Picking on Hughes was sport. Picking on me would be mean.

"Addison McGhee is an inspiration to all Americans," wrote an editor of the *Columbia Journalism Review*. "But, as much as it pains us to say this, she is not a reporter."

"Oh, la-di-da," Hughes had said to that, leaping to my defense in a way that flattered me. "As if that should matter."

But the thing is, no one cares about Columbia or its review of journalism. Hughes himself told me so, and I supposed he knew. (Readership or not, I still added it to the pile of magazine cover shots I discreetly kept in my desk. They had me pose wearing nothing but newspapers—which only goes to show how intellectual they are.)

Columbia's journalism reviewers could say what they wanted, but I was soon named "woman of the year" by more than a few women's groups, the newly formed American Academy of Cable Hosts, and, most famously, by the East Coast Association of Irish American Television Personalities— an honor that Hughes found delightfully ridiculous.

He gave me a playful nudge the morning after the Irish American award was announced. "And here I thought those red highlights you were sporting last summer were hair coloring," he said.

I shrugged and played along, making the self-deprecating wave that I had perfected when brushing off rude questions from customers at SI. "Oh please," I said, grinning at the camera. "Irish is a state of mind."

Hughes laughed and slapped his knee and Baxter frowned and shook his head in a bemused and world-weary way, as if this was just another of my wild antics, claiming to be Irish.

(I did not "claim" to be Irish. I dutifully talked about my heritage whenever asked, and it was reported many times over the years in various publications, both serious and trivial. But what can I say? The East Coast Association of Irish American Television Personalities did not have a lot of candidates that year. They could not afford to be particular about their definition of *Irish*. Or, for that matter, *American*.)

Of all the accolades piled on *It's Morning Now,* the one I cherished most was from a reviewer in *The New York Times* who said our show was "sort of like *Anderson Cooper 360,* only with more flirting and recipes."

It was the flirting that got the most attention.

Hughes and I were routinely linked on the gossip pages, and every winsome smile, every casual pat on the arm, every charming exchange, was analyzed and argued over by devoted fans on our Web site's discussion boards. This amazed the show's Web master, because we did nothing to promote the discussion boards, which were somewhat hidden on the site. "Who are these people and how did they even find the boards?" he would ask. But whoever they were, there were apparently quite a lot of them, and they enjoyed picking over every Hughes–Addison exchange. And there was, at the peak, a lot to pick over. I spent a little time pondering it all myself.

"Did you notice the way she patted his arm this morning?" Addifan wrote in a typical post. "The way she said 'now, now,' when he was getting all worked up about the World Cup. Was it just me or did it seem a tad too familiar?"

And FargoMama, a self-described feminist housewife and mother of three, admitted, with an appropriately self-deprecating tone, that she was in something of a snit for a week after Hughes complimented me for a particularly insightful interview of the director of a movie that was deemed the "new" *Animal House*. FargoMama nursed a crush on Hughes and appeared insanely jealous of my relationship with him.

("You know, I know a little about fraternity initiation rituals," Hughes had said after we ran the taped interview. And I had given him an admiring look, fanned myself as if I were feeling flush, and added in a mock Southern accent, "Now, Hughes, you know how impressed I get when you start talking about swallowing goldfish.")

"I never knew that the phrase 'swallowing goldfish' could sound so suggestive," FargoMama wrote. (This from a woman who repeatedly shared a fantasy about "pushing Hughes down on the futon and biting off his buttons.")

At one point, *Ladies' Home Journal* devoted an entire cover story to the question: HUGHES AND ADDISON: ARE THEY OR AREN'T THEY? They polled various body-language experts, fortune-tellers, and celebrity "commentators" about whether our chemistry was real. The nearly unanimous verdict? Absolutely.

But there were two notable naysayers. President Briarwood said that Addison McGhee, like his own bride, was a real woman and thus would need more of a "real" man.

Ahem.

And Baxter Bailey surprised us by weighing in as well. "I sit as close to Ada and Hewey as anyone," he told the magazine. "And they don't have a thing in common."

*Well, Baxter Bailey,* I said to myself when I read that little tidbit. *What business is it of yours?*

# Chapter 8

$\mathcal{B}$axter's comment irritated Hughes, too, although his reasons for being upset were different from mine. I was offended by the suggestion that I had nothing in common with the man I was fawning over. Hughes was peeved about being called Hewey.

At least that is what he said. But I wondered if he just didn't feel comfortable talking about our relationship yet. We were, after all, at a tender stage. We flirted like mad on air, but privately did no more than enjoy platonic and low-calorie dinners together. I would tell myself the dinners meant nothing, but we were eating together at least five nights a week. The staff at our favorite place, Emilio's Café, would save a table for us near the back. (Not that they really had to work hard to save it, as we always ate at 4:30 PM. Hughes was embarrassed by this, because he thought it sounded positively Midwestern. But when you've been up since 3 AM, 4:30 PM counts as a late dinner.)

We dined together even as our agents and publicists were setting us up on fantastic dates with hot young stars. I might be photographed on the arm of Orlando or Derek Jeter or that guy from the new show about ghosts, but Hughes and I kept having dinner together. Hughes might be linked to any of a series of scandalously young women—including a minor British princess or two—but we kept having dinner together. I was spotted dancing with Ty Pennington. Hughes was photographed holding hands with Kristen Bell and, to the delight of those fans rooting for him to be gay, holding a door open for Carson Kressley at a fashion show. But every worknight, or technically afternoon, we ate together at Emilio's.

The day *LHJ* came out, Hughes could talk about nothing other than Baxter's comment—which is saying something, given the president's remark. I should not have been surprised, though. I know he feels strongly about his first name. He hates it when people drop the *s,* so *Hewey* would naturally irritate him even more.

"It's just laziness," Hughes said. "It's as if Baxter can't be bothered to pronounce my whole name."

I nodded sympathetically, although I didn't really see his point. *Hewey* has more syllables than *Hughes.* So wouldn't it take *more* effort to pronounce, not less?

Besides, I don't agree that nicknames are about laziness. Perhaps it's because Slater Countians are big nicknamers, generally. I grew up with that. I understand it. My old classmates were forever calling me Addy, and when that "Hey Mickey" song came out in 1982, well, suddenly that was me, too. "Oh Mickey, you're so fine." It still makes me smile.

I *liked* it that Baxter called me Ada. I found it endearing. Although *Ada* doesn't even count as a nickname for me. It was my original name, the one that my parents and brother still use for me—the one I always assumed my husband would use as well. But I didn't want to get into all that with Hughes, especially since I assumed his real concern was the more pertinent one—Baxter dissing our relationship. It upset me, too.

So I just sprinkled more vinegar on my field greens and sighed in a vaguely supportive way.

Hughes wasn't looking at me. He was just aggressively picking at his hydroponic Bibb salad with lemon-infused salmon,
which I noticed was loaded with dressing.

"You know, that's what's wrong with America," he continued, jabbing his fork at me for emphasis. "Laziness."

I could see that he was pretty riled up about this. He usually
considers fork pointing vulgar. (Miss Liberty agrees.) Hughes
launched into a full-blown Baxter impersonation.

"Hey, Hewey," Hughes said, shrugging in an Eeyore-esque
way that he thought was a close approximation of Baxter's casual
weariness. "Hey, Ada. What's up? Got anything in common?

"I mean seriously," Hughes concluded, back in his own
voice.

I smiled. See? He *did* notice the *don't-have-a-thing-in-
common* line. It *did* bother him.

"Aren't you irritated?" he asked. (Apparently smiling had
been the wrong move.)

"Oh, you know." I waved my hand in a way that suggested *just a little*. "My mother calls me Ada," I said. "So I'm
used to it."

Hughes swallowed hard several times as he processed this.
His eyes made an *aha* expression as he finally figured it out. He
took another bite of buttermilk dressing with a bit of carrot in
it. "Yeah, well, my mom sometimes calls me her little Pooh-
bear. Doesn't mean I want Baxter to!"

I felt a surge of affection for Hughes. He always put on
a show of superiority. (Well, it's not a show, really. He is the
most well-dressed, well-connected, well-educated, well-spoken
man I have ever met.) But I think he feels threatened by people
like Baxter and me. I suppose that's the curse of being Hughes,
when you think about it. He's praised over and over for his
sense of style and his fashion risk taking. But then he wears a
lavender (excuse me, periwinkle) tie on television and loses his

job. Women swoon over him for being so sensitive and sophisticated, but then get bent out of shape to see that he spends more on shoes than they do. Or that he knows more about Danish fashion.

Don't get me wrong. Hughes enjoys being more suave—more dashing and dapper—than the rest of us. But I think he understood that there is a fine line for celebrities—especially male ones. You must be better than everyone else, but not that much better.

Just that morning, there had been an on-air "incident" illustrating this problem. It came during a conversation about my *Vanity Fair* cover shot. You know, the one with the cotton balls. (When in doubt, Cal said more than once that month, talk about the cotton balls.)

Baxter had obliged with jokes—asking for swabs to clean his map and so forth—but he had, until that morning, pretended not to have actually seen the cover. It was part of his Cal-mandated shtick. This cover may have been the talk of the country, but Baxter was too busy tracking the weather to actually check it out.

But that morning he finished up his weather report, then turned to Hughes and me and acknowledged "finally" seeing me in the grocery line. "I was there picking up bread and milk—you know, preparing for the winter storms." He smiled slyly. (Baxter puzzled me. I could never tell how much of his act was real.) "And there, between the *Farmer's Almanac* and *Organic Gardening,* was Addison in this . . . this . . . this . . ."

He didn't come up with a word, but gestured in a way that suggested something light and fluffy and small.

"You know," he said, with mock amazement. "I'd *heard* about it, but actually seeing it? I have to say: Wow."

I obliged with a blush.

"My blood," Baxter continued, "ran cold." And then he started whistling "Centerfold" by the J. Giles Band.

I laughed. That was the cutest thing Baxter had ever said on air. It cracked me up. But Hughes just sat there primly, looking confused. " 'Centerfold,' " I said. "You know, the song about the guy who finds his high school crush in a girlie magazine."

Hughes looked blank and somewhat uncomfortable.

"Oh, come on, Hughes," I said. Baxter and I sang a few verses.

"Ah well," Hughes said. "I can see that it's quite on point."

"You never heard the song 'Centerfold'?" Baxter asked. "What did kids in your middle school listen to? Classical music?"

"Of course not," he said, bristling. "We were into ska."

Baxter rolled his eyes.

"Oh, you were not," I said, sure that he was mistaken. "Not in middle school. Ska made its comeback in the nineties."

Hughes gave me a withering look. "Maybe in Nebraska." He glanced at Baxter. "Or California."

"Well," I said, with mock outrage.

"Well," said Baxter, with outrage that was not quite so clearly mock.

See, Hughes was smart enough to know those "common man" touches of Baxter's—his off-the-rack clothes, his nicknames, his weary bemusement about topics Hughes considered vitally important (celebrity gossip, fashion, the geopolitical implications of the latest Schwarzenegger film, that kind of thing)—were dangerous. Not dangerous in the normal sense of the word, but in the sense of "Who's the most popular guy on *It's Morning Now?*"

Suddenly, sitting there in the restaurant, Hughes looked, to me, fragile. He also looked to be taking solace in an overly generous portion of croutons—or, rather, what the menu called "herb-basted, dried whole wheat crumbs." *Poor Hewey,* I thought.

Hughes did not need to feel threatened as far as I was concerned. Baxter's common touches did not bother me, but they also did not impress me. I didn't want a common guy. Common guys are, well, common. You can find one anywhere. But how was Hughes supposed to know I felt that way?

I vowed to back Hughes up on this, to prove whose side I was on. I would not answer to *Ada,* I would not chuckle about '80s rock hits, and I would not even speak to Baxter the next day—other than on the air. I would have to speak to him on air to remain professional. Hughes would understand that. And I supposed I would have to engage in the minimal conversation needed to appear polite during meetings around the office. If I didn't speak at all, that would create an awkward scene. (Miss Liberty was very much against scenes.)

I would be civil, but there would be no more idle gossip between Baxter and me. I wouldn't ask about the weather or complain about the coffee. I would not even ask his opinion about whether my teacup matched my suit. (I love the Kate Spade Rutherford Circle pattern, but I find the green a very difficult shade to match.)

I would not even say yes when Baxter asked if he could fetch the news stories I sent to the printer. (I always made copies of the best pop-culture reports each morning so that I could keep them in a folder on the coffee table and study them during commercial breaks or, truthfully, the weather reports.) In fact, I thought, that would be a good way to rack up a few more steps on my pedometer. Every little bit helped!

I imagined with satisfaction that Baxter would poke his head into my office and offer to stop by the printer for me—it was on his way to the coffee machine. But I would say *No, no, I'll get them myself.*

I was wondering if I should tell Hughes about my plan for Baxter when my cell phone broke into song, embarrassing me. (Miss Liberty did not address cell phones, needless to say. But I'm quite sure she would not approve of them interrupting dinner.)

I dug my phone out to quickly silence it, but out of habit glanced at the caller ID. It said: "White House." I furrowed my brow, made a motion of apology to Hughes—who had started studying some art over my shoulder anyway—and said, "Hello?"

"White House operator. May I speak to Addison McGhee?"

"This is she," I said, fiddling nervously with my fork. I mouthed *White House* to Hughes, who marked his surprise by sitting up even straighter than usual, something I would not have thought possible if I'd not seen it with my own eyes.

"Yes, Ms. McGhee, please hold for the president."

I fumbled for a pen in my purse, grabbed a tissue, then a gum wrapper, and finally the wine list from Hughes's side of the table. I had no idea what was coming, but a good journalist has a pen in her hand and paper at her disposal when she talks to the president.

"Addison, Addison, Addison," the familiar voice said in his best *just-folks* accent. "Great little show you've got. The senator and I watch it every morning now, every single morning."

"I'm flattered, Mr. President," I said. (I wrote "great little show" on the wine list.)

Hughes grew another quarter inch at the words "Mr. President."

"It's on so early," I added.

"Yes, well, we don't always catch the beginning . . ." The president's voice trailed off. "Though I do like hearing you say 'Wake up, honey.'"

I'm ashamed to admit that I giggled at that. I mean, really. Giggling to the president? Especially after he'd insulted Hughes! Still, I wasn't sure what else I should do. Oblige him with a *wake up, honey*? Giggling seemed as good a move as any. He apparently agreed because he moved on without comment.

"So Mag and I—I mean, the senator and I—are having a little barbecue on Friday. Very casual, last-minute sort of thing. Telephone invites only. The etiquette experts are having fits. But I say if you can't call your friends up and say come on over for a burger, what's the point of being president?"

Was this a joke? First of all, it was hardly barbecue weather. It was the middle of winter. I glanced out the window and saw that, just as Baxter had predicted, there were flurries.

More to the point, I was not—by any stretch—a friend of the president. My four-minute interview with him before the wedding was the only contact I'd ever had with him, and his clumsy attempts to compliment me had always seemed more grating than anything. And did I mention that he'd insulted Hughes? I'm not even much of a fan of the president's politics, truth be told. But of course I never said so on the show.

I looked around the room. Could I be on *Punk'd*? (I'd suspected Ashton was out to get me ever since I went to a house-warming for him and Demi and we got into a debate about whether corn produced in Nebraska really was sweeter than that grown in his native Iowa.)

I couldn't think of a polite way to ask if this was a joke, so I decided to focus on the more obvious issue. "Barbecue?" I asked.

"Indoor barbecue, of course," the president said quickly. "Taste of summer in the winter. That kind of thing."

"Oh," I said. I glanced at Hughes and then said, "Ah."

"You know, Addison," the president continued. He paused. "You don't mind if I call you Addison, do you?"

"Of course not, Mr. President."

"You know, Addison, I thought your role on *ER* was groundbreaking for women."

"Really?" I said. I'd never heard *that* before. I think the word I had heard the most was *disgraceful*. Although that may have just been from my mother.

"Oh yes," he said. "It was inspiring to see a woman who wasn't hemmed in by society's sexual double standards, a woman who enjoyed sex as much as a man."

"Ah," I said. I was at a bit of a loss. I looked around the room again for the hidden camera. "Well," I said, "it was an interesting role."

"And that gauze bikini . . ." The president's voice trailed off, but then he suddenly found it again. "Yes, interesting."

I wondered if someone had just entered the room.

"So," said the president. "Bring that guy you're dating— Baxter, isn't it?"

I hesitated, looked across the table, simply froze. I could not, in good faith, say *No, no, I'm dating Hughes.* Because at that point, I was not at all sure that I was. Just friendly co-workers eating dinner together every single night of the work-week, that's all we were. At the same time, Hughes was staring at me, hanging on every word of this phone call, so I couldn't very well say: *I'm not dating anyone.* Because, well, I wasn't sure that I wasn't.

And did this mean that the president had misunderstood the question that *LHJ* put to him? Did he know which of the male co-hosts was Baxter and which was Hughes? Should I try in some way to correct him?

I swallowed again.

"Baxter *is* a good friend," I said, going with the safest option. "And I'll be happy to ask him if he's free to join me."

Hughes's eyebrows shot up at that.

I smiled weakly, being at a loss for any appropriate, silent expression. Not that I would have done much better if I'd been free to speak.

*"Friend,"* the president said. *"Gotcha.* Well, we'll see you both Friday at eight. I'll put someone on with the security details."

He did so, and after I got the detailed instructions from the Secret Service, I clicked off and laid the phone down gently on the table. Hughes was watching me with stunned interest.

"That was the president," I said.

Hughes stared at me, raised an eyebrow again. "I gathered."

"He wants Baxter and me to come over for a barbecue Friday."

Hughes took a long sip, dare I say, a *swig* of wine.

"Baxter and you," he said finally.

I shrugged. Leaned forward. "Do you think this is some sort of joke?"

Hughes smiled then in a familiar way. I think he appreciated my recognition of how odd it was. That the president would call me, rather than the child of a former chief justice, that the president suggested bringing Baxter rather than the man I flirted with every day in front of a nation of viewers. That the phone call had happened at all, frankly.

"No, no," he said. "I mean . . ." His voice trailed off. "Did it sound like him?"

I nodded. "It did."

"You're a star, honey," Hughes said. (And don't think I didn't notice the *honey*.) "People in power love stars."

"Yes, well . . ." There were a lot of ellipses in this conversation. "But Baxter and me? Why just the two of us?"

Hughes shrugged. He had his game face on now, I guess. "Oh, you know. The president probably hasn't gotten over my dad's vote on that constitutional crisis back in the eighties. For a guy who wasn't even in office at the time, he seemed to take that awfully personally."

(That was true. The president had mentioned Hughes's dad several times in his campaign, calling him "Ol' Sinister Sinclair" as often as not.)

Hughes took another bite of salad. "That's probably what his comment in the magazine was about, too. Man enough? Hrrmph. He just feels threatened by anyone with a sense of style."

"Well," I said again, and then paused awkwardly. "I suppose I'd better call Baxter."

"By all means," Hughes said. And then he excused himself to the men's room, a decent thing to do, allowing Baxter and me to golly and gee-whiz ourselves through the conversation without feeling uncomfortable about Hughes's uninvited presence listening to the whole thing. (Baxter gollied and gee-whizzed so much that he absolutely forgot to be grumpy. I still intended to be cold to Baxter, but this did not seem the right time to start.)

The next morning, Baxter and I were barely able to focus on the show—as we went on and on about why the president would have invited us. (I did not share with Baxter the president's incorrect assessment of our relationship.) And we further went on about what we should wear. The president had classified this as a casual, almost impromptu event, but we wondered if White House casual was the same as regular casual. I assumed that for Baxter the entire conversation was academic, because I thought it went without saying that he would wear one of his seersucker suits and his most patriotic bow tie—a star-spangled blue number. But I saw my decision, by contrast, as deeply, personally, exceptionally important. It was, I felt, a decision that would determine my entire future. And I guess in a way it did.

You know what I wore. It became, for a while, the defining

photo of me, and it was as wrongheaded as it could be. How much I wished, afterward, that I had asked Hughes's advice. But it had seemed cruel, somehow, to pester him for insight and help. So I called Ryan Seacrest, who was sleep-deprived as always and in a bit of a funk about a recent bad review. He was not at his best. He offered as his advice two little words. Two words that he would regret and I would regret and that a nation of women would regret.

Ryan said: "Parachute pants."

# Chapter 9

$\mathcal{I}$ do not blame Ryan. He's a dear. He's every bit as golden as his reputation and he's the only one who, during this ordeal, has never turned his back on me. He sent hair care products to me here in prison. And he has written me several times, just sweet little short notes, acting as if nothing was going on in my life at all. "Darling," he might write. "Did you see my show last night? Did I handle that tearful contestant well enough? No one understands how hard it is for me."

Needless to say, I didn't see the show, as it was not played on Lifetime. But it was still nice of him to ask. It is times like this when you realize who your friends are.

And anyway, really, the parachute thing wasn't that bad, I don't suppose. Setting off goofy trends is a celebrity's job. Ryan had read an article about a New York store that specialized in retro fashions and had argued that parachute pants, while obviously casual, would be casual in a way that made a statement, as opposed to just showing up in jeans. I thought this made sense. I repeated it to Baxter several times. I remembered that the girl who lived next door to me in Slater County, decades earlier, often wore a particularly impressive sea-blue pair. When I saw a pair like them at the retro store, I thought, *That's it*.

And, you know, maybe it would have been fine. Baxter did

say I looked nice, didn't he? And the whole thing did prompt a frenzy, didn't it? Yes, I'm quite sure the pants would have been fine if the president hadn't been drinking.

Baxter and I flew to DC on Cal's jet. We were very impressed. It had a little kitchenette, including a coffeemaker. Everyone who works on morning television drinks a lot of coffee and we were delighted to see it, though the coffee wasn't frankly all that good. Neither of us acknowledged that, though. We were just so impressed to be on a jet with a coffeemaker. I was momentarily relieved that I was with Baxter. Hughes would have certainly sneered about the quality of the coffee or the decor of the jet. (It *did* seem a tad 2002 to me, but 2002 was a good year, all in all. I personally thought it was fine. I was just surprised because Cal usually does not like for things to become dated.) Baxter allowed himself to be amazed. "Look," he said, after opening a small nondescript door. "There's a dining room in here!" We both clapped with glee, though we were not going to actually eat on the plane.

A limo picked us up at the airport and took us to the White House, where there were some drawn-out security precautions. But the White House is quite accustomed to carrying off security clearances with style and panache. There was a short consultation about my status as a permanent resident. They looked over my green card carefully and I gathered that I was the only noncitizen invited to this particular White House occasion. But they did so with enough discreet grace that even Baxter did not notice.

(They were not as discreet, I'm afraid, about my pants, which I saw a few Secret Service agents eyeing with raised brows.)

But once all that was over, we were ushered into one of the ballrooms, which had been decked out like a summer garden. "This is what the White House does on short notice?" I whispered to Baxter as he escorted me into the room of powerful party-goers. And he said he supposed it was.

Hillary Clinton looked overly pressed and hot (not in a good way) in a black pantsuit. Bob Dole was wearing wrinkled khaki shorts and a T-shirt that said I'M RETIRED—THIS IS AS DRESSED UP AS I GET. Elizabeth Dole stood next to him wearing, I kid you not, an evening gown. She looked exceedingly uncomfortable as she talked to Jenna Bush, who was wearing flip-flops and jeans with several artfully ripped holes in them. Jenna picked at one of the holes in what I thought was a self-conscious manner.

Tipper Gore wore a simple sundress that seemed as appropriate as anything, and she was the first to approach us. "Addison!" she said. "Baxter!" She shook our hands enthusiastically. "I heard you were coming."

She glanced at my clothes and leaned forward. "Excellent choice," she whispered. "It's casual, but it makes a statement."

Baxter grunted, allowed the corners of his mouth to twitch upward. "That," he said, "is exactly what she was going for."

Tipper smiled at him, then leaned toward me again. "I hear the president is quite a fan of yours."

"Oh," I said, making one of my standard dismissive waves of the hand. "I'm sure that's exaggerated."

She leaned even closer, lowered her voice still more. Baxter was standing right there and he couldn't hear her. "Watch out," she said. "That man is a pig."

"The president?" I said.

She closed her eyes and nodded.

I have often thought of her warning words. "That man is a pig." How differently things might have turned out if I had taken them literally. Because my fateful encounter with the president occurred just about an hour later during my attempt to avoid being photographed with the large hog hanging over a fake barbecue pit. *My parents would die if that photo got out,* I thought, and so—when the White House photographer had started shooting around the pit—I quickly extracted myself from a conversation with Clarence Thomas (denim shorts, Polo shirt) and pretended to be making a dash for a glass of water. "Something stuck in my throat," I (fakely) choked out.

If I had taken Tipper's comment literally, if I'd thought of the president as a pig, I would have taken the long way around, avoiding him as well as the actual farm animal. But instead I dashed from the pit to the bar, going straight by the bench where the president was sitting. Three or four empty beer bottles sat at his feet.

President Samson Briarwood glanced up at me and smiled. I smiled back politely, but then I noticed that his smile had sort of a leering quality. He appeared to think I was shimmying toward him in tight parachute pants, rather than running from a dead hog as fast as discretion would allow. Before I knew what was happening, the president had grabbed me, pulled me into his lap, and planted a kiss on my lips just as the White House photographer snapped his fateful shot. (The photo was really supposed to be of the hog, which was in the foreground. But you probably didn't even realize that because all the papers cropped the picture and zoomed in as tightly as they could on the president and me.)

It must have lasted only seconds. I cannot imagine that a full minute passed. But it seemed to happen in slow motion. First, I felt his hand yank my arm. I fell back into his lap, my legs shooting upward in an unladylike way. My blouse gaped open as the president slipped his arm around my waist. He reeked of cheap beer, bad cologne, and something else. (Barbecued pork, perhaps?) His lips were badly chapped. My thoughts came fast and incoherently. I remember thinking *No!* and *But my parents!* and, simply, *Yuck!*

I gasped, and then squirmed away and made a dash for the ladies' room. David Souter (dark suit) stepped aside, nodding in a solemn and knowing way. Christine Todd Whitman (little black dress) crossed her arms and put her hands over her eyes, as if trying to erase what she had seen. Ted Kennedy (horrible Panama shirt and unflattering cream-colored trousers) looked at me with an expression that was, well, hard to read.

I got to the ladies' room door, grabbed the handle, and glanced backward. I saw Baxter standing in the beer line and looking at me with a mix of sympathy and shared outrage. I was surprised. I had expected him, I guess, to be bemused. I think Hughes would have been bemused.

Perhaps that is unfair to Hughes. It's not that Hughes would have approved of what the president did. I'm not saying that. But I don't think, coming from the world he comes from, he would have understood my reaction to it. My deep-seated revulsion and horror.

I think Baxter did. Somehow. In some way that was hard to put my finger on, Baxter and I were from the same place, relative to Hughes. Baxter realized that I could not, at that moment, imagine a worse development for my life and career.

And then an arm reached out from the ladies' room and pulled me inside. It was the first lady. Or should I call her the junior senator from Ohio?

# Chapter 10

$\mathcal{D}$o I hate Senator Margaret Clemons-Briarwood, the junior senator from Ohio and the first lady of these United States?

Many people have asked me that. Susan Sarandon, Katie Couric, Michael Moore, to name a few. Although really, Katie was the only one who said, "Do you hate?"; the rest said, "Don't you hate?"—a critical difference of tone.

But honestly, I try not to hate anyone. Least of all, an inspirational woman like Senator Clemons-Briarwood. For one thing, Miss Liberty did not like strong emotions, and I'm pretty sure "hate" would qualify.

Besides, I try to maintain some perspective. It is true that Senator Clemons-Briarwood has very nearly ruined my life. But I think she would say that I very nearly ruined hers. I try to remain dignified. Living well is the best revenge and all that. Living well is, unfortunately, a bit difficult to pull off in a prison cell. But as Hughes pointed out, I have never looked better. And judging by one of those Lifetime biographies I saw about the good senator the other day, the same cannot be said for her.

I do not hate her. But I am not going to sugarcoat the truth. So I will reveal now for the first time what the first lady said to me on the night of the infamous barbecue where every-thing started to go wrong.

Senator Clemons-Briarwood (floral Capri pants and shiny pink wrap top) pulled me into the bathroom and told me that what she was about to say was off the record and if I told any-one about it, she would send my "skinny ass" back to "wher-ever it was" that I came from.

*Skinny?* I thought excitedly, distracted by the unintentional compliment. I glanced back over my shoulder and thought the parachute pants must be flattering indeed.

The senator/first lady ignored that. She lowered her voice in an apparently conciliatory way. She confessed that her hus-band had a drinking problem. "A bit of a bad habit" is the way she put it. At least I assumed she was talking about the drink-ing; maybe he habitually dragged unsuspecting women into his lap and planted unwelcome kisses on their lips. Or maybe it was the combination of the drinking and the dragging that was the habit she referred to.

At any rate, the nice tone did not last long. She went on to say I'd better not tell anyone about what happened or I'd be "using those pants to parachute into the desert with a foot-print" on my behind. (No flattering adjective that time.)

"I think," I said, "there was a photo taken."

"Are you *threatening me*?" the first lady said, veins bulging from her forehead.

"No." I began to feel truly rattled by now. "I'm just saying that I don't know what to do if the photo comes out."

"I'll take care of the photo," the first lady hissed. And then said: "You just take care of those big lips of yours."

Big lips? Was that a racial slur? I'm sure I don't know.

At any rate, I told the first lady she need not worry about me, my big lips, or my skinny ass.

She started crying then and grabbed a tissue to dry her

eyes. "I always cry when I get really angry," she said. I nodded and said that I did as well. She blew her nose, then took her eyeliner pencil out of her purse and started to work on the emergency touch-ups. She didn't look at me, but straight into the mirror. She said, "I really do love him, you know."

I said nothing.

"Sure, I started dating him for the political benefit. Why not? Everyone thought I was such a wacko radical. What could soften up my image more than hooking up with a radical from the other side? We both had to be more moderate than we let on, that's what people would figure. Our poll numbers went through the roof."

"I remember," I said.

"But then I went and fell in love with the big lug." She dropped her eyeliner pencil into her purse and snapped it closed. "Don't get me wrong. His fiscal policies are a night-mare. His tax plan is *insane*. But he's so sweetly sincere about it. I just love a sincere man."

"Ah," I said. That did explain it. The president always did come across as sincere, you know, in a badly dressed way. And women do tend to be suckers for some attribute or another. Sincerity is as good as any. "For me," I said, "it's laugh lines around the eyes. I can't resist a guy whose eyes crinkle when he smiles."

The senator/first lady stared at me and then continued as if I had not spoken.

"I violated my mom's first rule of relationships," she said. "Never fall in love with the guy you marry."

She washed her hands, then said: "Love is nothing but trouble, you know."

I nodded, made some vague sound of agreement, then excused myself and beat a hasty path out of the restroom and back to Baxter. He asked in a puzzled and polite tone if everything was okay. I waved my hand in a dismissive way and said: "Fine, fine."

He gracefully looked away and did not argue when I suggested leaving early. He even patted me on the back as we left. We did not say much on the plane ride home.

That night, I couldn't sleep in my luxury hotel bed. (I kept thinking Cal would ask why I was still living in the hotel room he'd booked for me back when I was only in town for a one-week show. But keeping a handle on expenses was never Cal's strength.) I tried to lull myself to sleep by spending even more time than usual "checking my e-mail"—a private code for reading the boards. Getting online at night to see what people were saying about you on message boards sounds kind of pathetic and needy, even when admitted only to yourself. Checking your e-mail, though? That sounds so professional and efficient. Why let an important message wait until tomorrow when you can reply today!

Sadly, no one had posted anything about Hughes or me on the boards since before Baxter and I had left for Washington—hours ago. I was disappointed, but it was a Friday night. I guess people had other things to do.

I considered going to bed, but then I found myself logging onto Baxter's discussion groups.

When I looked over the discussion, I felt bad for him. There were hardly any comments at all, and what was there was so harsh. I suppose all the boards had snarky comments. Mine certainly did. So did Hughes's. But the harsh comments were diluted, in our case, by over-the-top praise. There wasn't much of that on Baxter's boards.

The poster Baxterbasher called Baxter mean and ugly and bitter and, most inexplicably, "old." B-basher said that Baxter pronounced his *t*'s like *d*'s and dropped some of his *n*'s in a way that made him sound slightly drunk. "Sunny in Mahadden today." And B-basher further added that the talk of Baxter being mysterious was especially laughable as the only mystery was why Addison and Hughes didn't boo him off the set.

Moved by pity, I broke—for the first time—my rule about not posting on the boards. I had always thought that if I actually started writing on the boards, it would be a sign that I had completely lost control of my online life. I could justify *reading* the boards. That was just viewer research. I needed to keep in touch with what the fans thought. But joining the discussion by posting my own comments? That would be going too far.

I told myself that this was different. I was just sticking up for old Baxter, who had patted my back supportively as we hightailed it out of the White House and who had not acted bemused at my obvious discomfort. I logged on, giving myself the name *ObjectiveObserver,* a nod to how I always tried to watch the tapes later in a detached, objective way.

"I'm afraid," I wrote, "that I don't see where you're coming from, B-basher. Baxter's a sweet man. He's kind and patient. You can tell that . . ."

I paused there because I was not sure where, exactly, a viewer would see it, what with his brooding on-air persona. But after a moment's thought, the examples poured forth.

"You can see it in the way he lightens the mood whenever Hughes is being a little too hard on Addison. You know, the way Baxter chuckles wearily at the Irish jokes, so wearily that it takes the sting out of the moment. Haven't you noticed the way he talks about tornadoes and floods and the passion he brings to the subject?"

I sensed that I was edging into ridiculousness when I started explaining how Baxter's lack of fashion sense worked as a much-needed counterpoint to Hughes's obsession with being chic and that Baxter's clothes "served as a postmodern commentary on the nature of television as a visual medium."

But I didn't care about being ridiculous. It was liberating to post observations in this anonymous way. I had never felt so authoritative as when I was analyzing my own show.

That simple post about Baxter was the start of things, I suppose. I was thrilled to receive a reply to my first message almost immediately. A poster known as Weatherjunkie wrote: "Well said and welcome to you ObjectiveObserver. Hope to see you posting on the boards again soon."

Sad to say, Weatherjunkie did. In fact, I replied immediately and we exchanged four or five friendly posts that very night. I casually admitted feeling a little depressed after a "disastrous social encounter" and Weatherjunkie replied, saying 80 percent of social encounters left him depressed.

I was enjoying our "conversation" so much that I nearly forgot my embarrassment about the turn of events at the barbecue—until I briefly returned to the Addison McGhee board to find this post from someone called MorningFan.

"So," MorningFan wrote. "Addison went to the White House with Baxter? Hmm. Do you think she finally figured out that Hughes is gay?"

# Chapter 11

*E*arly this morning, Cassie came to see me again. She arrived at the visiting room all chatty and happy. I had not been expecting her. But when I said so, she scoffed at me. "I had to bring you some clothes, didn't I? It's Tuesday! The hearing is tomorrow!"

She carried with her a spiffy skirt and jacket from the Versace fall collection that Ryan Seacrest had shipped to her. She said the suit was fine, despite the shawl collar being a bit dramatic for the occasion. But she did not like—at all—the glittery tank top that Ryan had selected to go with it. Blazoned across the front were the words: BITCH FROM JAIL.

"I think it's supposed to be ironic," I explained.

"It's not," Cassie replied.

She said that she'd lend me a conservative ivory blouse to wear. (She always kept a couple of extras in her briefcase for coffee spills, lipstick smudges, and other emergencies. She was that kind of person.) I feared her blouse would be tight in the chest and big in the waist, but I just thanked her and silently planned to go without a blouse.

I did question the black pumps, which were low-heeled, devoid of detail, and boring in every sense of the word. I glanced at the tag. "You ordered these from Lands' End?" I said. I tried to sound upbeat about it, but I had once heard Hughes refer to Lands' End as "Fashion's End." I still can't help putting a lot of stock in Hughes's opinion. Even now. Even when he shouldn't matter to me at all.

"Yeah," Cassie said. "Lands' End has great deals on shoes. They hold up well and they look nice enough. No one pays attention to shoes, anyway."

I wasn't sure that "holding up well" was the primary consideration for someone in my particular situation. But I couldn't see how saying so would accomplish much. So I just fingered the shoes, absentmindedly.

"Now," she said, still breezy and happy. "Let's see what you've written." She plopped down next to me, put on her reading glasses, and held up my papers with a big smile. "Good, good," she had said. "Nice thick pile of papers. I'm sure this will help."

But the farther she read, the more she grimaced. At one point, her fingers moved up to the bridge of her nose, just as Hughes's had. Am I giving everyone a migraine these days?

"You don't like it," I said.

"Addison, Addison, Addison." She closed her eyes, rubbed her cheek wearily. "I didn't really need this much information about George Clooney or *Hollywood Squares*." She flipped through the pages again, looked at the ceiling, and sighed. "And I had forgotten about the gauze bikini and the 'wrapped in newspaper' cover."

She stood up, looked at her watch.

"Also, I'm obligated as an officer of the court," she said, "to point out to you that the conditions of your sentencing forbid you from speaking to Hughes."

I nodded.

Her voice softened. "I'm obligated as your friend to point out that he's been nothing but trouble from day one. Don't see him again."

"You're right," I said.

She stood up as if to leave. But instead she looked at me for a long moment. There was a touch of vulnerability in her face, something I had not seen for a long time—perhaps not since her Pork Queen effort.

"I'm so tired," she said. "I'm going on all these cable talk shows, waxing on about this stuff. I don't know why. Who cares what Geraldo thinks? Meanwhile, I've still got a big turkey dinner to plan. My in-laws are getting here tonight. The kids are all excited. But I don't even have time to think about it."

I had forgotten in the sterile seasonless world of prison that this is Thanksgiving week. Cassie had, I remembered now, argued against scheduling my hearing the day before the holiday, but the judge said he certainly hoped no one expected the testimony to last more than a few hours. "We'll all be home late Wednesday afternoon," he had said, looking at the lawyers in a pointed way. "Easily."

Suddenly I felt very bad for Cassie. I know how much big holiday gatherings mean to her. Even as a girl, she would get all excited about helping her mom make cranberry sauce. I didn't know what to say, so I just nodded.

There was a long pause, and then she added, "My mother-in-law claims I always overcook the turkey."

She glanced down at my stack of papers. "Also, as a point of fact, there were four contestants in the Pork Queen competition. Lindsay Martin came in fourth. She sang 'Over the Rainbow' and tap-danced."

"No, no," I said. "Remember she fell while tap-dancing? She ran off the stage—well, off the flatbed—crying and shouting, 'I quit.'"

Cassie turned and was on her way out the door. She looked over her shoulder and glared at me. "She still got fourth place."

There was a pause.

"Get your affairs in order, Addison." She didn't meet my eyes. Her voice was soft. "Say your good-byes."

I allowed myself to feel a little discouraged. *Getting your affairs in order* is, in and of itself, not exactly an uplifting thought. But it was the casual *Say your good-byes* that really got me.

I hadn't thought about it that way, somehow. If I get deported, I'll be leaving people—my parents, that cute guy at the Starbucks near the studio who always gave me a free upgrade to a Venti. Even Hughes.

Yesterday when he came to visit, I just treated it like the "latest" episode in our little ongoing saga. I didn't think about it being, perhaps, the last time I would ever see him. I didn't think about it being my last chance for "closure."

And Baxter. What about Baxter?

Cassie had left me a videotape with some of the media coverage of my case. The guard walked me to the audiovisual room, and I shoved the cassette into the player with a loud sigh. The tape did nothing to improve my mood.

Leno made a joke about the "good news" that I'd already landed a job in my new country—hostess of *It's Morning Now: The Desert Edition*. The bad news, he said, was that I'd be paid in chickens.

Lou Dobbs—not known for his concern for the problems facing holders of green cards—tossed to Anderson Cooper by asking, "Why on earth is this McGhee case getting so much attention?"

Anderson pointed out that no celebrity had ever been deported before, which segued nicely into the clip from Regis and Kelly. "Has anyone ever been deported before?" Regis asked. And Kelly said: "Not anyone I know."

The tape concluded with an immigration expert telling Greta Van Susteren that the result really looked inevitable. "Addison McGhee is going home," he said.

# Chapter 12

It says something about my naïveté and my misguided priorities that on the weekend that began with the first lady threatening to deport me, I became consumed with the question of whether Hughes Sinclair was gay.

MorningFan's simple question—"Do you think she finally figured out that Hughes is gay?"—caught me entirely off guard. I was sitting in an armchair, which I'd pulled up to the built-in desk at my Midtown hotel. I had been celebrating my extended conversation with Weatherjunkie—the poster who said 80 percent of social encounters left him feeling depressed—by eating an ice cream sandwich from the mini bar. (Fifty calories, no fat, no added sugar.)

I chewed slowly as I read MorningFan's comment. It still rings in my head.

*Do you think she finally figured out that Hughes is gay?*

I drummed my fingers on the empty space around the built-in mouse on my laptop. I took two quick bites of the ice cream sandwich—so much for savoring. I swallowed, hard. Harder than you need to swallow an ice cream sandwich.

Nah, I thought.

Then I thought more.

Actually, that would explain a lot.

I took another bite of my ice cream sandwich.

Curiosity got the best of me. "MorningFan," I wrote, tentatively. "Where do you get your information?" I felt I was crossing some great line. Not only was I continuing to violate my rule about posting on the boards, which were already sapping great wads of time that would be better spent working on my abs, but I also was seeking an anonymous and probably unreliable stranger's information about my own good friend.

I reread the note. And what struck me at that moment was not the legitimate concerns that should have stopped me. No, I thought the note was too confrontational, too journalistic, too formal.

I backspaced. Started over. "Gay?" I said, with calculated casualness. "Oh, come on. Some of you guys never will get over that lavender tie incident."

And I waited.

*You can't believe what you read on the boards,* I told myself. *These are people who don't know what they're talking about.*

Still, I wasn't about to shrug it off and go to bed. I clicked around, literally, all night, reading everything I could find about Hughes on the Web. Which was a lot, really. There was so much I didn't know about him. His grandfather was apparently quite the philanthropist, and his great-great-grandmother was a bit of a character, creating a stir by wearing pants and keeping her own name way back in the 1800s. And Hughes's father, the former chief justice, was credited with practically saving the nation during that constitutional crisis while he was on the bench. (At least he was credited with that by the people who agreed with him.) His mother, meanwhile, was believed by some critics to have performed "the world's most perfect fouetté." Yes, the Sinclair family, I learned with delight, practically defined America.

There was never a mention, in any of it, about Hughes having a girlfriend. *But not a boyfriend, either,* I told myself.

I clicked around in an increasingly frantic way, reading up on "gaydar"—to see if I could develop some. And further reading up on flirtatious body language, trying to see if he used any with me. ("You can lie with your words," one of the Web pages said. "But not with your body.")

I wasn't sure, really, why I was reacting quite so strongly. Certainly I was crazy about Hughes. I had clearly built him up in my mind as the embodiment of some sort of American ideal. I had, during our many platonic after-work dinners, entertained fantasies that our relationship was going somewhere.

Obviously, I would be disappointed to learn that my crush was hopeless. But sitting there in my hotel room, racing around the Web for hours that really should have been spent sleeping, it occurred to me that my behavior was not, perhaps, completely ordinary.

I realized I might have a problem of some sort.

But what sort? That was the question.

When the sun rose, I pulled the laptop over to the bed, where I could, at least, recline as I continued to surf. I eventually nodded into a restless, uncomfortable sleep. I woke at 6 PM, and the first glance in the mirror was startling. I had the imprint of a keyboard on my cheek and crumbs from the ice cream sandwich on my face. I looked—dare I say it?—absolutely haggard. On the bright side, I realized that sleeping away the day meant I had made my way through an entire Saturday without eating.

I spent the rest of the weekend in a fitful state, checking the boards over and over again, unable to understand why MorningFan had not responded to my message. What else could he be doing on a weekend?

Finally, I forced myself to go to bed early on Sunday

night—trying to get myself back on a regular work schedule. It wouldn't do to have bags under my eyes. On Monday, I "checked my e-mail" one last time before heading into the office. The only new post was from a site administrator who had not approved of Weatherjunkie and me chatting about our social encounters. We were admonished to, in the future, keep our discussions "on the topic of Baxter Bailey and his entirely new approach to weather." (I think that was partially sarcastic.)

I sighed, logged off, headed into work—where I was surprised to find everyone asking about my evening at the White House. By that point, it seemed like old news to me. I wasn't even worried about the photo. The simple truth is that I believed the first lady. She was powerful and confident and not afraid to take charge. She would not hesitate to threaten, or even blackmail, to get her way. I naively believed that if she promised to "take care" of a photo, especially one taken by a White House employee, then she could and she would. I didn't give it another thought.

I told everyone who asked that Baxter and I had a marvelous time watching a pig cook on a faux pit and eating its carcass at the president's home. And Baxter agreed that it had been spectacular. I don't know if he knew we were lying.

It did not take me long to realize I was in a bit of a downward spiral. I was totally losing control. I was posting all the time. I remember one night in particular when I ate *three* of those low-fat ice cream bars while waiting for replies from Weatherjunkie and searching, in vain as usual, for a response from MorningFan.

Three bars! That's 150 calories right there. And I found myself thinking, *If I had just one more, that would be two hundred calories. That's not so bad, for a snack. Just two hundred calories? That's hardly anything.* See. I was out of my *mind.* Then I slapped myself in the face and ran down the hotel hallway and into the stairwell, forcing myself to do five laps up ten flights of stairs. That undid the ice cream damage, but left me without any remaining willpower when it came to the Internet. I read *everything*. I posted *everywhere*. I didn't care. The Internet might suck up your time, exacerbate your worst tendencies, and lead you down a path of ruin. But it won't make you fat. At least not directly.

I started by poring over the boards where people discussed me, but quickly found that did not help my mood. Reading notes from people who are spending the wee hours of the morning talking about you—whether it be good or bad—does not exactly erase paranoia.

Besides, I had nothing in common with those people. The people who were fawning over Hughes, though—they were kindred spirits. I would giggle with them. I would share their enthusiasm. I could read long threads of discussions about, say, Hughes's suits, the general consensus being that he needed to dump the gray ones. *Oh, no, no, no,* I thought, but still I appreciated that they shared my interest in the matter. We discussed the vital issues of the day. "Has Hughes whitened his teeth again? Or has the lighting in the studio improved?"

It was several days before MorningFan responded to my "casual" question about why he thought Hughes was gay. MorningFan said only: "Oh, come on, ObjectiveObserver . . . *observe*. He's as gay as, well, as gay as that gay bar he frequents in the gayest section of Chelsea."

I laughed with glee at the note. I happened to know that a lot of straight celebrities frequented that bar. Vince Vaughn had been there just the other day. He's as straight as you can get!

So that bar meant nothing. MorningFan was just filled

with your typical ill-informed board bluster. I was ridiculous to get so upset. That is what I told myself.

Besides, that very morning, Hughes had confessed to me and all of America—or at least the small but big-spending segment of America that watched us—that for the past several years he had nursed an agonizing crush on Mia Hamm. It was a confession that filled me, in those long-ago innocent days, with relief and jealousy. "Oh please," I said, not knowing quite what else to say.

He said: "Surely you didn't think that you were the only woman in my life, Addison!" He gave me his warmest smile. And I said again: "Oh please." And moved the conversation gracefully to the recent flap in California over the right of homeowner associations to restrict the use of political signs in upscale subdivisions.

"You know, if you don't secure those things properly, they can blow away with the smallest storm," Baxter said in what I thought was sort of a clunker of an observation. But it's hard to fault him, really. Bringing a weather-related observation to a free-speech issue is hard enough. Who can ask that it be a good one?

"If you're not careful," he continued, "the whole neighborhood will be polluted with Nader signs."

"Oh," said Hughes, "the irony."

We all chuckled.

As we faded to commercial, Hughes turned to me and winked. "Dinner at Emilio's tonight?" he asked, quietly enough that only I could hear.

"Sure," I said. I winked back. MorningFan was forgotten. And things were back to normal.

*Except* for my use of the Internet, which was reaching alarming proportions. I had come to rely on the Internet for comfort, for company, for the compliments I felt I so desperately needed. Soon I was spending hours each day this way. I beamed with pride when people on the boards talked about my wit and wiles. I enjoyed having a place to say that I thought Hughes was the dog's bark and the kitten's purr. I defended Baxter and mostly I escaped the dreary confines of my life.

I know. My parents survived war and famine. I know. Most of the world lives in squalor and poverty. Even in the rarefied world of upper-middle-class America, I was at that point extraordinarily lucky, with my safe and glamorous job, with my paid-for hotel room with room and maid service. I had everything in the world going for me.

That is all true.

But I was still so lonely.

I would lie awake in bed at night, rethinking my social life. I was beginning to get the impression that—regardless of Hughes's sexual orientation—our relationship was stalled at Emilio's. So I would go back over long-ago dates and near dates. I would replay the scene where George Clooney asked me if I had dinner plans. I had said, honestly, that I couldn't possibly eat that day. But what if I had pretended that I could? I wondered if Pharm Boy and I could have hit it off, if I hadn't been so uptight. I even thought about the jerky boy I briefly dated in high school. And that always led me to think about Kevin Ford, the only person ever to ask me to play basketball.

It was pathetic. Even at the time, I knew these questions were pathetic. Pharm Boy? He had no redeeming qualities. George Clooney? I mean, really, the man could not remember my name. And Kevin Ford? Kevin Ford moved away after my freshman year of high school. I couldn't even remember what he looked like. Not really. I remember he had sandy brown hair and really nice eyes. But I was fourteen the last time I saw him. And fourteen was a long time ago. Besides, why him? His brother, honestly, was nicer to me. His brother didn't laugh so much when I missed a basket. Thinking about Kevin Ford now was crazy.

The only reason I was thinking about him, I realized, was because I'd never known him well enough to know his flaws. *That's my problem,* I thought. *I am totally enamored with guys unless and until I actually get to know them. Then I find out their stomach is soft or they bring up pro wrestling too often or they hog up the sofa they're renting out or, well, something.*

My fixation on men from long ago was a sad manifestation of my loneliness. So were my long discussions with strangers on the Internet. But I didn't realize exactly how sad it all was until the day some of us at the office were going to lunch together, celebrating three pregnancies on the staff. We were supposed to meet outside Hughes's office at 11 AM—a late lunch for us—and walk together to a nearby salad bar. I was thinking of doing something wild like loading up on croutons.

As we were about to leave, I said I needed to dart into my office and check my e-mail. And Hughes acted surprised. "You do?"

I looked at him, a tad defensively. "Well, yeah. Don't you?"

"Unless I'm expecting something important, I just check mine once a day," he said.

"Once a day?" I asked incredulously.

Baxter rolled his eyes. "Good grief, Hewey," he said. "Once a day?"

One of the administrative assistants snickered. A producer nodded his head solemnly. "It's no wonder Hughes is so productive," he said.

I just gulped. The sad truth was, I wasn't even really going to check my e-mail. I was using my private shorthand for checking the boards, only I was now using my private shorthand publicly. (Which is worse? Lying to yourself or to others?)

I was stunned by Hughes's reaction. I knew that going to check the boards again would be an embarrassing thing to own up to, but I had thought checking my e-mail sounded perfectly legitimate. But Hughes's comment was a wake-up call. I realized, suddenly, how twisted my view of the online world had become. I was no longer capable of distinguishing between obsessive and normal.

At least that is how I felt, standing there. Hughes was looking at me in his amused way while the other lunchgoers glanced at their watches. I suddenly saw myself through their eyes, and from that vantage point I realized that I spent a *lot* of time on the Internet. Just the other day, in fact, one of the pregnant staffers had told me an exhausting story about her previous evening, in which she had attended a Lamaze class, childproofed her home for the coming baby, cooked seven casseroles to freeze for harried postbirth meals, cleaned out her hall closet, and had a dinner date with her husband. "One last hurrah," she said. And then she smiled at me and asked what I had done. I pretended to have a coughing fit to avoid telling her that I had surfed the Web all night, chatting about my own show and reading up on ways to increase your pedometer count.

I had told myself she was just engaged in some crazed hormonal behavior, but now . . . I wondered. I looked at her and the rest of them, waiting for me to answer Hughes and explain why I needed to check my e-mail.

"Well," I said, with feigned breeziness. "I suppose if you only check once a day, I can wait until after lunch."

I acted as if everything was fine. But it wasn't. All during the chatty, happy lunch, I felt distant from the crowd as I picked at my salad of butterhead lettuce. As I ate, I looked around the room and I suddenly realized with absolute conviction that none of these people were spending hours a day reading about themselves online. I felt, for the first time, like someone with a shameful secret. I was, arguably, sick. It was as if I was addicted to reading about the show. *Wait a second,* I thought. *I've heard of that. Internet addiction. I'm quite sure I read something about that once.*

I couldn't wait to get back to the office to get online and read about it again. And that impulse alone, the impulse to turn to the Internet for more information, *proved* that I had an Internet addiction. I felt a surge of panic, and then something very much like excitement. Cal will let me have a whole month off for treatment, even during sweeps! I could sleep, possibly, for days.

*This Internet obsession,* I found myself thinking, *is quite possibly the best thing that has ever happened to me.*

When we got back to the studio, I closed the door to my office so that no one could see what I was doing and found a Web site devoted to Internet addiction. I scrolled through the questions. "How often do you spend more time than you intend to online?" Well, always! Didn't everybody? I thought everybody did! Apparently not! I'd only done one question and I'd already gotten five points!

"How often does surfing interfere with your work?" Well, there you go. See? Right at that very moment it was interfering with work. If I didn't have Internet access, I would have had to wait until I left the office to read up on this. But here I was, in the middle of the workday, taking this test rather than doing something productive. Score another five points!

A couple of the questions were a bit difficult because they didn't really apply in my case. "Does surfing get in the way of doing housework?" The hotel maids did all the housework, but I figured that if I had housework to do, I would surely do less of it because of the Internet. So I gave myself the highest score. Then it asked if loved ones ever complained about my online usage. *I don't have any loved ones who know about it,* I thought sadly. *I live alone. In a hotel. Still, I'm quite sure that my mother would complain if she knew.* "You can't write a decent letter, but you spent two hours yesterday looking for baby shower gifts on RedEnvelope?" I could just imagine her saying that! I gave myself another maximum score.

The next question was about whether I ever comforted myself with "soothing thoughts of the Internet." I giggled a little. *Well, that's just silly,* I thought. "Soothing thoughts of the Internet." The Internet isn't soothing.

But then I remembered that rough day just last week when Cal made us leave straight from work for an embarrassing team-building exercise in Central Park. (The real objective was not to build our team, but to look picturesque for *Business Week,* which was doing a story about the GUP network's superb morale and its employees' "intense loyalty" to Cal. They needed photos.) So Hughes, Baxter, and the rest of us ran around the park, doing ridiculous stunts while wearing, in my case, a really uncomfortable pair of Fendi pumps.

Cal suggested I take them off, but I was embarrassed by a slipshod pedicure I had received the day before. (Add that to my rules of life: Just because a pedicurist "once" did John Cusack's nails does not mean you should let her do yours. Note the word *once.* Never consider a pedicurist who can't boast of repeat customers. Also, in retrospect: John Cusack?)

At any rate, I remember quite clearly climbing a portable rock wall in those stupid shoes and thinking: *I cannot wait to go home, kick these shoes off, and mess around on the Internet.*

There it was! A "soothing thought" about the Internet!

*I am sick,* I thought.

And when I made my announcement and there was the press conferences and everything, I would give credit to Hughes. If he hadn't expressed his surprise that I was going back to check my e-mail, well . . . I never would have known. (Of course, if he hadn't been rumored to be gay, I may not have gotten addicted in the first place. But I didn't plan to go into that.)

I hoped giving this public credit to Hughes would deepen our relationship. Little did I realize how much it was about to deepen anyway.

# Chapter 13

The eye-opening Internet quiz had been on a Thursday. But I decided to take the weekend to read up on Internet addiction before making my announcement. Good thing I had decided not to do anything rash.

During a story-idea brainstorming session, I casually suggested a story on Internet addiction and Cal said it was quite a good idea. "Maybe we can interview some of these loonies who are talking about our show online for hours every day," he said. Hughes and Baxter and I each cringed. I assumed that they were cringing for the implication that our fans were unhinged. I was cringing at the suggestion that *I* was unhinged.

The Web master used this as an excuse to launch into his favorite topic, the lack of publicity for our discussion boards. There was some tedious back and forth and Cal finally said, "Fine. Publicize them, redesign them. What do I care?"

The meeting ended and I told Cal I was feeling ill, though I didn't explain it was from hearing him talk about "loonies."

I raced back to the hotel and went straight to bed without logging on—not even for a moment. I considered it something of a test and was very impressed with myself for doing it. I wasn't sure I could. But I was lucky I did because the extra sleep came in handy on Friday.

That morning I headed into the office as usual, getting there a little early to check the boards once before going over the scripts. (I thought since I had gone without the night before, I was entitled.) I was pleased to realize that my absence on the boards had not gone unnoticed. Baxterbasher posted several times, saying, "Are you out there, ObjectiveObserver?" And when he finally gave up, he said: "I suppose if my online friends are going to disappear like this, I'm going to have to do something to get an actual life."

And Weatherjunkie had posted: "LOL, B-basher. Me too."

I smiled with satisfaction at that. Weatherjunkie and Baxterbasher were my best friends on the boards. The only ones whose comments on the show seemed insightful and on point. But I liked Weatherjunkie better. B-basher had a mean streak. (Hence the name.)

Anyway, I was sitting there, grinning a little and wondering how on earth Weatherjunkie and B-basher would get by when I had to give up the boards to treat my addiction, when Hughes startled me by popping into my office, flashing some theater tickets, and asking if I wanted to join him for what he called a "wickedly avant garde" theater production. It was, he said, a postmodern, edgy take on love and marriage by an up-and-coming playwright who was all the rage in the circles that rage about such things.

"Really?" I said. (It was hardly Miss Liberty's approved response to an invitation, but I was frankly stunned. Hughes had never, ever asked me to an event other than dinner.)

"Oh yes," Hughes continued, apparently misunderstanding my question. "They say it's simply shocking."

He went on to describe the play, which was about a woman's decision to leave her emotionally abusive husband for her lover. I confess I was skeptical. I supposed leaving an emotionally abusive husband would have been considered edgy at some point in history or in some places in the world. Miss Liberty was, for example, not a big worrier about emotional abuse. (I specifically remember a passage where she said that domestic servants should not be so silly as to get their backs up about employers mispronouncing their names or using "so-called derogatory slang.") But Miss Liberty lived in 1910. Now? In Manhattan? Leaving an emotionally abusive husband struck me as an edgeless concept.

But who cared about that? Hughes was asking me to join him for a play. This meant that unlike our dinners, which were always conducted in empty restaurants, there would be witnesses. People might actually think we were a couple! On a date!

I'm not ashamed to admit that this thrilled me. I was atwitter all the way to the theater. On the cab ride over, Hughes even asked me why I was drumming my fingers in such an agitated way, but I passed it off as a weight-maintenance thing. "People who fidget are slimmer than those who don't," I said.

He nodded solemnly. "I've read that, too," he said, and began tapping his toes to the beat of the cabdriver's music.

When we arrived at the theater, I felt self-conscious and alive. I looked around and wondered how many people recognized us and, if they did, what they thought. Just co-workers out for a social night?

And was that all we were? Co-workers who often ate together or shared play tickets or gave each other career or fashion advice?

As we settled into our seats in the left balcony, the big lights dimmed and a woman took the stage, a spotlight illuminating her as she gave us the usual reminders about turning off phones and not expecting an intermission. Then she walked off and the regular stage lights came up. I looked across the theater, and directly opposite me in the right balcony, a tall, agile man was slipping into his seat, the only one taken in a couple of rows near the back. He was wearing crisp-looking chinos and a black T-shirt. His hair was tussled in a Kurt Cobain sort of way. He laughed at something the usher said as he lowered himself into his seat. He was still chuckling as the light from the stage illuminated his face and I realized, with a start, that it was Baxter. Where was the bow tie? And he looked so, well, happy.

He adjusted his long limbs awkwardly, looked up at the stage, and then, almost magically, looked right at me. An entire theater of people and when he looked up, he looked up right at me.

He was clearly surprised. He jumped a little. His face broke into a smile and he waved.

And then I did something that still puzzles me. I put my hand down at my side, so that it was blocked from Hughes's view by my own body and by the program I was holding in my lap. And I waved back.

Why did I do it that way? Why did I hide from Hughes that I was waving to our mutual co-worker? Why didn't I nudge Hughes and indicate for him to wave, too? What was my impulse toward secrecy?

Baxter apparently noticed the discreet move I'd made. He looked at me, then at Hughes, then back at me with an amused, questioning look. Cocked his head a little, turned the corners of his lips up, but most importantly he locked his eyes on mine. I took this as a challenge. He was daring me to look away.

I didn't.

The first scene of the play was filled with tortured dialogue, inexpertly delivered. The review the next day tore it apart—tore the whole play apart—but was especially hard on the first scene, which the reviewer noted was so stilted as to be painful to listen to.

And listen to it was all that I could do because I was still staring into Baxter's eyes across the crowded theater. I could see the actors moving in my peripheral vision. I could hear the words. That was all.

One of the actors on stage moved over to the side to deliver a tortured monologue about the anguish of being involved with a man who treats you badly. The lights shifted and for a moment—no, for longer than that—I could barely see Baxter and I assumed that he could barely see me. But even then, neither of us looked away.

Soon the actors on the stage were rolling around, thumping about on the floor in a love scene that the review called pathetic and icky. But Baxter and I just kept looking at each other.

As the minutes passed, I began to feel giddy and reckless. I was tempted to up the ante in some way. Blow a kiss? Unbutton the top of my blouse? I felt like I should do something wild and outrageous. But then, as this little stare-down continued, I came to feel that this was the most wild and outrageous thing I could do with this man whom I talked to every day. I would simply allow him to stare into my soul for as long as he would.

Toward the end of the play, there was a gloomy scene in which most of the characters in the play got drunk in the dark and some of them killed themselves. The scene was, in the words of the reviewer, "as long as hell and a good deal more painful." The stage was dimly lit; no light at all escaped into the crowd. For the entire ordeal, twenty minutes at least, I could not see Baxter at all. But I continued looking into the dark space where I had been able to see him before, aware of the play in only the most vague and incidental way.

And then, finally, it was over. Light once again flooded the theater seats, and it seemed to me that time moved so slowly that I could see the glow spread row by row into the audience. It seemed to take an hour to reach the place where Baxter had been sitting and when it did, it was as if not a second had passed.

He was still looking toward me. He cocked his head toward the stage and rolled his eyes. I smiled and then, finally, looked at my shoes. And when I looked up again, he was gone.

Hughes leapt to his feet then, calling out "Bravo!" and whispering in my ear about how marvelously risqué the whole thing was. It was a subject he was able to go on about throughout the curtain call and during the slow walk to the lobby. He used the word *brilliant* several times. I think he said it was a "tour de force."

"I don't know about that," I said. I didn't normally argue with Hughes, but this play had not been, at all, my kind of thing. "Didn't you think the dialogue was a little stilted?" I asked.

Hughes sighed in an exasperated way. "Intentionally, honey," he said. "It reflects the stilted age we live in."

"I suppose," I said. I had, after all, given the play less than half my attention, so I didn't want to be too dogmatic. I must confess that I wasn't absolutely certain it was terrible until I read the review the next day.

Hughes was going on some more about our stilted era as I looked around the room. I gathered that Baxter had left. He had disappeared so quickly, he surely must have been dashing off to meet someone. Probably a woman, I found myself thinking sadly. And this surprised me, for I had never found myself wondering about whom Baxter spent time with before.

But then I saw him. A clump of people standing nearby broke up and suddenly there he was, walking toward us from the elevators. His coat was casually draped over his shoulder. He looked more relaxed than he ever did on the set. He looked more relaxed than anyone I had encountered in my adult life, I guessed. He looked like a relaxed Midwesterner. He reminded me of home.

"Well, well, well," Hughes said, when he saw Baxter approaching. "The whole gang is here." He looked Baxter up and down and added, "And you're dressed like Shaggy Doo! No bow tie."

I winced. First of all, I don't think Shaggy's last name is Doo. He's not Scooby's brother, after all. And I don't recall him ever wearing a black shirt. He always wore green, didn't he? More importantly, why did Hughes always have to bring up the ties?

Baxter ignored the whole thing. "Hello, Hewey," he said. He nodded toward me then but didn't meet my eyes. He simply said: "Addison."

I noticed that he said my whole name. He did not call me Ada, as he normally did. I wondered what that meant.

"I had no idea you were here," Hughes said. "Did you, Addison?"

The question surprised me and made me feel guilty. I wondered about it days later. It was a strange question to ask. I would have expected Hughes to ask if I had known Baxter was coming. But asking me if I had known Baxter was there? It was a very specific question. Not as specific as *Have you been staring into this man's eyes for the past two hours?* But specific nonetheless. Why did Hughes ask that, particularly?

Still, live television prepares you for surprising moments, and I handled it. "I saw him just now coming across the room," I said. (It was an absolutely true statement. I had seen him just then coming across the room. I did not say it was the first time I saw him that evening.)

"And I saw you," Baxter said, which made me blush, but by that point Hughes had started glancing around the room again to see if he was being recognized. He did not notice the blush.

"I wasn't aware that you liked theater," Hughes said, without making eye contact.

Baxter said, "I'm trying to branch out."

"Well, you picked an excellent one to start with," Hughes said. He yammered on for a while about reflecting our stilted times. I looked at my feet again. I wished I had worn higher heels.

Baxter eventually interrupted. "I guess I didn't appreciate the significance of the stilted dialogue," he said while looking directly at me for the first time since approaching us. "They were rolling around on the stage, talking about the 'handcuffs of marriage' and the 'ethics of love.' The whole play I was just thinking of lines like: 'Dump the jerk, run away with me. Push me down on the futon and bite off my buttons.' "

I gasped. I was terrified and, well, thrilled. I was also slightly appalled to realize that the futon-pushing, button-biting fantasy was common enough to be some sort of catch-phrase. When FargoMama had used it on the boards, I thought it was original. I took a moment to chide myself for not staying up on pop culture. Hughes didn't bat an eye.

"Ah, Baxter," he said. "Charming as usual." Then he excused himself to get another drink and Baxter and I stood there, uneasily shifting from one foot to the other.

"You look nice," I said. I meant this as idle chitchat. It's one of the sorts of things co-workers say when they encounter each other in nonprofessional settings. But I immediately cringed. After having stared at him for so long, it seemed like a more meaningful comment than I had intended.

But he accepted it gracefully. "The bow tie thing is an act, you know," he said. "My agent came up with it. Bow ties are big with weathermen."

"Ah," I said. Then: "Oh."

I don't know why this surprised me so much. *Other people have agents, too, don't they?*

"The agent picked out the name *Baxter,* too—after Ted Baxter on *Mary Tyler Moore,*" he continued.

"And the curmudgeonly thing?" I asked, a bit hesitant.

"All an act," he said. He winked, leaned toward me. "Most of the time, at least."

I smiled and, inexplicably, blushed.

"You know," Baxter said, "the little speech I gave Hewey about what I was thinking during the play? That wasn't really what I was thinking."

"Oh?" I asked. I was now definitely tilting more toward terrified.

"No, I was really thinking *Dump the jerk, run away with me, let me love you.* But I thought button biting sounded more avant garde."

He leaned over then and whispered in my ear. "Your move." And he turned and walked out the door without looking back.

And that was the night Hughes finally kissed me.

# Chapter 14

$\mathcal{M}$en.

I suppose women are the same, really—loving the unattainable more often than not. But men seem particularly transparent about it. Not that I was ever unattainable to Hughes. But it did not escape my notice that he did not make a physical move in our relationship until the night that Baxter flirted with me.

I learned this lesson about men early enough. My high school boyfriend and I had been taking what should have been a romantic stroll when I was fourteen. It was summer and dark out and we were walking around the block of his leafy, suburban neighborhood. We were holding hands, but he was telling me that he wasn't really interested in a relationship just then and that he thought we shouldn't spend so much time together. Our relationship was, he explained, getting in the way of his pro-wrestling viewing.

I was about to drop his hand—understandably, I thought. Who holds hands while breaking up? Just then, in the distance, I saw a red Toyota pickup turn on the street, engines gunning in a typical teenage-guy fashion. For a moment, I thought it must be Kevin Ford, who sometimes borrowed his brother's truck though he wasn't old enough to drive. (Not a strongly enforced law in Slater County—at least not then.) I was, by this point, admitting to myself that I rather liked Kevin Ford so I dropped my boyfriend's sweaty palm even more quickly than I'd originally intended, a move that did not go unnoticed.

"What's going on?" my boyfriend asked, glancing at the pickup and then back at me. By the time the truck got close enough for me to realize it was not Kevin, but his truck-owning brother, my boyfriend was looking at me with admiring new eyes. "You *like* him," he said, incredulously. "One of those Ford boys."

I shrugged. There was a long silence, and then my boyfriend revealed an amazing bit of self-awareness and honesty.

"I feel completely different about you," my boyfriend said. "Now that I know you like someone else."

Yeah, well. Yeah.

We dated for another three months and those three months were as satisfying as you would expect, given that little story.

Anyway, I suspect that the same sort of thing happened with Hughes. I don't think he saw Baxter and me staring at each other during the play, for Hughes was obviously enthralled with what was happening on stage. And he clearly did not hear Baxter telling me that it was now my move.

But I suppose that night when Hughes returned with his drink, I was distracted and disinterested. I hung on his words less. My gaze was a little less admiring. I actually was, in some small way, less "available" to him. He picked up on that and, suddenly, he could not get enough of me.

"You smell great," he said at one point. And a few moments later, he added: "You look great."

As we were leaving, he placed his hand on the small of my

back. And when I pulled my skirt up a little to get in the taxi, he whistled in a sweet, boyfriendish way.

"Want to get a drink?" Hughes asked. I was surprised: It was awfully late for people who worked our kind of hours, and besides, even Hughes had to watch the alcohol. The camera adds ten pounds to men, too.

There was a basement bar near my hotel, and we settled into a discreet corner. He got a gin and tonic. I got a glass of water. "For now," I told the waiter. As if I was just a little thirsty and wanted to get my hydration levels up before blowing a day's worth of calories on sugary mixed drinks.

Hughes and I had fallen into a companionable routine by then. On camera we were often extraordinarily flirtatious, but in real life it was far more toned down. You can talk about swallowing goldfish all day on television and what's the harm? But it feels dangerous and scary and, you know, *real* to say the same thing in the darkened corner of a bar. (Or even in an empty restaurant at 4:30 PM, which as I've said was our more typical date.)

Our private conversations were normally—well—friendly, yes. Comfortable? Undoubtedly. Occasionally even flirtatious. But for people who were, by that point, celebrated for their public chemistry, our private conversations were rather inert.

Usually.

That night Hughes kept grinning in a boyish, impish, charming way, laughing at everything I said, and slinging his arm along the back of our shared bench in an intimate gesture. There was an awkward moment when we finally ran out of conversation and just grinned at each other for what seemed like a very long time. His dimple quivered. His smile wavered, and he finally looked away. A couple of times, he set his hand down on my thigh to emphasize a point.

Yes, his eyes crinkled. Often.

During my third glass of water, he started talking about how "refreshingly down-to-earth" I was and how "genuine" also. Looking back, I should have known then that something had changed in my relationship with Hughes. You would have to be delirious with infatuation, I think, to consider me "genuine."

And I was feeling pretty infatuated myself. When we left the theater, I had been distracted by my interactions with Baxter, but after a couple of hours with a flirtatious Hughes, I had forgotten all about that. And then we started yawning. It was 2 AM—we'd each been up about twenty-three hours. "I guess I should get home," I said.

And Hughes said he supposed he should as well. He offered to walk me to the hotel, just around the corner really. I followed him up the narrow stairs that took the bar patrons to the street level, and a blast of cool misty air hit us in the face. "Wow," he said. "It's gotten cold."

He popped open his James Smith & Sons umbrella. He always had that handy, being the sort that sweats the details. I murmured something and leaned into him. It was an instinctive reaction—seeking shelter from the drizzle and the chill. But I immediately realized that this spot—my head on his chest, just under his chin—was a nice place to be.

His arm slid around me and for many months afterward I swore to myself that I could remember each individual step we took, hunkered together, until we reached my hotel. But time has erased some of that. Now I remember only the general feel of it.

I do remember that as we got closer to the lobby, I felt an impending panic. I didn't want the night to end yet, obviously enough. And I didn't think he did, either. But this was one of the moments you realized how odd it was to be living in a hotel. If I'd been in a regular apartment, I would have asked him to come up for some herbal tea—something warm and noncaloric to sip while he called a cab. I do not know if any hot drinks would have been consumed or any cab called, but it would have been at least something to say.

But there was a taxi in front of the hotel and there was a bank of phones in the lobby and there was a cafeteria, presumably with tea, next door. And there was nothing in my room except a television, a laptop, and a bed.

*What should I do?* I asked myself. What can I say?

As it turned out, though, I didn't need to say anything. We stepped into the lobby, shook ourselves free from the wet air, laughed at some silly weather joke the bellman made, and then Hughes gave me his arm and walked me straight into the elevator as if he had no need to be invited, as if that was simply where we all knew he belonged. There were several other people on the elevator, a group of five or six conventioneers—all loud and laughing. Hughes and I stood side by side, our backs to the side wall of the mirror-lined elevator. We stood there looking straight ahead into the opposite mirror. Without turning toward each other, we could still make eye contact, and there was a long unbroken glance. Somehow our pinkie fingers became intertwined.

On the eighth floor, the raucous group exited, apparently headed for a balcony bar. We stood there for a beat or two, waiting for the elevator doors to close. From the bar, we could hear the wailing sounds of Marvin Gaye's "Let's Get It On." We stood like that for a long time, the doors to the elevator still open. Finally, I realized with embarrassment that I had never pushed the button for my floor. So I giggled and reached across Hughes to do so. I swore I could hear his heart beat.

The elevator doors closed and we were silent, looking at

our feet, our pinkie fingers swinging a little. Then his hand was on my face and his lips were on mine and my arms were around his neck and his tongue was in my mouth and my heart was in my knees.

After that, it is all a blur.

# Chapter 15

It's hard for me to remember how I felt those next few weeks. Obviously, everything that has happened since then has colored those days in my memory. At the time, I was exhilarated, ecstatic, and enthralled. But now I look back and am skeptical about every moment of it. I'm not sure, to this day, what I think of Hughes or of our courtship.

The next morning was the blending of comfort and awkwardness that you'd expect. We'd been talking and sharing meals together like an old married couple for months and now we were ordering breakfast from room service and dividing up the morning paper like new lovers.

"Is this awkward?" he said at one point, employing his boyish grin to full effect.

"It's like *When Harry Met Sally,*" I said, shrugging a little. "We already know each other's stories."

He said he'd never seen *When Harry Met Sally,* which amazes me to this day. What had he been doing for the last fifteen years?

I tried to explain Harry's theory, expressed in the middle stages of the movie, that the reason his relationship with Sally fell apart was that they had been friends so long, they already knew each other's stories and thus had nothing to talk about after sex.

I challenged Hughes then to tell me something I didn't already know about him.

"I just did," he said, with a wink. "I've never seen *When Harry Met Sally.*"

"Something else," I said, smiling into my breakfast fruit cup. It was mostly cantaloupe, thankfully. Strawberries are so terribly caloric.

He looked out the window for a moment, as if he was thinking very seriously, and then he said, "My dad says that after all those years on the bench, he can immediately spot a lie. He says that everyone has a 'tell'—a gesture or an expression or sound they make when they're lying. Mine," he continued, "is that I always blink three times after a lie."

"Blink?" I said.

"Yeah," he said. "Three times. My dad said it might be a second, or five seconds, or nine seconds after the lie, depending on how determined I am to keep my secret. But before I say the next thing, I always blink three times."

*Well, Hughes Sinclair,* I thought, *don't think I won't remember that.*

And then he smiled and acknowledged the usefulness of the information. "My dad also told me that I should never share that information with a woman—at least not if I intended to lie to her."

He chuckled, looked at his hands. "So I guess," he said, in what I took to be a meaningful way, "I'm never going to lie to you."

I nodded. "Or at least, you'll get caught if you do."

He dipped his head and lifted his palms in an expression that seemed to say: *Fair enough.*

"On the other hand," he said, eyes still sparkling with playfulness, "everyone blinks."

Our eyes were locked. He smiled. I smiled. He pushed his chair back a little, propped his bare feet into my robed lap. And we went back to our papers.

Hughes left my room at 2 PM that Saturday, all dimples and meaningful glances. He said he had family plans on Sunday, apologized for not being available. I made all the appropriate comments. "Don't be silly. I understand. Of course, your family is important. I think I can live a day without you."

And so forth.

But I was, as you might expect, mad with relief and delight when he called the next morning anyway, saying he couldn't stand another of his cousin's sing-alongs and asking if he could sneak away and meet me for a movie and a meal. And then he showed up at my door with a DVD of *When Harry Met Sally* and take-out Thai food in boxes. We never left the room, until he made a great show of peeling himself away from me at 10 PM, six short hours before we would see each other again at work.

# Chapter 16

*I* arrived at the studio at my usual time, although more giddy and gushy than usual. I had chatted with my driver all the way into the station and chirped "good morning" as I passed the doorman, the various overnight producers, and the administrative assistants who were already in the studio. (This may not sound particularly giddy to you, but compared with my usual 4 AM demeanor it was positively over-the-top.)

"Well, you're in a good mood," one of the lighting guys said. "You and Baxter must be drinking the same coffee. He's all bouncy, too."

I turned then and saw Baxter at his workstation across the newsroom. I suddenly realized with horror that he might interpret any appreciable change in my mood as being about him and the stare-down we shared in the theater on Friday evening. I had not, I am embarrassed to admit, given him another thought since Hughes kissed me in the elevator.

It was a surreal moment, standing there—looking at Baxter whistling at his computer, expecting Hughes to appear at any moment and hoping that he would seem similarly happy. After months, years really, of loneliness, two very interesting things had happened that weekend. And for the first time, I focused on that coincidence and thought about how briefly thrilled I had been by Baxter's attention and how quickly I'd forgotten it. It didn't speak well of me, I was afraid.

I would have been a little nervous about how Hughes and I would handle ourselves in the office and on the air anyway, but that morning as I watched Baxter, I felt the stakes being raised noticeably. I cleared my throat, smiled at the lighting guy, and said by way of explanation: "It's a beautiful night out there. I suspect everyone will be in a good mood."

Sure enough, Hughes bounded in moments later—with doughnut boxes no less. He was handing out glazes—I had a quarter of a doughnut hole—and acting uncharacteristically chummy with even the lowliest of interns.

I was flattered out of my mind at the thought that his weekend with me was apparently doing so much for his spirits, but also a little concerned. I finally gathered myself to enter his office, where I mustered all my professionalism and dignity to say that though we'd had a lovely weekend, I hoped he shared my belief that we should not speak about it with any of our co-workers. He came around his desk then. He was wearing a four-button suit, one that I always found impossibly sexy. He perched himself on the beveled edge of his Amish-crafted, hickory desk. (Every time I looked at that desk, I thought I really should talk to Cal about my own, which appeared to have been salvaged from a 1970s Dumpster. Little hints like this left me with the impression that Hughes was valued more and— dare I think it?—paid more also.) He folded one leg under him as he eased himself onto the desk. It was a smooth, strong, agile move—one that showed off his ballet mother's influence.

He grinned.

"Not ready to shout it from the rooftops?" he said. I had no idea how to take that—a complaint? a challenge? a sarcastic joke?

I ignored it.

"I just think it would be better if we were discreet," I said. I looked at my shoes, which struck me suddenly as being *so* six months ago. I decided on the spot to go shopping after work.

I looked back up and he was still grinning. "Secrets are very sexy, you know," he said.

I grinned back. "It depends on how you wear them."

"Indeed," he said. "It *always* does."

More grinning and foot watching. "Well," he said, finally. "Back to work for me."

On the air that morning, we engaged in our usual friendly banter. I was shocked, frankly, at how easy it was to settle back into business as usual after the weekend we'd had. In fact, only two things about that morning's show were memorable for me. At one point, Baxter asked Hughes if he'd had a nice weekend. And Hughes said that it was nice enough. "Uneventful really," he said. "Not a single important thing happened."

And then he blinked three times.

The other moment was when Hughes was interviewing a music critic about some new album or another and finished up the interview by saying: "I understand you've a book coming out this spring."

"Yes," said the music expert. "It's a critical look at sexual imagery in R-and-B music. It's called *Let's Get It On.*"

Hughes blushed, right there on camera for anyone to see.

I blushed as well, but I was off camera at the moment and no one saw me. Except for Baxter. He raised an eyebrow and looked at me in a questioning way, and I did the worst thing I could have done, for secret keeping. It was not yet seventy-two hours since I had spent an entire evening staring into Baxter's eyes, but when he glanced at me just then, I immediately looked away.

I think he knew at that moment. I thought I detected a noticeable souring of his mood.

And he was not the only one with a worsening mood. I learned later that it was just about that same moment that the first lady of the United States/junior senator from Ohio received some disturbing news. She was informed that the *National Enquirer* had an incriminating photo of her husband and Addison McGhee.

"How did they get their hands on that photo?" she said to her top aide, seething with rage. (This was widely reported later by *Entertainment Weekly* and other respectable news outlets.)

"In the future," the aide said, wearily, "if you're going to make dramatic staffing cuts at the White House to gain publicity for your little dispute about the federal budget, here's some advice." He leaned toward her, as if about to whisper, then startled her by screaming: *"Don't lay off the photographer!"*

# Chapter 17

That night I went shopping, which I think threw Hughes for something of a loop. We had eaten dinner together every weeknight for the past several months—more than a year, really. Then we spent a romantic and sensual weekend together and suddenly I was begging off from evening plans, saying I had errands to run.

I had been putting aside money every month into a special savings account—telling myself that what I saved by living in a hotel room paid for by Cal ought to go to good use at some point. But I blew it all that night on a stunning collection of new clothes, shoes, and lingerie. It's funny to think about that now, as I sit here in prison wearing the same outfit I've worn every day for six months.

I shopped frantically, then went back to the hotel and called my mom and giggled more than usual as I talked to her. I did not say anything about my weekend —obviously. I mean, she would have been shocked enough that I'd gone to a play where people rolled around half naked on the stage. Knowing that I made eyes with Baxter and made out with Hughes would have killed her.

I hung up and noticed with disappointment that I still had no messages—I confess I had called my mother in part to pass the time quickly rather than staring at the phone and hoping for it to ring. But soon the front desk called to say a florist had a delivery for me. I told them to bring it on up and I, thankfully, checked my makeup in the mirror as I waited, because it turned out that it was Hughes himself who came to the door, his face hidden behind the bouquet of three dozen roses. I did not realize it was him until he had set the roses on the table and I had reached into my purse for tip money.

I changed course quickly, pretending I didn't have any money in my purse and whatever was I going to do? Hughes said we would work something out. The look he gave me at that moment . . . I'll never forget how playful and spontaneous and, well, real it all seemed. It's impossible for me to understand how we got from that place to the one it all came to.

I feel a little silly writing about the rest of this. Because, well, because it's just embarrassing first of all—and well documented in the media, second. But my marriage to Hughes is, after all, part of what Cassie told me to write about. So I guess I had better start.

It was just a few weeks after our relationship took its sudden and somewhat unexpected turn that Cal Gupton sent us to Las Vegas. The Supreme Court of Nevada had ruled that banning gay marriage was unconstitutional and gay marriages would be performed there starting the next morning. Cal said that Las Vegas would be the news capital of America for at least a week and he thought that Hughes and I should broadcast live from there.

Hughes and I each protested this decision with rather halfhearted passion. Putting on a three-hour live show from outside the regular studio is tougher than people realize, and hopping across time zones when you're already sleep-deprived and off schedule is tougher still. We each said as much to Cal, but did not really push it. For one thing, we didn't want to seem unenthusiastic about his big idea. And for another, a trip to Vegas together sounded like fun.

"Cheap, tawdry fun," Hughes said, as we were settling into our first-class seats. "But isn't that the best kind?"

And I said I supposed it was.

But the truth was, I will now confess, that I didn't really understand Hughes at moments like that. I could appreciate on some level that a man of his background and upbringing and pedigree did not see Vegas as a particularly glamorous destination. He'd rather be flying off to Monaco or Tuscany or Hong Kong. I knew that. But from my perspective, Las Vegas was a perfectly exciting place to visit. The girls of my high school class had voted it their number one dream honeymoon location. I don't know if I would go that far. For one thing, I long ago had to give up the appeal of budget-priced buffet meals. (Give me a place where I can only afford the salad, please.) But still, I couldn't quite muster the sophisticated disdain for the place that I knew Hughes expected. He thumbed through a Vegas brochure and made a crack or two about the fake Venice you can visit there. I smiled and nodded, but really I looked forward to seeing it.

It was times like this that I wished again that someone would write an updated Miss Liberty book, one that addressed issues like this, rather than all that old stuff about calling cards and servant–employer relations. It seemed to me, while growing up in Nebraska, that Las Vegas and Wal-Mart and cruising in old cars were the essence of America. But as an adult, I was spending time with the likes of Hughes Sinclair, whose family *built* America, and learning that I was apparently supposed to sneer at such things. It made no sense at all to me. I read a couple of books about it—red and blue America and all that—but I still didn't get it.

Anyway, it didn't matter what either of us thought of Las

Vegas, because we were both going only at Cal's insistence and had no time for a prolonged debate on its merits anyway. We were frantically reading up on the gay rights movement on the flight. I pressed my knee against Hughes's while I read an entire *New York Times* article about a controversial school in Oregon that claimed to "cure" homosexual youth through a diet of brussels sprouts and onions.

"It certainly ought to cure you of something," Hughes quipped, looking over my shoulder once. And I giggled, though honestly I love brussels sprouts and onions. They have hardly any calories!

I don't think any of our programs that week—broadcast from an all-night wedding chapel—were particularly good. Thanks to the time change, our show started each morning at 4 AM Vegas time. Not many people are getting married at 4 AM—even in Vegas. Plus, at moments like these, it became apparent how much Hughes and I played off Baxter. The more I'd defended Baxter on the boards, the more I had come to see him as instrumental to the whole show. Hughes and I were airy and flippant and fun—I say this with more shame than pride—and Baxter was the necessary grounding element. He was the one who rolled his eyes and chuckled wearily and served as sort of a Greek chorus to our little act of silliness and saltiness.

But it was hard to provide this sort of grounding from several states away. We couldn't even see each other and that threw the whole show off more than I would have predicted. Hughes and I became less flirty than usual. In part, I think, this was because we were even sleepier than normal—and in part because, given what was going on in our real lives, we felt uncomfortable casually flirting around wedding bells. And ultimately, I think it was Baxter's absence that reined us in. We normally relied on him and his bemused shrugs and appalled glances to let us know when we had gone too far. Without him, we just felt unsure.

That Friday, Hughes and I were discussing the discomfort at the hotel buffet. (I kept going back—to the spinach bowl and the vinegar bottle. Another rule of life: Kirstie Alley never would have had problems in the first place if she had stuck to spinach and vinegar.)

I was sort of surprised that Hughes and I could discuss our on- and off-air chemistry with such professional detachment. I wondered if that said something quite good or very bad about our relationship.

"You know," he said, startling me by pointing his fork at me for emphasis. Utensil pointing was becoming a habit for him. "There's only one way to avoid all this awkwardness. We should just do it."

I raised an eyebrow, not sure exactly what we should do that we had not already done.

"We should just get married," he clarified.

I broke into a smile. (With my mouth closed—I did not want to run the risk that his memory of this moment with his new fiancée would include spinach in her teeth.) "Okay," I said.

Any serious accounting of my marriage to Hughes ought to include my emotional reaction to his proposal, I suppose. But when I try to replay that moment in my mind, what strikes me is that I was not nearly as surprised and blown away as I should have been. I was pleased. I was excited. More than that, I was ecstatic. At that moment, I felt and believed that the only thing I had ever wanted to do was marry Hughes.

But I wasn't *surprised*. I had, I guess, somehow thought that Hughes's proposal was inevitable. My gut feeling had told me this long ago. The only surprising aspect was that it came at an all-you-can-eat buffet in Vegas. It's as if I'd always known that this was where we were headed and wasn't it nice that we were finally there?

I don't know why I felt that way, in particular. It's not as if I believed that any romantic relationship would naturally end in marriage. I certainly had evidence to suggest otherwise. I read *People* magazine, you know. And there was the high school boyfriend and Simon Cowell. But Hughes and I were different. I believed marriage was our destiny.

We did not go to the all-night wedding chapel, I am proud to say. No need to on a Friday afternoon, for one thing. And besides, Hughes Sinclair may have been acting uncharacteristically impulsive and romantic, but he was still Hughes Sinclair. We slipped back to his room and he worked the phones while I worked the Internet and in two scant hours we had a lovely ceremony planned in a small chapel in the Vegas suburbs. We stopped at an outlet mall—"Aren't all malls retail outlets?" Hughes asked—and I quickly found a pale pink sundress at Coldwater Creek while Hughes picked out a new tie at, of all places, Eddie Bauer. (Looking back on it, I should have seen that as an omen. If Hughes Sinclair buys a tie at Eddie Bauer, he is clearly not himself. And if he is willing to marry someone wearing Coldwater Creek, he has lost his mind.)

But I thought the clothes looked lovely. It was like that time Sharon Stone went to the Oscars wearing a Gap T-shirt. I made this rather immodest point to Hughes, who said that it was indeed like that. "Only less matronly," he said. "And without the complexion issues."

I carried a bouquet of baby's breath—breathtaking in its simplicity. "A blooming tumbleweed" is the way Hughes described it.

We were both barefoot, which was much commented on, but it was perfectly simple really. I had not been able to find matching shoes and Hughes said that if I was barefoot, then he should be, too. "If we were on a beach, no one would think anything of it," he said. "And what's Vegas if not a beach without water?"

Even after everything, I still smile when I see a copy of our wedding photo, the one *It's Morning Now* sent out with the press release. Hughes is standing straight and tall, facing the camera. I am turned toward him, my perfectly flat belly pressed into his side, my arm reaching around his neck, my dark hand in his gray hair, and my head lying on his shoulder. I am facing the camera and my face looks, to me at least, the very picture of security and comfort, as if I'm right where I belong. Our bare feet—all four recently pedicured, of course—are touching one another in a note of whimsy and familiarity. Several people told me that if Hughes and I had been married in some fancy New York cathedral, with a huge reception and exquisite clothes and shoes, they would have been highly skeptical of the whole thing. But when they saw that photo with those bare feet—my long dark toes jumbled with his paleness—then they knew, they said, that it was "real."

That's what a lot of people told me.

Baxter wasn't one of them.

# Chapter 18

$\mathcal{I}$ kept telling myself that my sheepishness around Baxter was ridiculous. I had done nothing more than engage in a single flirtatious evening with him—most of it spent yards and yards apart. I had offered him no words of encouragement or promise. I had merely refused to look away. He had said the next move would be mine and I had not made it. What apology did I owe?

But I dreaded going into the office on Monday. My honeymoon with Hughes was that Friday and Saturday night; we flew back to New York, as scheduled, on Sunday. I slept in his apartment near the studio Sunday night and was amazed to realize I had never been to his home before, although I was honestly somewhat relieved to know that was something I could tell my mother. ("I never even saw his apartment, Mom, until I walked in as Mrs. Hughes Sinclair.")

The wedding photo made the appropriate splash in the papers, magazines, and tabloids. The *National Enquirer* promised "more sensational Addison photos soon," a remark that puzzled me but that I naively did not think much about.

When I called my parents, I was surprised that they greeted the news with a sort of guarded pleasure. I had expected a more negative reaction, and the conversation with my parents made me realize two things: (1) I had severely underestimated their concern about my lack of maternal progress. (2) Marriage was really the easiest thing I could have done.

I hope that what I'm about to say does not seem to blame my parents for my obviously ill-considered and much-too-quick marriage. But I think it must be noted that if you are wondering why an eager-to-please girl from a conservative refugee family would, with two hours' planning, marry a man no one knew she was dating—in Las Vegas, of all places—then think about this: Which call is easier to make to a mother like mine? Would you rather call her and say that you've been spending nights and long, lazy weekend days with a somewhat snotty celebrity widely rumored to be gay? Or would you rather just say that you married him?

So my conversation with my parents had gone well. Better, really, than the conversation with Hughes's family had. Hughes's mother was politely gracious and his father was jovially congratulatory, but they seemed stunned and a little disappointed. Hughes assured me they were just regretting missing out on the big rehearsal dinner and an opportunity to show off to political cronies and former fellow dancers. "It's nothing to do with you, Addison," he said, giving me a quick peck on the forehead as we rode into the studio together on Monday morning.

When we arrived, I realized I wasn't sure how to act around Hughes in the office or on the air. And I was more nervous still about Baxter. I supposed I would have to say something, but I could not imagine quite what.

Baxter made it easy on me, however, bursting toward me with smiling good wishes. "Congratulations!" he said. "Or is it Best Wishes? I never could remember which you're supposed to say to who. One's to the bride and the other the groom, isn't it? I'm sure Hughes could straighten us out."

He was talking quickly but passing it off as effusive, rather than nervous. I wasn't sure whether to be grateful or a tad disappointed.

"Actually," I said, "I know all about this." (Miss Liberty's book was full of this sort of useful etiquette information.)

He put up a hand to stop me. "Don't tell me now," he said. "This will be perfect chatter for the show." He hugged me again, a bit loosely really, and headed off down the hall repeating things like "Congrats!" and "Can't wait to hear about the honeymoon!" as he disappeared.

Baxter was right about the show chatter. He repeated his "Best Wishes/Congratulations" confusion for the audience. Hughes cheerfully supplied the answer: You congratulate a groom, but merely wish a bride well. "Although I have no idea why," he said with good-natured bemusement.

"I know," I piped up. "I read a book once. It was called *Miss . . .*" I hesitated. Would Hughes Sinclair really want his wife to admit on national television that her entire knowledge of etiquette was based on a book on cultural assimilation from 1910?

"Um, 'Miss Somebody's guide to, um, cultural stuff,' " I blurted out. Hughes raised an eyebrow in a subtle way that the cameras didn't pick up. He knew that whatever my faults, I had a good memory. Miss Somebody's Guide to Cultural Stuff? I felt a pang of guilt. Miss Liberty had helped me so much and now I was brushing her off as if I was too good for her. But, after all, I was no longer a little immigrant girl with crooked teeth and dorky Old World parents.

I got the teeth fixed years ago. Sure, I still had the dorky Old World parents, but I also had a husband, a very sophisticated, very American, very establishment husband. I didn't need to go babbling on about outdated advice from Miss Liberty.

"Anyway, Miss, um, somebody or other, said it's because of the historic inequity in divorce law."

As I said this, I realized for the first time that Miss Liberty was making a political statement, a rather radical one for her time. Why do you wish a bride well, but congratulate a groom? "Because of the inequity in divorce law." Hee. The old gal had a bit of spunk, I guess. And here I had treated her as if she was simply an objective arbiter of etiquette.

"Ah," said Hughes. "But we don't need to worry about that."

He patted my knee. I patted his hand that was on my knee. Then I said: "Enough about us."

That night when I watched the tape over, I thought, *That's it, that's the moment the rest of my life begins.*

I was either quite right or very wrong, depending on how you look at it.

Then I turned the tape off, even though we were just ten minutes into the three-hour show. Now that I was living with and loving Hughes, I did not have as much time for endless tape analysis. Or surfing the Web. Or counting my steps, for that matter. Marriage had turned my life upside down!

But if I *had* continued watching the tape, I might have wondered about the next news story, the one that Hughes reported while I was off stage getting my makeup touched up. He told our viewers that there were rumors that the first lady/ Ohio senator was locked in a fierce battle with the *National Enquirer* over some sort of photo they wanted to publish. Hughes noted drily that some bloggers were speculating that the photos had something to do with the first lady's previous and much-mocked relationship with Latin singer Ricky

Martin. "The first lady's office says, however, that she is not actually pictured in the photographs," Hughes said.

He turned to Baxter. "Well, that doesn't make any sense at all. If she's not in the pictures, what does she care what they show?"

And Baxter said, "I have no idea. But everybody will care about this weather we're having."

# Chapter 19

My life story, I suppose, can be summed up by four photographs. The cotton ball one, naturally. The barefoot wedding photo, unfortunately. The one of me in handcuffs, almost certainly. And most importantly, the one of me and the president.

Two of those photographs were released within days of each other. I was, in fact, hanging a framed wedding photo in my office at the moment I heard about the release of the presidential photo. I had kicked off my shoes and hiked my skirt up a bit to crawl up on a bookcase to hammer the nail, and I had asked an office assistant to hand me the frame. He shocked me by saying the first negative thing about the happy turn of events my life had taken. "I'm afraid," he said, glancing at my bare feet in the office and my bare feet in the photo, "that I'm not wild about the shoeless element. Is it supposed to be like the Beatles?" He altered his voice to sound spooky and conspiratorial. " 'Paul is dead. Paul is dead.' "

I snatched the frame from him a little roughly but did not respond, not knowing exactly what to say. (I was a little fuzzy on the whole *Paul-is-dead* phenomenon. It happened before I was born, first of all. And then there was the cultural issue.)

Still, the suggestion that Hughes's and my bare feet were

something sinister and death-related, rather than refreshing and real, startled me and gave me a chill. And before I could recover, Hughes walked into the room and said: "Addison, honey, we need to talk."

The office assistant excused himself, and I climbed down from the bookcase, slipped my shoes back on, and plopped down on a chair. I had a sick feeling. *Something has happened to my family*, I thought. What else could it be?

Hughes blinked three times. (I remember that quite distinctly and still wonder what it means. He was not lying, obviously.) "Cal thought I should be the one to tell you," he said.

He looked at his hands, then folded them in his lap and sighed. "I don't know that he's right."

"What is it?" I asked.

"Did you . . ." He looked at me, but then away. "Did you . . ."

This was the most inarticulate I had ever seen him. Suddenly, though, he simply spit it out. "Did you have a relationship with the president?"

I am quite glad that Hughes looked again at his shoes at that moment, because the look of realization and horror that swept across my face could have been easily misinterpreted as guilt or shame.

"Of course not," I whispered finally.

Hughes nodded. "No, I wouldn't think so." He flicked some lint on his leg. "The suits alone would be a turnoff."

I didn't respond.

"And the chin," Hughes said. He shuddered.

"But there's this photo," Hughes said. He pulled a torn newspaper page from his pocket and unfolded it carefully. It was the *Enquirer*.

You know what it looked like. There is no need for me to go into detail about my skintight parachute pants splayed across the president's lap, his mouth open on mine, my eyes flashing him a horrified look that an alarming number of people mistook for feisty flirtatiousness. My shirt gaped at the neckline and apparently, judging from the commentary later, no decent woman had ever before been betrayed by a gaping shirt. (Ann Coulter, in her typical fashion, later wrote that if a lady's shirt gapes open it's because the lady *wants* it to.)

I glanced at the photo and put my hands up in front of my eyes. "I don't want to see it," I said, though I already had. I told Hughes the whole story then, starting with my desperate attempt to escape being photographed next to a pig and ending with the first lady pulling me aside to discuss my skinny ass and my big lips.

"Baxter saw the whole thing," I said. "At least I think he saw most of it." I paused. "I think David Souter did, too. And Christine Todd Whitman. And maybe Teddy Kennedy."

"Teddy Kennedy was there?" Hughes said. "Great."

A moment of silence. Hughes looked hurt and sad. He seemed to believe me. Why wouldn't he? I don't think he could imagine that any woman he knew would ever consider a dalliance with a man who buys suits off the rack—even if he is the leader of the free world.

For a moment, Hughes looked smaller to me, and I realized with a start that he was, ever so slightly, slumping. *He must be really upset,* I thought.

Suddenly I was filled with a steely resolve. I think if the photo had come out a month earlier, right after it had been taken, I would have collapsed in humiliated despair. I would have resigned on the spot and just hoped for a gig on *Celebrity Mole*. I would have run back to Slater County and begged my parents to take me in, despite the shame.

But I had married the love of my life that weekend and now I was a fighter. I was a married woman, by golly, and though I would not have predicted that my marital status would matter in this situation, I realized at that moment that in some way it did. I had internalized at least two cultures' worth of sexism and I thought that the president could mess with Addison McGhee, but Addison McGhee *Sinclair* was a whole other matter.

(That was how I was thinking of myself, though my name on the show did not change. Cal had urged me to keep my maiden name professionally. "At least until we see how long this lasts," he had muttered. I was terribly offended, but Hughes laughed it off. "Oh, Cal," he had said, then laughed some more.)

I was ready to stand up for myself because it wasn't just about me anymore. It was about my husband and—well—our children. (Hughes and I had not talked about whether to have children, but I assumed that we would. I had started taking a vitamin each morning and had quietly switched to decaf coffee in an effort to prepare my bones for pregnancy.)

I was the plucky immigrant kid who grew up to do well for herself, but it had mostly been a story of good luck and good timing and forgone meals—until that moment. At that moment, I became what any good immigrant kid should be—I became a fighter.

"This is the president's problem," I said. "It's not mine. I'll be damned if I let it hurt me."

"Well, okay then," Hughes said. He seemed surprised by my fierceness, and he patted my head as he hugged me. "Well, okay."

That afternoon, I held a small press conference, making what I naively said would be my only statement on the matter. Hughes and Baxter both accompanied me to the front steps of the GUP building, where I stood before my colleagues in the press corps. My hair whipped a bit in the breeze, a couple of times blowing right into Baxter's eyes. But he did not react. He and Hughes stood on each side of me with solemn dignity. And it was reassuring for me and for the nation, I think. My husband believed me. Good ol' Baxter was my witness. There was nothing to worry about here.

"I think the president was feeling playful and silly," I said. "And though it made me uncomfortable, I decided to merely remove myself from the situation and leave everyone in peace. I'm sorry the tabloid has decided against a similar philosophy.

"This is the sort of thing my family would chalk up to a cultural misunderstanding," I concluded. And Hughes and Baxter nodded solemnly behind me.

Looking back on it now, it seems spineless to me. Why did I excuse the president's behavior as "playful and silly"? Why did I pretend there could have been some sort of "cultural misunderstanding"?

But at the time, it was the most forceful thing I had ever done. I dared to offer my own version of events—albeit a fictional one. I did not laugh or make a joke. And I did not do what someone told me to do. It was, perhaps, spineless spin. But it was *my* spineless spin. And I was actually proud.

For the first time since my marriage, I logged onto the boards that night. I couldn't believe how many people were posting now. Those publicity efforts for the boards must really be working. Plus, there had been a lot of news to discuss lately. The boards' newcomers had analyzed everything from my blooming tumbleweed to Hughes's slight hammertoe, which was evident in the wedding photo. They also went on and on about the photo of me and the president. But I couldn't bear to read any of that. I just skimmed through the posts looking for anything from my buddies, Weatherjunkie and B-basher. Both were strangely silent. Weatherjunkie had written nothing at all lately, and B-basher only had one short post, saying that he didn't understand why Baxter stood with me during my formal statement. "Who does he think he is?" B-basher said. "As if her husband weren't support enough?"

I sighed, logged off. It was a rough few days. My brother reported that my parents started wearing disguises in public. My father, he said, would ask over and over again: "We came to America to live with this shame?" And my mother would reply: "I suppose we did."

My new in-laws rather pointedly did not mention it. Unfair things were said about me—Why had I brought Baxter instead of my husband? Why had I worn such tight pants? And come on, could I really have been that afraid of a dead hog?

But it's amazing sometimes how these things turn out. Soon the subject was neither my supposed "easiness" nor the president's quite-real drinking problem. Somehow in the twisted way of the media age, the issue became the first lady. Why did she marry this guy? What was she thinking? Can she really be trusted to represent the good citizens of Ohio when she dates Latin singer Ricky Martin for two-odd years and then ups and marries a big loser like the president?

"I've seen the president up close," *The View* co-host Elisabeth Hasselbeck said rather famously. "I don't think he flosses."

Barbara Walters gasped and replied: "No decent woman marries a man who doesn't floss."

It was terribly unfair. And I, of all people, probably should have said so. But I was too relieved that the discussion was no longer centering on me. So I kept quiet. Besides, I soon had another problem.

There had been some news from Vegas. A higher court had overturned the gay marriage ruling, and all the gay marriages of the past few weeks would be forcibly annulled.

I would like to say that I had some great opinion on this,

being as I was a commentator on our society, an informed resident of the nation, an outspoken and thoughtful human being. But my mother-in-law was planning a reception for us, and I was overwhelmed with the details of the seating chart. I greeted the news with only passing interest. The images we were sent from Nevada seemed properly solemn. The clerks in each county scoured through the licenses, removing those of gay couples, and sending them before local judges. The judges were required by the higher court ruling to review the documents, stamp them ILLEGAL MARRIAGE, and mail them to the couples with a long-winded letter filled with legalese.

I knew this. I made some small talk on the air about it. But I confess I didn't really think much of it—until I opened the mail and saw that Hughes and I had gotten one of those letters.

# Chapter 20

Hughes had been nothing but a doting husband, but sometimes you have a sense about these things. A normal bride, I told myself, would laugh off this confusion. But I feared, somehow, that this would be more than just a minor annoyance.

In fact, I didn't initially mention the letter to Hughes. I wanted to get it straightened out before I troubled him with it. Using all my journalistic savvy, I had within an hour or so tracked down the clerk who had culled our license and gotten him on the phone.

"I'm calling about the Hughes Sinclair–Addison McGhee marriage," I explained.

And the clerk chuckled nervously. "I've been expecting this," he said. "I knew the media would pick up on it."

(Apparently, the clerk was paying more attention to the caller ID, listing my call as coming from GUP News, than he was my own stated identification as the bride. I decided not to say anything at this point; perhaps being in the media would prove advantageous in getting this straightened out quickly.)

"I don't understand why this marriage was annulled," I said.

"There was a court ruling," the clerk said, continuing

incredulously. "Surely, you've heard? They're all being annulled."

"All the gay marriages are," I said. "Not all the marriages in the state."

"I don't know where you're from, honey," the clerk said. "But around here when a guy famous for wearing a lavender tie to the Super Bowl marries some dude named Addison, that's a gay marriage."

He paused, then added in a pointed way, "Oh wait, excuse me. I believe the tie was *periwinkle*."

Now I was the one to chuckle nervously, but hopefully. Obviously, this would be easy to straighten out. "I'm Addison McGhee," I explained. "I know *Addison* was once a male name; so were *Ashley* and *Leslie* and *Madison*. I wore cotton balls on the cover of *Vanity Fair*. I'm on this month's *Celebrity Gourmet* wearing a bib apron. I assure you, I am a woman."

He stammered a bit, asked if I was joking, murmured something that approached an apology, then patched me through to the judge.

"That's terrible," the judge said. "Positively terrible. But still, easily fixed. Just hop down here and I'll remarry you myself. No harm done."

"We live in New York," I said. "Can't you just un-annul our wedding the same way you annulled it?"

The judge sucked air through his teeth in a *that's-a-tough-one* tone and gave me some legal mumbo jumbo about having the authority to annul, but no authority to rescind an annulment.

"That doesn't make sense," I said.

"Of course it doesn't, honey," he replied. "It's the law."

That night, I sat at the end of Hughes's long dining room table, picking at my arugula and radish salad. It was a lovely salad, but come on: radishes? You simply can't eat them if you have any hope of breathing near a man.

At any rate, when I remember that evening, I always picture Hughes seated at the other end of that long table, like half of a cartoonish, clichéd rich couple. But Hughes was, in fact, sitting right next to me. Just like a normal couple at dinner.

He was chewing slowly and smiling at me in sort of a goofy way and commenting between bites about how quickly the presidential thing blew over and how well it had worked out.

"Honey," I said finally. "There's a little problem."

# Chapter 21

*H*ughes said all the right things. He called it an outrage and an affront. I particularly remember his use of the word *atrocity*. His eyes got all crinkled up and he shook his fist a lot.

"And we should take a moment," he said, as he pulled himself together and took a sip of wine, "to remember all the couples that do not have the resources and legal rights that we do."

Giddy with relief, I agreed that we should. We even rose from our chairs for a moment to bow our heads and remember them.

Then Hughes said: "I'm sick of arugula. Let's go to bed."

"Well, Mr. Sinclair," I said, pretending to be shocked. "We're not even married anymore."

And he said, "No, Miss McGhee, we most certainly aren't."

Later, we lay there, intertwined and breathless, and he stroked my hair and asked how I thought we should handle it. "We could just get married again," I said. "It'd make your mom happy. Have a little ceremony before the reception."

Hughes didn't say anything for a long moment. But then he said he thought we should take a stand. We should announce to the world what had happened to us, he said. And we should point out that we weren't any different from the gay couples this had happened to.

I propped myself up on one arm, squinting at him in the darkness. *My parents would not like that, at all,* I thought. Not that my parents' politics were my main concern. I had just ordered some new monogrammed towels, AMS, Addison McGhee Sinclair. Suddenly I wasn't even sure if that was my name.

"Yeah, so we have a press conference," I said. "And *then* we'll get married again?"

Hughes sat up now, too, and reached over to the bedside table for a pad and pen. He started scribbling notes—a draft, I later learned, of what some people believed was a stunning and moving pledge of allegiance with gay couples the world over.

"If we were to just drive up to the courthouse and get married," he said, "we'd be saying we agreed that it was okay for them to annul all those other marriages, but not ours."

My heart was beginning to sink. I realized suddenly that this was something very much like what I had feared. This was the reason I had hesitated to tell Hughes. "I don't think *we're* saying that, honey," I said, trying not to grit my teeth. Was this the first time I ever really argued with Hughes? "I think the Supreme Court of Nevada is saying it. And if you're going to say that it's wrong for heterosexual couples to marry just because homosexual couples can't, then the whole world is filled with people who are wrong."

"Maybe the whole world is," Hughes said solemnly. "And maybe we're the ones who've been called to point it out."

"Called?" I said. I didn't like the tone of that. I wasn't interested in launching any sort of crusade at this point. I'd been in the news enough lately, what with the president and the parachute pants and all.

"Look," I said, "Hughes, honey, I already ordered monogrammed towels—AMS. They're going to look great. And your mom, she's planning that reception and we've got all these wedding gifts . . ."

I gestured vaguely behind us, toward the direction of the study, where we'd been piling the packages that were arriving by the hour, mostly from people we didn't even know.

He looked up when I mentioned the gifts and smiled roguishly. I realized then that had been a tactical mistake. Hughes was, actually, not at all wild about the gifts. He had rather minimalist sensibilities, first of all. So watching the bellman bring up multiple sets of toasters and Crock-Pots and dish towels was more than he could stand. Second, he was rather particular and he did not understand that other people would not be. He would look at wine goblets and say something like, "Why would anyone give such a personal item as a gift? You can't possibly predict what sort of wine goblet another person would like!"

(He himself tended to give what he called consumables as gifts. He figured that even if you didn't like the particular style of goat cheese that he gave you, you could at least serve it to guests who might and, at any rate, it would go bad eventually and then you could throw it out, so it would not be burdening your closets for years to come.)

He started scribbling more furiously on his pad of paper.

And I rolled over and pretended to go to sleep.

# Chapter 22

$\mathcal{H}$ughes and I, perhaps pointedly, did not discuss the subject at hand the next "morning" as we got ready for work or during the drive into the studio. After we arrived, though, Hughes pulled the studio staff together and announced that "Addison and I have something important to say at the top of the show." He did not want to give the specifics now, because he wanted to talk about it only once, but he wanted everyone to be prepared for an emotional conversation.

I mostly looked at the ground while he made this little speech, but once I glanced up and caught Cal's eye. Cal looked worried, and I understood why. He was concerned about Hughes and me—first the marriage, then the presidential photo. Now there was something new. He exhaled sharply, and I fully expected him to pull Hughes and me into his office and demand a full explanation of what was going on. But he didn't.

So the theme song started and the credits rolled and I looked over my Royal Copenhagen Flora Danica teacup, winked, and said: "Wake up, honey. It's morning now." (That teacup and saucer, I will have you know, cost an astonishing twelve hundred dollars. For one cup and saucer! What can I say? I was, in those heady brief days of two incomes, a bit of a spendthrift.)

164

Hughes gave a quick overview of some headlines of the day and then turned to Baxter. "But before we go further, Addison and I have something we'd like to say."

I would later learn by reading the board discussions that a lot of people thought Hughes was going to announce I was pregnant. Weatherjunkie said, in a short post, that a pregnancy was what he had suspected, and it was a thought that made him "depressed and ill." He did not explain why he had that reaction, but I had often thought that Weatherjunkie seemed to have a bit of a crush on me. (*Me* meaning Addison McGhee the television hostess, not *me* the person who posted messages under the name *ObjectiveObserver*.)

Anyway, the pregnancy fears or hopes were dashed when Hughes instead announced that our marriage had been mistakenly annulled and that we had decided "by mutual consent"—whatever that meant—to let the annulment stand until every other couple who'd had their marriage annulled could also remarry.

"Wow," Baxter said, not knowing really what to say and rather resenting, I think, not being given more of a detailed idea of what to expect. Here he was, being asked to react for the whole world, in front of the whole world.

There was a moment of silence. Baxter said "Wow" again and then asked: "How do you feel about this, Addison?"

I smiled, in a way that was meant to be brave but struck me as a little weak when I viewed it back later. "I'm happy to be able to make a statement, I guess," I said, looking at Hughes for approval. (In retrospect, I spent a lot of time looking to Hughes for approval.) "And I'm happy to do this until we've made our position clear."

"And our position," Hughes said, as if clarifying my point rather than basically contradicting it, "is that we won't get married until everyone else can."

Then he patted me on the knee and introduced the cooking segment. Our marriage was not mentioned again during the show, but when it was over we had long lists of media calls to return. Hughes handled all the meaty parts of the interviews, and I talked about the "hurt that I now know firsthand."

A *New York Times* reporter asked what we would do in the meantime, while the issue was being fought in the courts. I looked at Hughes, curious myself for the answer. He seemed surprised by the question, but didn't hesitate. He slung his arm over my shoulder and pulled me close. "I suppose we'll do what all the other couples are doing," he said. "We'll continue being married, whether Nevada knows it or not.

"This is," he added, "a battle over public policy. Our private lives won't change."

He blinked. Twice.

I gasped quietly. The reporter was standing to leave and didn't notice my gasp, but Hughes did. He glanced over at me with unblinking eyes, kissed my forehead, *then* blinked. Did that count as blinking three times? I wasn't sure.

When I got back to Hughes's apartment that afternoon, I saw that the monogrammed towels had arrived.

# Chapter 23

A few minutes ago, the woman in the next cell—the embezzler I mentioned earlier—had a visitor. It turned into a bit of an incident. The visitor was a guy, a former boyfriend or husband, I guess. Or current boyfriend and husband, I suppose. I don't know why I should presume that people have broken up just because they appear to hate each other.

The visiting room is way down the hall and on the other side of two big prison-style lock-down doors. But still we could hear the shouting here in our cells. The guards apparently threw the guy out, and the embezzler was returned to her cell in tears. She grunted several times and walked laps around her cell.

I caught her eye and smiled in what I hoped was an encouraging, supportive way. "Pacing is the best thing to do," I said finally. "I've always believed in it myself."

She looked at me suspiciously then looked away. "I just never thought we'd ever be so mean to each other," she said.

I reached through the bars to pat her on the shoulder. She looked up at me then and asked me a personal question that made me gasp.

I was struck at that moment by the fact that while my mistakes and my marriage were being discussed daily in the world outside prison, no one here had ever asked me about them before. I am not sure if it's due to politeness or disinterest. But the embezzler asked. She said: "What on earth did you ever see in that Hughes guy?"

I hesitated and then blurted out what I think is the truth, something that is much like the truth at least. "Well, he's good looking," I said, but I realized this was lame. "And he's smart. And sophisticated. He's not like the guys I knew at home. He's urbane. I remember when Peter Jennings died, all the obits called him *urbane*. And I realized that growing up in Nebraska, with my accent and my teeth and my acne, all I ever really wanted, even before I knew the word for it, was to be urbane."

I sighed. "Or at least, you know, to date someone who was."

The embezzler nodded.

"Anyway," I continued, "I certainly didn't meet anyone urbane in Nebraska or LA. It's a very rare quality, you know. But then, Hughes entered my life. He was sophisticated and suave. He really *is* dashing and dapper. He's like a young Peter Jennings. He's the epitome of America. I guess that's what I liked about him."

The embezzler looked at me for a long moment and then chuckled a little. "Peter Jennings was Canadian," she said.

"Nah," I said.

"Yeah," she said. "He was."

We sat there in silence, and then soon she was watching Lifetime again and I was busy with my marker, deleting several pages that I had just completed, pages that gave a rather detailed account of the latter days of my marriage to Hughes. (If they can technically be counted as "days of my marriage," since legally the whole thing was already all over.)

But today, after listening to the embezzler and the man she loves and hates, I've decided that really, there is nothing to be gained from going over the details. Marriages end for a million different reasons, but they end—ultimately—in the same way, with tears and sorrow and disillusionment and suspicion.

Things were said that will never be forgotten, but at least for my part of it, they will never be shared. Nothing was said that would help Cassie, I'm sure.

I don't know how much of it was true anyway. As I've already said, I do not feel even now like I know what happened in Hughes's and my marriage. On the day of our wedding, I believed with all my heart that our relationship had been building toward that moment, perhaps with uneven and irregular pacing, but that was only because of erratic schedules and cultural confusions and sleep deprivation.

But by the time we were taking our "stand"? I will confess that I wondered, still wonder, if our marriage had been planned from the get-go as a publicity stunt. Depending on the day, I can concoct a scenario in which Hughes planned the whole thing, either for the simple pleasure of being the most-talked-about name in the news for a few days, or to "prove" he was not gay, or to, ultimately, acknowledge that he was, by aligning himself with a cause he had not yet publicly embraced. You can put together all sorts of interesting and contradictory scenarios and the one thing they share is this: I was the patsy. But that's crazy, isn't it? That's what I always decide.

It's just like me to come up with some grand and dramatic scenario rather than simply admit that I'm a two-bit Hollywood actress with an all-too-Hollywood marriage. Except that I didn't even work in Hollywood anymore. Hadn't in a long time. But you know what I mean.

You may wonder if I ever asked Hughes directly. *Of course,* I asked him. And while I will not give you a blow-by-blow account of our final days together, I suppose I owe you at least that much—to tell you the firsthand account he gave of himself to me.

Unfortunately, this key question of mine came during a somewhat heated confrontation. I shouted it at him and I slammed a kitchen cabinet door for emphasis. (I had been looking for the balsamic, which his cook had stashed in the far back reaches of his pantry.)

To Hughes's credit, he took a moment to cool off and answered me in a serious and solemn way, which made me feel better. But he also answered in a rambling and confusing way that simultaneously made me feel worse. "You were the one, Addison. The only one," he said.

Whatever that meant.

Then he blinked three times and confused matters further still.

"You just blinked," I said. "You're lying."

Hughes sighed.

"Everyone blinks, Addison."

I guess really I'm in no position to judge. Talking to the embezzler just now, I realized that my desire to marry Hughes was less than pure. I was crazy about him. Still am, I guess. But it was a craziness fed by a need to escape a lifetime of people smirking at my name or my avoidance of pork products or my parents. Even when people were being nice, complimenting my English or taking honest pleasure in my family's dramatic triumph over adversity, it was grating to me. I didn't want to be special or different. I just wanted to be American, to be part of the establishment.

I wanted to be the daughter of a former Supreme Court justice and a ballet dancer, the grandchild of a couple who built half the country's libraries. I wanted, at least, to be the in-law.

Being the daughter of a pig-blood mopper and a Wal-Mart greeter wasn't the same.

I really loved Hughes. But I see now that my panting pursuit of my co-host was the natural extension of what I'd been chasing my whole life—I just wanted to fit in. Besides, Hughes looks so boyish when his eyes get crinkly. I've always been a sucker for crinkly eyes. Have I mentioned that?

Suffice it to say, no matter how valiantly I fought to save our marriage or at least to understand it, I realize in retrospect that, for me, the marriage really ended on the morning that Hughes made his little announcement to the world about our annulment. Baxter had absorbed the news and said: "How do you feel about this, Addison?"

At that moment I had realized with a sharp ache that Hughes had never himself inquired.

Soon I moved out of Hughes's apartment. I checked back into the Ritz and brazenly told them to bill Cal. I was unreasonably upset and disappointed to learn that the room I'd lived in up until my marriage had now been given to another guest. I understood they would have. They would have to. But I was still disappointed, even though they made a big point of giving me a better room and a nice welcome basket with fruit.

The porter patted me on the back as he unloaded my bags. "I knew," he said, "the moment I saw your face when Hughes started talking about 'an opportunity to take a stand now and forever,' I knew there was more going on."

I bit my lip and tried to hand him a tip and he waved me off. "No, no," he said, as he turned to go. "It was my pleasure . . ." He stopped then, turned back to me. "Should I call you Mrs. Sinclair?"

I took his hand in my right hand and patted it with my left. "No," I said. "Just call me Addison. Addison McGhee."

He nodded and I nodded. I can't tell you how touched I was by that exchange—a bellman refusing my tip, asking me how I would prefer to be addressed. It struck me at that moment that no one had ever before asked me what I wished to be called, and I realized that maybe that is the reason I was so excited about those monogrammed towels. Women have fought over the years to keep their "own" names and I have, in principle, supported that fight. (I *begged* Courteney not to add *Arquette* to her name. I said, "Really, it's not like it's helped Patricia. Or Rosanna. Or, for that matter, David." But since I was just a waitress at SI at that point—Courteney was visiting with the Alabama relatives—she just looked at me uncomfortably and asked for more raspberry-infused vinegar for her salad.)

But taking Hughes's name was, for me, a feminist move itself. A lifetime ago, a stranger named me. A man no less. Now I would decide for myself what I was to be called. So if Addison McGhee Sinclair wasn't going to work out, perhaps I should choose something else. I could become Miranda Marlin or Darcy Sanchez or Seville Chan.

Or maybe I should go back to Ada Sinmac Ghee. Or at least Ada McGhee. Baxter already calls me that. I've always sort of liked it.

I unpacked my laptop and plugged it into the wall and started reading the boards. I had given them up, basically, during my marriage. But that night, I was on a board binge. Isn't that the way with addiction?

I was surprised and heartened, I suppose, to realize that most people thought I was the victim in the whole thing. There were all sorts of conspiracy theories, similar to the ones I had already created in my own mind. Hughes was the bad guy in just about all of them, thank goodness.

Weatherjunkie and B-basher were still out of commission. Perhaps they had gotten bored with the whole thing. Who could blame them? All their witty insights and informed opinions didn't really matter in the current climate, where the discussion was all about innuendo and smear.

But I enjoyed it. I did not go to bed at all, reading the lively chatter about Hughes and me and our "shamarriage"—people on the boards just love those sort of coined meldings.

I was shocked when I finally glanced at the clock and realized it was time to get dressed for work.

And despite how low I felt when I checked into the hotel, despite not getting a moment of sleep, I felt surprisingly frisky that "morning." I dressed in a snug suit that was particularly becoming and I delivered my signature sentence with more than my usual flirtatious charm. I had selected a Lenox teacup of the Solitaire pattern for the occasion. I thought the name was appropriate and, at about fifty bucks, it was a particularly frugal choice for a single woman.

Cal had a glint in his eye off screen. I could tell he was thinking: *She's back. She's back.*

Hughes had a glint, too. "Well, you're in a good mood, Addison. Must have slept well, I guess. Hotel living suits you."

My face froze. I turned toward him, slowly.

You think of a television studio as being a quiet place during a show, but it's not really as quiet as you think—not for the anchors. There are the people talking in our ears and the cameramen's grunts and shuffling. All of that is filtered out from the audience, but there are, at least on a low-rent show like ours, deliveries being made and production problems being solved in stage whispers all around you. Still, when Hughes made his comment about hotel living, the entire room went silent. Even the producer—who had been blathering some information about how we were going to replace the Pilates demonstration with some trained seals—stopped midsentence. Hughes had recently said publicly that we were still married, whether the state of Nevada knew it or not. But now he had just casually acknowledged to the whole world that his wife of a few weeks was no longer sharing his bed, that he had no idea how she had slept, that she had moved into a hotel.

Except I wasn't legally his wife, but you know what I mean.

I glared at him. I tried to convince myself later that it wasn't really a glare, but when I watched it back on tape, it most definitely was. I cleared my throat. I said: "Well."

I turned away from him then and said: "And how about you, Baxter? What did you think of this new controversy with the gold standard?"

"I think," said Baxter, dependable as always, "that the Gold Coast is in for a terrible storm."

And we muddled through the rest of the show.

I suppose it is possible that Hughes just blurted out his comment without realizing how revealing it was. Or furthermore, that he just thought the truth needed to be broached and the sooner, the better. But it fell so obviously and painfully flat that I never could believe that. Surely someone of Hughes's charms and grace would have attempted to apologize in either case. Instead, he merely acted for the rest of the day as if nothing had happened, including our marriage.

But the viewers could tell that something had happened. Icy asides and snippy exchanges were analyzed and debated, even at times when no icy or snippy intent was meant.

Much was made, for example, of Hughes using the word *corny* to describe the latest Ben Stiller movie. Some thought it was a putdown to the corn-producing state of Nebraska and everyone who once lived there. I think they were seriously overestimating how much thought Hughes had given to my ties to Nebraska. In his heart of hearts, I don't think he truly believed that I ever lived there. I'm not sure he believes anyone does. He thinks it's sort of a quaint pop-culture invention—like a Norman Rockwell painting or the city of Mayberry.

My own comments were also scrutinized. The most cited exchange involved a particularly harsh putdown of Hughes when he steered our conversation about a small fashion flare-up in an unexpected and unwelcome direction.

We were going to discuss the unfortunate movie premiere at which Ewan McGregor and Jude Law appeared wearing identical Union Jack bow ties. I thought we were going to talk about the identical part, which seemed to me to be the central embarrassment. But Hughes got hung up on the bow tie concept itself.

Baxter was, that day, wearing a blue-with-white-polka-dots tie, and he tugged it in what I took to be a self-conscious way when Hughes used the phrase *finicky dandies* about Ewan and Jude.

"Hey, Baxter," Hughes said, turning toward the weather map, as if suddenly realizing there was someone else in the room. "You're one of those bow tie guys. Maybe you can explain the appeal. I, myself, don't get the look. It's so positively George Will!"

Baxter looked mortified, and I was filled with dread. There was no good way this conversation could end.

"Oh, Hughes," I said, nudging him with my elbow. "You're just jealous. You know how bow ties drive women wild." I looked over my shoulder then, glancing at Baxter. I gave him my "devilish" grin—the one I had perfected during a short stint playing a substitute teacher/demon in *Buffy the Vampire Slayer*.

Hughes looked at me, incredulous. "Bow ties drive women wild?" he said. "Really?"

"Heard of the Chippendales?" I said, turning back toward Hughes and giving him a meaningful look. "They're not wearing bow ties because women think they're frumpy."

"I suppose," Hughes said, seeming to give this serious consideration. "But those ties are solid colors. And they match their cummerbunds."

I furrowed my eyebrows. "Do they?" I asked. "I don't remember any cummerbunds."

Hughes made a *there-she-goes-again* face, as if this was some sort of sexual remark. I rolled my eyes. But neither of us went down that conversational path.

"I don't know what it is about bow ties," I continued. I looked directly at the camera. "I guess we just want to untie them." I made a gesture with my hands that looked something like pulling a tie apart. Then I clapped my hands together and laughed.

"Those ordinary things you wear." I reached over and tugged at Hughes's tie, which happened to have muted red stripes on a silver background that day. (The women on the discussion boards never had cared for it.)

"We don't even understand how this sort works." I was on a roll. "If we started tugging on one, we might just choke you."

I smiled, then looked back at Baxter.

"Not that choking Hughes doesn't have its own kind of appeal." I winked.

Hughes pursed his lips in mock sheepishness. Baxter smirked and looked as if he was about to break into an honest-to-goodness grin.

By that point in our relationship, all friendly on-air banter was a show. I assume you know that now. But my comment about choking Hughes was nevertheless entirely innocent. I meant no harm to Hughes. It was all about the show. Hughes had made a mistake by broaching this subject with Baxter. He was not going to score points for himself by publicly picking on the unfashionable unfortunate. I never asked, but I think Hughes realized that. He did not seem angry at me, afterward. It was just the way we were on air. It didn't faze him at all.

Still, that comment was cited often, including most famously in the special issue of *People* magazine titled: WHAT'S WRONG WITH ADDISON AND HUGHES? The Coalition Against Office Romances was quoted far and wide saying that we were an example of why interoffice flirtations should be banned by company policy and the law itself. The religious right said it demonstrated how gay marriage would destroy the very fabric of a nation and ruin the lives of God-fearing young couples like Addison and Hughes. The liberal left said look what happens when the government gets involved in people's sex lives.

George Clooney was asked about it on his way into a movie premiere. "Ah, Madison and Hugh," he said. "Wish them both the best." He turned to his date. "We went to their wedding, didn't we?" And she said, "No."

Meanwhile, the gay rights movement in Nevada picketed with signs that said: SAVE OUR MARRIAGE—AND ADDISON'S TOO.

But it was obvious to everyone that it was too late for that. Nothing that happened in Nevada would change anything now. Our personal story had an all-too-predictable plot. Anyone could see how it was going to end. The state of Nevada was not going to restore all those marriages, and neither Hughes nor I was going to do anything about it.

I even allowed myself to think a little about my post-Hughes future, wondering wistfully if Derek Jeter was still single, if Clooney had worked on his abs, if Baxter would still stare at me in a theater.

Over on the boards, the conversation, not surprisingly, had been followed with more than average interest. The people posting things on the boards all day wondered how often I'd been to Chippendales (never!), whether I was a good tipper or not (generous is more like it; I was, after all, a waitress once), and if, really, it was Hughes who frequented Chippendales. And Weatherjunkie said that perhaps the reason I mentioned Chippendales was that was what "really" happened to our marriage.

That was a theory that B-basher did not like at all. "Let's not engage in spreading wild and unsubstantiated speculation," he wrote. I thought his reaction was a bit odd. I mean, that's all we ever did there on the boards. Why protest it now?

This launched a rather animated discussion about the pleasures and pitfalls of unsubstantiated speculation. It was the kind of conversation that would have normally gone on for weeks. But it was interrupted by the momentous and violent events that occurred the next day during a Cal-mandated segment on flexibility, which our guest, the author of a series of books on stretching, called the "fountain of youth."

The author, a frighteningly agile man, said your true age can be determined in large part by how flexible you are. I was not thrilled about helping with the demonstration because flexibility had never been one of my strong suits. In high school, I could not have considered cheerleading, even if my parents would have allowed it, because there was no way I ever could have done the splits. And high school was a long time ago. And, perhaps proving the expert's theory, things had not improved.

But Cal insisted the segment needed a demonstration and that Hughes, Baxter, and I must all participate.

The expert trotted Baxter and Hughes and me out to the middle of the stage and put us through a short workout of stretching, as he took measurements with an odd instrument featuring spikes and sharp points. He made notes and tsked and tutted at us. Hughes was whizzing through them all with a ballet dancer's grace, while Baxter and I were grunting and so forth. I, more than Baxter, truth be told, even though the expert said women are usually better at this.

But it's not all about gender. It's also genetics and culture— my parents' culture believed all your limbs should be kept close to your trunk, thank you very much. And besides, I was wearing control-top hose during the entire ordeal, an obstacle that Hughes and Baxter, as far as I know, did not face.

The expert did a few calculations during the commercial break and then gave us a live, on-air report. Baxter was first, and he was proclaimed to have the flexibility of a thirty-four-year-old woman. "Ah," he said, looking very pleased. "I turned thirty-six last month. And, as you know, I'm a man."

Hughes and I gave him high fives. Then the expert turned to Hughes. "You, sir, have the flexibility of a seven-year-old boy." Hughes leaned back into a yoga bridge position to celebrate. There were gasps and cheers from the production staff. Baxter whistled, and I applauded with good-natured glee.

Then the expert turned to me.

"I'm sorry to say, Ms. McGhee, that you have the flexibility of a seventy-eight-year-old arthritic patient."

I blinked. I had been prepared for mild embarrassment, which I planned to gamely shrug off in a charming and self-deprecating way. In my most paranoid moments, I could not have fathomed such humiliation was possible from this stupid segment. (I still think he got his calculations wrong.) I looked at Hughes and realized that since the happy day I got married barefoot, there had been nothing but humiliation and regret.

"I've never seen numbers like this," the expert continued. "And I evaluated Pope John Paul the second." The expert hesitated and then added, "Just before he died."

My dimple started quivering.

"Oh, don't worry," Hughes said, patting me on the back.

I looked up at him, suddenly consumed again with the old fondness. We had just gone through a wrenching and mysterious marriage. He had broken my heart and forced me to waste money on monogrammed towels. But here, on this show, on *our* show, we were still a team. I could trust him again. He would help me out of this mess. He would save the day.

"I'm sure," Hughes said, "it's just a temporary condition. You've just been all brittle and crispy since that court ruling thing."

My budding fondness shriveled instantly. Brittle? Crispy? Not to mention: Court. Ruling. *Thing?* I turned and looked at him incredulously and noticed that the production staff had fallen quiet again. "You mean, the ending of my marriage?" I said in a husky whisper as I placed my hand over my mike. (The people on the boards caught only the word *marriage,* and so were not quite sure what I said. They proposed several theories—all of which, I'm afraid, were more clever and striking than what I had actually said.)

But the question of what I said was overshadowed by what happened next. Without thinking it through, I grabbed the sharp, pointed flexibility measurer and heaved it at Hughes.

My high school neighbor, Kevin Ford, and Slater County's glamorous PE coach said I had terrible aim. And for all those years I believed them. But if I have terrible aim, then angels (or devils) must have carried that flexibility device, for it hit Hughes square in the left temple and skidded down his face, leaving a deep gash and briefly knocking him unconscious.

# Chapter 24

$\mathcal{A}$l Sharpton was on the phone within the hour. "Addy, baby," he said. He sighed in what I think was supposed to be a sympathetic way but rang with a note of excitement. "Girl," he said, clucking his tongue a little. "You got to watch yourself with the white people."

I confess that it took me a moment to make sense of that sentence. I did not immediately connect it to the on-air incident with Hughes. I didn't really think of Hughes as being "white people." I thought of him as my husband, or ex-husband, or, you know, something.

And secondly, I did not really perceive racial issues in the same way as Al Sharpton. I suppose that goes without saying. I'm not sure anyone sees racial issues exactly as Al Sharpton does.

But in a broader sense, being an African refugee in America is much different from being a traditional "African American." And being an African refugee of Middle Eastern descent, with a rather undefined appearance and a career in television, is even more different.

It's not that I cannot understand, intellectually, where the Al Sharptons of the world are coming from. Being forcibly brought to America and enslaved? It is quite obviously a horror that can be erased only after many, many generations, if at all. And every time Al Sharpton reminds the world of that, well, it's time well spent, I say.

But it's different for me. My family's arrival in America was, you see, our salvation. To use a sports analogy, I watched the Al Sharptons of the world the way baseball fans might follow the labor problems in hockey. They can sympathize with the hockey fans. They can see the parallels to their own painful experiences. They can understand, in a deep intellectual way, that they're the same exact issues and that this will play itself out in ways that will leave no team, in any sport, unchanged. But really, when it comes right down to it, they don't care about hockey.

Al Sharpton was making a clicking sound with his tongue. "This is going to be huge, you know? *Huge.*"

I gulped. *Was it?*

I looked out the door of my office, saw everyone working. It seemed quieter than usual. Hughes was holding an ice pack to his head with more drama than was strictly necessary, I thought. But people were not exactly gathering around to commiserate or check on him. In fact, once Hughes was conscious and okayed by the paramedics, people had hardly spoken to him at all. Or to me, either, come to think of it.

I'll never forget how I had felt as a schoolchild, sitting at my desk, in my Goodwill clothes, my body smelling of spices my classmates didn't eat, my words—even after a year or two—awkward and slow compared with theirs. Utterly apart is how I felt. Completely different.

But for several years now, that had not been my experience at all. I was on the cover of *Vanity Fair*. I was eating nightly with the son of a former chief justice, an American hero of sorts. I was going to barbecues at the White House. (Well, okay, one barbecue.) I had shamed my parents, wasted years looking at a computer screen, and starved myself because of a television-induced fear of food. I was married for the lesser part of three weeks and my marriage began and ended in Las Vegas. How much more American could you get?

But at that moment, as Al Sharpton was excitedly relaying to me the racial ramifications of what I'd done, I looked out through my office door and felt absolutely lost again—the way I had as a young child. More than two decades in America and I had still not mastered this basic tenet of American life. I still didn't understand race.

"I don't think it's going to be huge, A . . ." I started to call him Al, instantly thought better of it. "Um, Reverend Sharpton. I'm not really black and Hughes . . ." I don't know where I'd been going with that, because Hughes was certainly white. He was about the whitest white guy in television. I paused, then offered: "It's different for celebrities."

"Oh, you're black all right," Sharpton said. "Especially now that you nearly killed a white guy."

I gasped. This was the first time the *nearly killed* line was used on me.

But Al didn't hear or, at least, didn't care about my gasping. "We're going to have to get your story straight and get it out quick. I'm assuming you've been Hughes's target a few times or you wouldn't have had your technique down so well."

"Oh no," I said. "Hughes never . . ."

But Sharpton wasn't listening, just continuing on his own beat. "I'd say you learned from the master."

He half chuckled. "Heh, the master. Sometimes I amaze even myself."

"This has nothing to do with any of that," I finally said. I pulled out the drawer of my desk where I'd stashed our wedding photo. I looked at Hughes and me. I realized that in the entire time we had flirted and dated and married—the flirting time being the longest—I had never heard anyone mention that we were an interracial couple. I had never thought about that. Did I need to think about it now?

"Thanks for your concern," I said, a bit briskly. I hung up and noticed the other line bleeping. The caller ID said: JESSE JACKSON.

And in what was either my shrewdest or most idiotic move, I didn't answer.

If you want to make a case for shrewd, then this is it. In the entire tortured series of events that followed, much was made of almost everything, but Al Sharpton was wrong—not a whole lot was made of race. Perhaps it ran in undercurrents throughout the whole thing—as I said, I'm not well tuned to such matters. But if it did, it at least did not dominate the conversation.

On the other hand, if you want to make the case for idiotic, then this is it. Here I am, sitting in prison. And tomorrow, I very well may be deported.

# Chapter 25

Our ratings skyrocketed. They were already higher than usual as people tuned in to get a glimpse of our train wreck of a marriage. It was all so delightfully surreal. A show built on the flirtation of its hosts suddenly sees, in the course of a couple of months, the two get married, then unmarried against their will, and then the whole thing falls apart into an awkward spectacle. And then I knocked him out and gave everyone what they wanted. The video clip was posted all over the Web and was, later that year, named by *People* magazine as the "only frequently viewed Internet video of a clothed couple."

You can't buy that kind of publicity. I tried to make that point to Cal once, and his response was, "I wouldn't want to."

He believed the whole thing had ruined his show. "My show, my show," he said, laying his head on his desk in a dramatic way. "My favorite show."

He threatened to put me on the channel's new late-night (and so far poorly rated) competitive gardening show, *Iron Thumb*. I didn't believe him for a second. Cal might love his "favorite show," but he loved his favorite show's ratings even more.

All those new viewers were sorely disappointed, though. Hughes and I gamely and professionally carried on. It was stilted, but never overtly hostile. There was one awkward moment when Hughes stumbled over the word *falafel* a few times and then said: "I don't know what's wrong with me, it's like I've been knocked in the head or something." I gulped and looked embarrassed. Hughes twisted his face in a pained and sheepish way. Baxter leapt in and started babbling about low-pressure systems.

I turned toward Baxter, listening to him babble, and I thought, really, it was the sweetest thing I'd ever seen and I realized that after everything that had happened, he still stood as the only person who had asked me how I felt about it all.

*Baxter's a dear,* I thought. I think his agent is quite wrong about needing bow ties. The "Shaggy Doo" look he demonstrated at the theater that night could be a very popular weatherman image.

We went to commercial break and Cal, who was hanging out on the set all the time now, put his head in his hands and moaned loudly. "Knocked in the head? Did you really freakin' say 'knocked in the head'?"

"It's a common phrase, Cal," Hughes said testily.

"That's it." Cal put up his hand to stop Hughes, as you might a whining child. "We've got to do something." He turned to his producers. "I want Hughes and Addison apart tomorrow. Do you hear me? Tomorrow! Addison is going to have to broadcast from the Pella, Iowa, Tulip Festival or the National Cornhusking Championships in Missouri or I-Forty Days in Amarillo, Texas, or *something*. Give me anything. What the hell is going on *tomorrow*?"

The producer gulped and looked down at his notes for the next day, which as usual had nothing of the festival variety. But the producer was from Louisville, Kentucky, and so he knew one thing that no one else in the room did. It was Kentucky Derby Week.

"There's always the Kentucky Derby," he said.

"*Horse* racing?" I said, a bit haughtily. I didn't see why I was the one being sent off someplace when it was Hughes who had put his foot in his mouth. "I don't think so. My parents would freak out. Gambling? On horses?"

Cal met my eyes. He looked mean and serious. "Oh, but assaulting your husband on TV—this is okay?"

I blanched. I had tried to put the *nearly killed* line out of my head, but now Cal was using the word *assault*? I said simply: "He's not my husband."

"Ten seconds to air," called the producer, tapping his watch.

There was silence for five long seconds. Then Baxter said, "Oh come on, Ada. It'll be fun. I'll go, too."

I looked at him, then Cal, then Baxter again.

"Okay," I said.

"One second . . . air," said the producer.

Hughes looked into the camera and said, "And we haven't even told people about your big trip, Addison."

"We basically just found out," I said, with an exaggerated shrug. I looked over at Baxter, smiled in what I fancied to be my most winning way. "Didn't we, Baxter? It's the Kentucky Derby for us."

"Go Smarty Jones!" Baxter said, pumping his fist in the air in a goofy and endearing manner.

"I think Smarty retired," Hughes said, but he laughed when he said it.

"Baxter and I are going to learn all about this horse stuff," I said. "We'll be broadcasting live from there starting . . ." I hesitated, but then saw Cal mouth from off stage, *To-mor-row.*

"Starting tomorrow!" I said, in an excited and breathless way. I could always fake it when I had to.

"I suppose I have to hold down the fort here," Hughes

said, with obviously feigned glumness. "I'm going to be lonely and jealous."

Baxter wasn't in the camera shot at that moment and it was a good thing, because I could see him from my place on the sofa and he definitely rolled his eyes.

# Chapter 26

The flight was still boarding, but Baxter and I—seated in the back of first class—were already sorting through the files of newspaper and magazine clippings that our producers had put together to educate us about the Derby. I was looking at an interesting clip called HOLLYWOOD SOUTH—LOUISVILLE'S WEEK AS A CELEBRITY MECCA. Baxter was reading about the actual horse race.

Out of the corner of my eye, I saw a slightly overweight woman wearing sweatpants and a TALK DERBY TO ME T-shirt coming down the aisle, seemingly carrying more baggage than the law allowed and making more noise than she ought to. She had an efficient haircut and a friendly smile and she looked to me like the motherly sort that was prepared for anything.

Suddenly the woman stopped. "Oh my word!" she said excitedly. She dropped her large shoulder bag, the better to wave her arms about. "I can't believe this! I'm your biggest fan!" She was jumping up and down and pointing at Baxter.

He smiled at her, murmured, "Thank you."

"I watch you every day," she said. "Especially, you know, when there is a hurricane or something."

"Oh," Baxter said. "Do you live on the coast?"

"Well, no," she said. "But I like to stay informed on the weather."

Baxter smiled. "As do I," he said.

"Are you going to the Derby?" she asked.

"Yes, yes," Baxter said. I noticed that Baxter had mastered the same technique for fan small talk that I had. Answer in the most concise way possible, in order to give them little to elaborate on. But repeat the answer often, so it seems longer and more polite.

"Yes," he said again, glancing pointedly at the long line that was forming behind her. But she did not seem to notice. She smiled at me. "Are you his wife?"

Baxter chuckled softly and looked at his feet.

I hesitated. The word *wife* was a painful one for me at that particular moment. Besides, was this woman joking? She was Baxter's biggest fan and she didn't even know that he wasn't married?

"No," I said, turning back to my magazine. "No, no."

"Well, you ought to be," the woman said and nudged Baxter. "You're so cute together." She pronounced *cute* in a cutesy way, overemphasizing the *t*.

"Well," Baxter said. He looked down at his paper awkwardly. "Well, well."

A man holding a large suitcase cleared his throat, and Baxter's fan finally moved on down the aisle.

Baxter looked at me then, raised an eyebrow, and shrugged. "Does she really watch the show?" he asked. "Or, you know, anything at all?"

I was, I confess, grateful for the acknowledgment that failing to recognize me was awkward—and not just because I was the star of the program she professed to watch daily. My marital problems were big news. I was on Fox News those days more than I was on my own show—in clips, I mean; I did not give interviews on the matter. And if you saw any of that coverage at all, it would be quite clear to you that I was not, as a matter of law, married at all, and certainly not to Baxter.

I gave him one of those charming, self-deprecating waves and said: "Weather is the most highly rated segment of the show, Baxter. You know that. There's got to be tons of people who know you, but not Hughes or me."

He made a skeptical expression, then seemed to think seriously for a moment. "I think it's more likely that she was thrown off by your hair"—he made a gesture toward my hair band. We'd had to race from the studio to make the afternoon flight, and I had few hairstyling options at that point. I could never stand to leave the studio with my hair so totally encrusted with hair spray, but I didn't have time to restyle it. So I snagged a hair band from the cosmetics office and hoped it would look "trendsetting."

"You don't wear it that way on the air," said Baxter. "It's different and, you know, 'cute.'"

He pronounced it the same cutesy way the fan had.

I grimaced. "Cute is a *different* look for me?" I said, in what I can confess now was a pathetic play for a compliment.

"Oh, Ada," Baxter said, exasperated. "You know better than that." He leaned toward me. "Sometimes it looks beautiful, sometimes it looks striking, sometimes it looks simply luxurious. Cute is not the opposite of how it normally looks, but only a particular sort of attractive that it happens to look today."

I leaned back—as far back as I could lean in the crowded confines of the plane. I gave him an appraising look. Written down like this, the words sound flirtatious. But they were delivered in an agitated, irritated way—so I wasn't sure.

"You're a smooth talker," I said, finally.

Baxter snapped his finger and looked back at his clippings.

"Darn," he said. "Here I'm doing my best to be gritty and you call me 'smooth.'"

# Chapter 27

$\mathcal{T}$he Derby puts the *D* in *D list*, I'm afraid. My agent told me that years ago, and I was a little disappointed to find out he was right. I had thought he was being harsh, but there are some unlikely "stars" who turn out for this thing. The "Hollywood South" article touted Donald Trump's cousin, and Lynda Carter, and Mary Ann Mobley. (A former Miss America, she appeared often on *Love Boat, Fantasy Island,* and *Love, American Style,* and if you don't remember that last show, well, join the crowd.)

I loved *Wonder Woman* as much as anyone. And Donald Trump's cousin is, legitimately, *related* to a celebrity. But all in all, even I had to admit it was sort of unimpressive.

Not to belittle the event. It draws more stars in a weekend than most midcontinent cities do in a year. Omaha certainly doesn't attract this kind of crowd. I don't think Mary Ann Mobley has been there once.

And the Derby does sometimes lure a real star. Ed Harris has shown up on occasion. Jack Nicholson did once. Pamela Anderson counts, I suppose. And when Louisville gets real stars, Louisville remembers. The residents talk about it for years afterward. And at that particular moment in history, with my face all over the tabloids and our ratings higher than ever, Baxter and I counted as real celebrities.

My star-crossed and controversial wedding had made me a household name, and my plight as a ditched wife had made me popular with just about everyone. Liberal observers thought my plight mirrored that of gay would-be spouses everywhere; conservatives thought I was a good wholesome girl who just wanted to get married and have children and would have happily done so if my husband had not been led astray by the "gay agenda."

I was the victim in all versions of events. And for those few days, even the "assault" had not hurt me. It would take the first lady another day or two to work with that. At the moment I was arriving in Louisville, people were watching the video of me chucking that thing at Hughes and saying, "Yes, well, but . . . think what she's been through."

I was at the height of my fame and celebrity. I had the nation's sympathy. But the TALK DERBY lady recognized Baxter and not me—that pretty much sums up my career, I suppose.

At any rate, Baxter and I rather enjoyed the Derby, enjoyed being the hot young stars. The local newspaper was all abuzz with the news of our last-minute arrival, and the hottest "celebrity events" in town—the big parade, the diabetes fundraiser—were clamoring for our attention.

The mayor of Louisville even intervened on our behalf, giving up the suite that she normally reserved for her father-in-law, so that we could stay at the prestigious and otherwise booked-up Seelbach hotel in downtown Louisville. Baxter and I were swept into the two-bedroom suite with great fanfare. Although really, I thought even that was a bit awkward. People like Baxter and me do not share hotel rooms, even two-bedroom suites. I mean, come on. Even if you did not realize the way we had shamelessly flirted once at a play—and of course they didn't—you might realize that two co-workers of the opposite sex would like a door with a lock between the two of them at night. But people don't think of Baxter and Hughes and me as co-workers. That's what's so strange. They see us work together every day, but they don't realize it's work and we may not be as buddy-buddy as we seem on television.

Still, we could hardly complain when they were treating us with such fanfare as they whisked us around to all the pre-Derby activities. Even the cabdrivers gave us pointers on what horse to bet on. And a local boutique owner was summoned to bring me all her best Derby suits and hats, so that I could choose among them without troubling my celebrity self to leave the hotel. I told the owner that I wasn't sure about the headgear. "I'm not a hat person," I said. She told me that everyone says that at first. And I found, actually, that I looked rather nice in a hat. All the other women did, too. And it was great fun. I wore one every day on the air and it always matched Baxter's bow tie. We were just adorable. Everyone said so.

Each morning we sat elegantly on the side of the track not open to the general public—it was, we soon learned, called the backside. We had all sorts of fun with that. "We've got our backsides perched here on the backside," Baxter said once. And we both giggled a little, in our lovely finery, as beautiful thoroughbreds performed their workouts behind us.

(I learned later that Hughes complained to Cal about this, asking who'd decided that Baxter would suddenly be chipper. "I'm supposed to be chipper," Hughes said. "He's supposed to be sullen.")

But Cal said nothing to Baxter and me, who were each rather taken with the whole Derby spectacle and gushed about it on the air in a way that pleased the locals and shifted our show's cosmic energy from New York to Louisville. Baxter and I were suddenly the stars of the show and Hughes a dutiful handyman, helping us out with news tidbits we'd been too busy to read about.

Baxter got so blasé about things that he even seemed to forget he was the weatherman. At one point, we were going on and on about the beautiful spring when Hughes broke in from the New York studio to ask Baxter if it were safe to assume that a snowstorm so late in the year would not accumulate much. And Baxter was unable to hide his surprise.

"It's *snowing?*" he said. "In May?"

He laughed a little, then added: "Where?"

*"Here,"* Hughes said, impatiently. "In New York!"

Baxter replied, in what sounded like a slight Kentucky accent, "Well, I'll be."

I grabbed his arm, in a panicky gesture. "It's not going to snow here, is it?" I asked. "That could totally change what I've planned to wear to the race!" And Baxter, who normally couldn't tear his nose out of a weather map, shrugged.

"I have no earthly idea," he said. "But I'll surely find out."

"Oh good," I said. "I really need to know. I was going to wear my new Prada sandals. I don't want my little toes to get cold."

"No, no," Baxter said. "Not your little toes. I'll check during the next commercial break."

"You do that," Hughes broke in, obviously irritated. "And if you could find out about the forecast in the rest of the country, that would be nice, too."

Cal was not happy about that whole exchange, and he gave Baxter a serious talking-to later. Baxter nodded seriously and made apologetic sounds on the phone even as he watched some of the horses working out, nudging me at a particularly fast one.

Baxter and I fed off each other's irreverence. One morning on the air, Hughes was blabbering on, trying to be a part of his own show by telling me his personal picks for the big race, and I put my hand to my ear and said breezily, "I guess we're having technical problems, Hughes, I can't hear a thing you're saying. So we'll just skip you for now and go to Baxter."

At the next break, Baxter asked if I needed my earpiece replaced; he could hear Hughes perfectly. I smiled in my most mischievous way and said, "Yeah, I could, too."

Friday was our last show before the Saturday race, and Cal casually suggested on the phone that we just come on back after the morning broadcast. "You must be kidding," Baxter said. "There would probably be a riot. We're huge here!"

He handed me the phone, and I picked up the argument.

"Besides," I said, "we can't go on and on about this for four days on the air and then not even be able to tell people on Monday how it all turned out."

Cal snorted. "Well, you could use some of your reportorial skills and find that out, Addison. It's sure to be in the paper. Or the Web," he added.

*Does that mean something? Is he implying I spend too much time on the Web?*

"I don't mean who won the race, Cal," I said in a pointedly dramatic fashion. "I mean what people wore, how it felt—the sights, the smells, the sounds."

I was using all my most dramatic gestures to illustrate the senses, but that was all lost on Cal because, well, we were talking by phone.

"Oh for heaven's sake," he said. "No one cares about the Kentucky Derby. I was just trying to get you off Hughes's sofa for a few days."

I bristled at the reference to Hughes's sofa. I was suddenly consumed by what has become the one lasting regret about my marriage to Hughes. Why did I not take advantage of our short period of intimacy to find out if Cal was paying him a lot more than me? I mean, really. Hughes's sofa? The sofa certainly belonged to me as much as Hughes. I was the one who had to constantly worry about it clashing with my clothes.

Cal could not see me bristle. He sighed. "What do I care? If you and Baxter want to cavort about the barns, be my guests. But listen to me, Addison, don't get married and don't knock anyone unconscious. And tell Baxter to keep up with the weather!"

We hung up.

Baxter had collapsed on the small couch in the living area of our suite. His tie was undone and he had a bemused smile on his face.

"What?" I said. He could not have heard any of Cal's advice or his reference to Hughes's sofa, so I didn't see what he could be smirking about.

"The sights," he said, in a Zsa Zsa Gabor voice, his hand over his eyes as if pantomiming a ship captain. "The smells?" He took a huge exaggerated sniff.

He was mocking me!

"The sounds!" He spoke in the same silly breathless voice, but now he was cupping a hand around each ear.

I threw a pillow at him.

"She's resorting to violence again!" he yelled—a bit too loudly, I thought—but I laughed despite myself. He threw his hands up. "Just don't call Al Sharpton on me!" he continued.

I plopped in the armchair, gracelessly, and my skirt got pulled up a good two inches higher than I would have normally allowed. I'm actually fairly modest when I'm not on television or, you know, magazine covers. I started to jump up and straighten myself, but Baxter was continuing with his shtick and it was all so comfortable and familiar that jumping up for the sake of two inches of modesty didn't seem worth the bother. Lots of women wear their skirts this short all the time. At least, a lot of models do.

"You know, the first lady will be on my side about this," he said. "She thinks you're setting a very bad example, you know."

He was laughing, but it didn't sound like he was just making that up. "The first lady?" I said. "She's weighed in about this?"

Baxter, who was acting so silly as to seem a little drunk, now took on a serious, political spin-master tone. "The junior senator from Ohio, Ms. McGhee, weighs in on everything, especially something as vitally important as the feminization of violence and the glamorization of a crime."

"Oh come on," I said, kicking my feet up on the coffee table. My skirt rode up another half inch. "Be serious."

Baxter sighed, from honest tiredness, I think. Not boredom. Or exasperation. "I am serious. She's all 'out to get you'—that's the way they put it in the *Post*."

He took off his tie, tossing it toward the dining room table. He missed, and it fell to the floor. He just sighed again.

"Out to get me?" I felt the faintest stirrings of fear. I hadn't read the *Post* lately. I wasn't reading much of anything. Well, except for the *Daily Racing Form*. It had all sorts of valuable information. For example, one of the horses was from Asia and had always trained running uphill. I rather liked that. It seemed very Addison McGhee to me. Why run on flat land if you can run uphill? Why walk ten thousand steps if you can walk twenty?

But honestly, I liked the *Racing Form* mostly because I wasn't in it. Every time I picked up a regular paper, it seemed I saw something about Hughes and me. It was making me sick. I had stopped reading for my own mental health.

Still, if the first lady was reportedly out to get me, I should know about it. I remembered the look in her eyes when she threatened me and my "skinny ass." She couldn't do that, could she? I'd have to commit a crime or something.

"Bax," I said. "She couldn't get me deported, could she?"

He had one leg on an ottoman and was popping breath mints like they were popcorn. "I'm starving," he said, when he noticed me eyeing the breath mints. "And of course not. She can't deport a US citizen. You know that."

"I'm not a US citizen." The words came out fast. I was shocked he didn't know this.

Another breath mint.

"You're *not*?"

"You know I'm not a citizen," I said, in a voice more pan-icky than the situation called for. I tried to tone it down a bit. I feigned a light, breezy manner. "I'm a permanent resident. It's a green card for me. You know that. I'm fresh off the boat." I made sort of an airy motion with my hand. "Or, you know, the plane."

"Yeah, well, not that fresh," Baxter said. "What's it been, three decades?"

I bristled a little. How old did he think I was? Did he think I was in my late thirties or something? I was in my early thirties. Or at least my late early thirties. It had not been three decades. Not quite.

"I'd have thought you'd have become a citizen by now," he said. He chewed the last mint slowly, as if to savor. "Hmm. Wow, Ada. Hmmm."

He finished chewing. Neither of us spoke.

"You probably should do that," he said. "You know, be-come a US citizen."

I nodded. I probably should. My parents and brother had. I thought I would get started on that when I got back to New York.

I got up from the armchair and slid into a narrow spot on

the sofa with Baxter. I put my hand on his arm. "Baxter," I said. "Am I going to be okay?"

He brushed my hair back from my face and pulled my head into his shoulder. "Sure you are," he said. And he kissed me on the forehead.

We sat there like that, unmoving, for a few minutes. "I should make some broth," I said. He didn't answer. I looked over and he was asleep. I laid my head back down on his shoulder and soon I was, too.

When he woke me up, my head was lying on his chest. It was the deepest sleep I'd slept in a long time, and I was disoriented when he nudged me. "Ada," he whispered. I looked up at his face. He had some serious stubble. How long had we slept? "Wake up, Ada," he said. "It's morning now."

I laughed.

"Seriously?" I asked. "How long did we sleep?"

"A long time," he said. "It really is morning. Let's go to the track."

# Chapter 28

$\mathcal{I}$ would like to say that the previous afternoon's discussion had cast a pall over Derby Day, because that would suggest that I had the good sense to know when my world was being threatened. But in fact, Baxter and I were laughing and giddy as we got ready for the race. I wore a red striped suit with a matching hat, purse, and shoes. Baxter shaved, which sort of disappointed me actually, and put on a crisp four-button suit—strikingly similar to the one Hughes often wore that always drove me wild. Baxter set his off with a red polka-dot bow tie.

I tugged on his bow tie, straightening it in a familiar way. "We look like Easter eggs," I said.

"Yummy," he said.

Among the other things I had enjoyed about being at the Derby was the ability to hobnob with other journalists and to hear their stories and theories. The previous morning, during a commercial break, I had chatted it up with a local newspaper reporter who had explained to me, somewhat suggestively I thought, that the wonderful thing about the Derby is its unbridled sexiness.

"Sexy?" I said. I glanced down at the manure-y mud. He caught my glance.

"Oh sure," he said, "there is that problem. But on Derby Day, the place is teeming with people, overcrowded and understaffed. The drunken college boys in the infield are pleading with women to pull up their shirts and the millionaires on the Skye Terrace are leaning too far over the railing with their breasts leaning too far over their bras. The whole thing feels as if it's about to teeter madly out of control," he said. He kicked the mud and then looked up at me.

"And everyone's wearing their beautiful hats and talking about the studs and drinking their mint juleps and spending too much money on a horse they've got a gut feeling about."

"I never trust gut feelings," I said.

He quickly glanced up at me, and a kind look swept over his face. "Yeah," he said. "I would think not anymore."

Then he had walked away.

But when the cab dropped Baxter and me off at Churchill Downs, I saw immediately what the reporter meant. I had never seen a fashion display quite like it before. Women were dressed in wonderful pastel suits that looked positively Easter-pageant-esque, except for the sexy shoes and the low-cut tops. And the men? The men were dressed in a way that took male fashion seriously. Bright ties, hats, seersucker suits. You have never seen so much color in men's clothes. Baxter's colorful bow ties wouldn't even be noticed here.

When Baxter and I arrived at our box seats, we found that we shared the box with some other celebrities and their companions. The stars were legitimately familiar. Erik Estrada, Lynda Carter, and a guy who I think was on *Celebrity Poker* with me. He was a country singer and he had one of those geographic names. Denver? Dakota? Dallas? Des Moines? Yes, I thought that was it.

Maybe.

I wasn't sure. I suddenly sympathized with George Clooney's

panicked face when he saw me coming at the post-Oscar party.

"Hi, Addison," said Des Moines, or whatever his name was. He glanced at Baxter, then back at me. "Good to see you on the prowl again."

Well.

Baxter shifted uncomfortably. I bristled, but covered well. I gave Des Moines and the others my most engaging smile and said, "Let's leave all that stuff behind for the day, shall we? We're just folks watching the races."

Lynda Carter rolled her eyes and stuck her nose back in her racing program. I don't know what she was rolling her eyes about. I wasn't even talking to her! Not specifically. But I held my smile until I was sure she was back in her program, then I turned to Baxter and cocked an eyebrow.

He cocked his as well. And I felt we shared a secret joke. He then put his hand on my back. It was tight quarters, there in the box. It would be anyway, with eight people. But Lynda was wearing a larger-than-average hat and Des Moines's date was wearing some sort of hoop-skirted outfit that took up more than her allotted room. (Was this skirt the next big thing in country attire? I mean, it certainly qualified as *big*. No doubt about that.)

Des Moines was yammering on, too loudly to be ignored, about his strategy for picking horses. It was all about the name and the trainer, he said. A horse with a good name suggested that there was something inspirational about the horse when it was being named. But you had to allow for the trainer, he said, because a bad trainer could suck the inspiration right out of an animal. Des Moines said that with great importance, as if we would all be very grateful for the insight.

Instead, Baxter shrugged. "It's a horse race," he said.

Des Moines looked at him suspiciously. "Yes," he said,

with a tone of sarcasm that smacked of insecurity. "I think we're aware that it's a race involving horses."

Baxter ignored him, turned to me. "You know the old saying—*It's a horse race*—what we say if a political race is close. It means the outcome can't be predicted. Handicappers realize it's no trite cliché. Because the brutal truth is that even if your horse is the best to come along in thirty years, even then it can be beat. The only ones that are undefeated are the ones that retired early."

I was sort of impressed. I didn't think Baxter knew anything about racing. Not that what he said really amounted to much, I guess. But he said it with an air of authority.

"The secret," Baxter continued, "is to find the value bet."

We all looked at him. *Value* is not a word that gets used a lot in celebrity circles.

"What you're looking for is a horse that has a better-than-average shot of winning but is for some reason being overlooked by the bettors."

Blank stares all around.

"Say he's got a bad trainer." Baxter looked at Des Moines, then away. "Or an unknown jockey. Or he's imported from some country where they don't even time the races so no one is exactly sure how fast he is.

"Bet for value," Baxter continued, "and no doubt about it, most of the time you'll lose. But that's true no matter what. If you go for value, then at least when you win, you'll win a lot."

Lynda Carter rolled her eyes again. *What's her deal?* I found myself thinking. I myself thought Baxter's little speech was quite impressive. And I became even more impressed over the next few races as he quietly whispered in my ear about speed numbers and track records and dosage indexes.

"Where did you learn all this?" I asked at one point.

"Oh, online," Baxter said. "I've been reading up."

At one point, the other people in our box went off to make their bets at the same time, and Baxter and I were alone. I slipped off my sandals and stretched my legs out into the other seats for a moment, leaned back to look up at the warm sun, placing my hand on the top of my hat to keep it from falling back. I cocked my head and looked at Baxter sitting there. His face was soft and serious as he pored over the *Racing Form*. His bow tie was slightly crooked.

"Baxter baby," I said. "Tell me something. If you're only wearing those silly ol' ties because of your agent, why do you wear them when you're not working?"

There were nearly two hundred thousand people in the stands. I had never been in such a crowd, but Baxter and I were, somehow, alone. Once again, I was struck by how familiar Baxter was to me, by how much he felt like home.

"I don't," he said casually. He looked up and caught me raising an eyebrow. "Except," he continued, raising a finger like a professor explaining a technical point. "Except when accompanying a woman who is on record as saying they're sexy."

I laughed, a bit too loudly, and looked up at the sun again. I just loved doing that, looking up at the sun and holding on to my hat. I decided then and there to wear hats more often. Though as it turned out, my days for selecting my own clothes were numbered.

"You know I lied about bow ties that day on the air," I said. Baxter feigned a crestfallen look.

"Not about them being sexy," I quickly clarified. "They're definitely sexy. But that whole business about how they look easy to untie. That was a total lie."

I was still looking up at the sky. I'm not sure I could have talked about this to Baxter if I'd been looking at him. "I haven't the faintest idea how to untie one of those things," I said.

Baxter's nose was back in his *Racing Form,* but he peered over it. "I can show you sometime," he said. He winked.

I laughed too loudly again.

I gestured toward the paper. "You're really into this," I said.

"Yeah, sort of." He looked a little sheepish. "I had no idea it was this fascinating. It's all about odds and weighing different variables and making assumptions about future outcomes based on past outcomes. It's like doing the weather," he said. "It's wonderful."

"Except," I interrupted, "that horse racing is impossible to accurately predict."

He grinned and leaned toward me so that the people in the next box couldn't hear. Not that they were listening. "So is the weather," he whispered.

We both laughed. And I looked up again at the warm sky while Baxter pored over the *Racing Form* some more. Finally, he glanced up at me. "So," he said, softly. "Who do you like, Ada?"

I looked over at him, warmly.

"You," I said. And then I realized with horror he had been asking me which horse I liked. Luckily, my experience with live television saved the day. "Decide," I added quickly. Then I repeated myself. "You decide."

# Chapter 29

$\mathcal{B}$axter came up with some sort of exotic bet in which he grouped multiple horses in various first- and second-place combinations. We split the cost of the bet, each contributing twelve dollars.

The energy at the track had been building all day, and when the crowd paused to sing "My Old Kentucky Home" before the race, I looked up at the stacks and stacks of people, leaning out of the track balcony above me, and felt dizzy. All the big hats. All the colorful men's suits.

A crowd like that alters your sense of personal space, so that Baxter and I stood quite close to each other during the entire day. When the big race finally started, he whispered "They're off" in my ear, and it seemed so intimate. We screamed and yelled and stood on our chairs as the horses came thundering down the track. We each had twelve bucks at stake, after all.

And we cheered some more when we saw that one of Baxter's combinations had come in, to the tune of eight hundred dollars. I thought about buying myself a large supply of expensive monogrammed towels, with my own initials. AM.

When the race was over, I picked up my bag, slipped my sandals back on, and stood up with Baxter. We stepped into the torrent of the crowd and were pushed along by it. I walked directly behind Baxter and put my hand on his back, so as not to lose him. We tried to head in the direction we had come from, but missed our trajectory somehow and ended up in line for the express buses, which would take us downtown for ten dollars each.

"Too good for the bus?" Baxter said.

I laughed and said I was not.

For the next forty minutes, we stood in a loosely formed cattle line, set up between tall chain-link fences. We were pressed in from all sides as we shuffled toward the buses. At one point, he reached back and took my hand as the crowd turned a tight corner, but when the line straightened, he dropped it again.

When we finally climbed aboard the bus, it, too, was jammed and hot. We were among the last ones on and so we were standing, I just in front of Baxter. I could feel his breath on my neck. Each time the bus stopped, he lurched into me. And each time it started again, I fell back into him. The first few times, we apologized, but then we stopped.

People began getting off; by the time we reached our hotel, there were plenty of empty seats and we were the only two left standing. We had turned now so that we were facing each other, each holding on to the pole, giggling a little when the bus's movements knocked us, particularly me in the stiletto heels, off kilter. The driver was messing around with the bus's interior lights, which went off for a second. In the darkness, I leaned toward Baxter and said: "Do you know, in the whole mess of my life, you're the only person who ever asked how I feel?"

He nodded. "Do you know you never answered me?"

"I feel like this," I said. I leaned forward and kissed him. Then the lights came back on.

# Chapter 30

$\mathcal{I}$'ll never know what, if anything, would have happened that night in the suite Baxter and I shared. We were cut off at the lobby. We were pulling up to our stop near the hotel and Baxter was saying there was something he needed to tell me and I was thinking of all sorts of romantic things he might be needing to say, when we noticed the live television trucks parked up and down the street. There had been media outside the hotel all week, what with all the "celebrities" going in and out. But this seemed a bit excessive. I wondered in a vague way if someone big had shown up at the last minute. There had been a rumor all week that Teri Hatcher was going to drop in. She had been to the Derby once before. "But that," our bellhop had explained to us, "was back when she was still washed up."

As soon as we stepped off the bus, Baxter and I realized that we were the celebrities the crowd of cameras were looking for. "There they are," a cameraman yelled. "She's wearing red!" All the lights turned toward us, and the reporters all started talking at once. I couldn't understand what they were actually saying, but the vibe suggested this was not the friendly *who'd-you-bet-on* sort of questioning that we had grown accustomed to. There were scowls and shouting and some of the more aggressive ones pushed toward us. I saw Bob Costas in the crowd and realized that he'd been pulled off the post-Derby coverage for this. That was pretty impressive, given that I wasn't even sure what "this" was. It seemed to be about me getting off a bus.

Then I heard a voice say: "Addison McGhee! What's your reaction to this criminal charge?" And I heard a man say: "Ever been to the track with a fugitive before, Baxter?"

I crinkled my nose, not consciously, but it was evident in the tapes when I watched them back later. I used my hand to shield my eyes from the camera lights. "I don't know what . . ." I was going to say that I didn't know what they were talking about. But Baxter grabbed my arm and dragged me inside while a friendly bellhop shooed the cameras away from the door. We stepped into a coatroom—another friendly bellhop—and Baxter called Cal on his cell phone.

Cal asked to speak to me, and that's how I heard that I'd been indicted for felonious assault.

"Felonious assault?" I asked incredulously. "Why? Because I threw that thing at Hughes?"

Cal sighed. "Well, I certainly hope so. You haven't assaulted anyone else, have you?"

I didn't answer.

"The prosecutor has the studio surrounded and your room at the Ritz staked out, and he's calling me every fifteen minutes to see if I've heard from you." Cal was breathless. "I said, 'Look, she's not on the lam, for heaven's sake. She's at the Kentucky Derby.'

"But he seemed to think it was very suspicious that all at once you 'up and go to a horse race.' "

I sighed.

Cal continued. "I told him that I thought it was suspicious that there are fifty zillion unsolved murders in the city and he's got four SWAT teams looking for a woman who chucked a glorified tape measure at a guy. A woman with good reason, truth be told."

I suddenly flushed with pleasure. Cal was on my side? I had not realized!

"Hell, I want to throw things at Hughes and I wasn't even married to him!" Cal continued. "So I told the prosecutor that just because the junior senator from Ohio is from the same political party as he is and controls the national committee funding, that doesn't mean he has to do every stupid thing she gets into her head. We know what this is about! Margaret Clemons-Briarwood wishes she could knock the president in the head with something and she can't, so she's taking it out on you."

"Cal," I said, "I'm flattered! I never knew you'd stick up for me like this."

"They're messing with my show, Addison," he said. "This is going to be the death of my show."

"Oh," I said, a little disappointed. And then added: "Surely not. It will be okay, Cal."

I was comforting *him*.

"Look, Addison, I promised him you'd be here by midnight. I've got a plane waiting for you at the airport. Can you and Baxter come right now?"

I looked at Baxter, handsome and composed, worried and supportive. "Sure, Cal," I said. "Whatever you say. I appreciate you handling all this."

It was a long ride back in the plane. Baxter and I looked out the window at the changing patterns made by the lights on the ground. Neither of us said much. "It'll blow over, Ada," he said. "You'll laugh about this someday."

But I thought I detected a weariness in him that had not been there before. I decided to address this directly. At least, you know, directly for me.

"My life is a mess, Baxter," I said. "Being my friend is a thankless task right now. I've screwed it all up. Every bit of it. You'd have to be a fool to get involved in my life."

He looked out the window for a moment longer, then took another sip of coffee. "This stuff is horrid," he said with a sigh. "You'd think a guy with Cal's money would stock some decent coffee on his plane."

"Yeah, well." I had started picking at my nails. "If you sleep at night, like he does, coffee's not so important. We're the ones who have to become connoisseurs."

We sat in silence for a moment. I finally said, nervously, that he had been about to tell me something on the bus. And he said it was no longer important.

"It seems so unfair," I said quietly, to no one in particular. It was the only time in the whole ordeal that I allowed myself a small degree of public self-pity.

Baxter did not commiserate. "What can I say?" he told me. "You married a jerk."

We sat opposite each other and leaned back, away from each other, and pretended to sleep for the rest of the flight. Perhaps he was sleeping. I was definitely pretending. What I was really thinking was that I had just said that anyone would be a fool to get involved with me, and Baxter had not argued.

# Chapter 31

*I* was arrested at the airport in New York. I still had my Derby finery on and I insisted on wearing my Derby hat, which was much mocked later and eventually listed by Joan Rivers as one of the fashion mistakes of the year. Please. I had been wearing that hat all day. If I had taken it off, people would still be talking about the hat head. Sometimes, Joan, you have to go with the lesser of two evils.

Cal said he would get a lawyer for me and Baxter offered to call my parents, a gesture that touched me. When I was finally alone in my jail cell, I cried and cried and cried. It all came out then—my anguish over my failed marriage, my wrenching heartbreak, my bubbling anger, my resentments, my regrets, my fear. I really wanted to log onto the boards and see what the people there were saying, but I couldn't. And that made me cry some more.

By the time my attorney, a grizzled old guy Cal went to college with, arrived, I was a blubbery mess.

If I had allowed Al Sharpton to help me out, he would have undoubtedly found a committed, self-righteous attorney who would have fought my case to the bitter end and would not have been deterred from doing so by any force of nature—not exhaustion, not public opinion, not even an internal sense of decency. Al Sharpton's attorney, I am sure, would have fought until I was free, if he had to embarrass me, himself, and everyone else in the process. Al Sharpton's attorney would not have taken anything for granted, least of all the photographic evidence, the live footage of my chucking a sharp implement. "What is the definition of *sharp*?" Al's attorney would have asked. "Can we really believe what we see on that video?"

But the lawyer Cal called had a less aggressive defensive posture. Clem Fuget just handed me a tissue and recommended that I plead guilty.

Even in my defeated state, I balked for a moment. "Assault?" I said. "You want me to plead guilty to assault? A felony? Can't I plead guilty to disturbing the peace or . . ." I struggled for another legal term. "Or setting a bad example or, you know, excessive rowdiness?"

Clem Fuget smirked.

"I didn't think I'd actually hit him," I continued. "My old PE teacher can testify! I have terrible aim!"

Clem Fuget waved me off as if not wanting to touch my silliness. "Oh sure," he said, "we could quibble about this for weeks, months. Is that what you want? Drag this thing into next year? You knocked the guy out. *Permanently scarred him.* Pure and simple. I saw it myself on television, turned to the missus and said: Did you see that?

"I guarantee you," Clem Fuget continued, "if the situation had been reversed, he would have been charged before nightfall. A man hits a woman on TV, that's a felony. A woman hits a man and everyone's all concerned about how *she's* doing? Bah!"

I was taken aback. *This* was my legal representation? I'm not a lawyer, but I was under the impression that they were supposed to try to put things in a positive light for their client. What was Cal thinking, getting this guy? Was Cal intentionally setting me up? But the sad truth is that when Cal said he would find me an attorney I'd used my one call to telephonically cry on my brother's shoulder.

I looked at Clem Fuget. "What kind of sentence will I get?"

"No guarantees," he said. "But under the circumstances? For a chance to put this thing behind them quickly? I think we can get you eighteen months with work release."

"Eighteen months!" I said. "In prison?"

"With work release!" he said. "Hell, you're at that dumb studio all night. This way, you'll sleep in the prison all day. What will you be missing, really? It's not like you've got a husband waiting for you at home."

I did not like this man at all. But the truth is the truth. So I signed some papers that Clem Fuget gave me and when I appeared in court later that day, I stunned the world by pleading guilty. And the judge stunned the legal community by going along with my lawyer's request to sentence me on the spot. It was unprecedented and it was eighteen months in prison, with work release.

I thought it was terrible, but I also thought it was over.

It wasn't.

Those papers I signed, the ones I didn't read, turned out to be rather important. Cassie tells me that, among other things, I was swearing that I had been counseled about the potential consequences of this plea on my immigration status. This time, it would take more than a gauze bikini to fix the mess I made by signing something without reading it.

# Chapter 32

All the legal experts interviewed on CNN and Fox thought that Clem had led me terribly astray. While I had undoubtedly hurt Hughes and while it was probably criminal and possibly even technically a felony, it was so out of the realm of what is normally prosecuted anywhere in the country, and particularly in New York City, that I surely could have pleaded to a lesser charge. Failing that, I could have taken my chances with a jury, which likely would have been sympathetic to me and my broken heart and might have acquitted me outright.

Even if they had ultimately convicted me of a felony anyway, it's hard to imagine that I would have ended up with more than eighteen months in prison. "Do murderers get eighteen months in prison?" Howard Stern memorably asked, and one of his callers said that he thought not.

What the experts did not say is that whatever the outcome, the spectacle of the trial would have, in and of itself, served the unstated purpose of the charges against me. Even if the outcome of the trial had been the same, it would have, at least, satisfied the first lady by providing my thorough humiliation. (I thought I had been humiliated enough, but the catastrophic nature of the arrest photo was lost on the first lady, who wouldn't know a fashion faux pas if it knocked her in the head. So to speak.)

She would have, perhaps, gotten bored by the whole thing, or at least distracted by the president's continuing habits. After the trial, she may have been able to move on.

Furthermore, the media itself would have been tired of the story and would have exercised their subtle pressure against further legal actions by beginning to talk about vendettas and so forth. But with me arrested a few minutes before midnight on Saturday and pleading guilty before noon on Monday—well, they hadn't gotten to sink their teeth into it at all. They were still quite hungry. They wanted more. I knew this. I could see it in their eyes.

What I did *not* know, as I was being booked into the Bayview Correctional Facility in West Chelsea, was that they would get more. I thought I would commute from prison to the GUP studios every workday for eighteen months, that Leno and Letterman would have great fun at my expense, and then it would be over.

I was unaware that a bureaucratic process had begun. The wheels of government turn slowly, but they do turn. In a matter of weeks, the Bayview authorities notified the Department of Homeland Security that a noncitizen was serving time in prison.

The notification sat on the desk of a lawyer in a department that I now know is called ICE for another week or two before he finally picked it up and read it. The first thing he did was notify the White House that a celebrity had popped up on the list of potentially dangerous immigrants. I suppose he thought there was a chance that there would be political pressure to look the other way. He was wrong. The first lady, in fact, publicly lobbied for my quick "removal" from the country.

"We can't be giving sanctuary to criminals from sinister countries," she said, rather famously. It may be the only sentence ever uttered that managed to simultaneously insult my father's homeland, my mother's homeland, and Turkey to boot.

I was sitting on the set of *It's Morning Now* when this news came over the wire. Hughes and I were laughing it up about the latest voting scandal on *American Idol*.

(Hughes had been extraordinarily friendly on the set—the only place we were allowed to talk under the terms of my work release. But I thought he gave me several meaningful looks during the days and weeks immediately after I pled guilty, something I mentioned to the makeup artist. I also mentioned that I saw him blink three times after telling Larry King that he was "relieved and grateful" that I pled guilty. That was a sign he was lying, I explained. Hughes was not really grateful or relieved. The makeup artist displayed her usual sensitivity by laughing at me, muttering something that sounded like the word *delusional,* and then saying, "Everyone blinks, Addison." I don't know why I had bothered attempting to explain it to her. I never liked the woman. She had some sort of contract with Chanel and insisted that if I wanted her to apply Amber Glow foundation—the only foundation that truly matched my skin—I had to pour it from my tiny CoverGirl bottles into her empty Chanel bottles. You cannot imagine what a tedious exercise that was.)

Anyway, there Hughes and I were, laughing it up about the voting scandal on *American Idol,* when I noticed the producers gathered around a computer screen off to my right. One of them whistled in a *wow, this is terrible* sort of way. Another one grabbed something off the printer and went running for Cal's office.

Hughes tossed to Baxter for a weather update, which meant

that the camera was turned away from us. I could watch Cal's office with undisguised interest. Cal was throwing his hands about in an animated way, and the producer was nodding. Cal picked up the piece of paper and tossed it across the room. It was one of those gestures of rage that never works when I try it. I can't get enough muscle behind the light paper to create any impressive velocity. But Cal's picked up a current from the air duct and got bullied about the room in a dramatic way. Then Cal sat down and put his head on his desk and began to weep, which was more dramatic still.

He was not crying for me. I can see that now. I understand with the passage of time that for all Cal's good-natured friendliness, he never cared one way or another what happened to me, where I lived out my remaining years, whether I found happiness. Whether I was safe.

If I had been hit by a bus, instead of being killed off symbolically by a slow fizzle of a public relations disaster, Cal probably would have worked up some almost genuine sorrow for a co-worker lost in her prime. But even then, he would have been thinking about how to replace me on the way home from the funeral—if not sooner. I see that now. And this demise, being neither quick, nor sudden, nor blameless on my part? He had no sympathy at all.

At the time I was sitting there watching him though, I did not even know what the paper he threw across the room said. Someone came over and whispered in Hughes's ear and he looked startled and then glanced at me, then the floor. Baxter, obliviously doing the weather, finished up with a report about flooding in Missouri and tossed back to me and I tossed to a commercial. "Up next," I said, "a new study shows that mouthwash maybe does replace flossing."

I turned to Hughes. "You know they said it did, then it didn't, and now maybe it does again."

"Science!" said Hughes, all goofy and enthusiastic. And then we went to commercial.

I leaned back in the sofa, ready for the makeup person to come touch me up as usual. But Hughes took my arm and said: "Addison, Cal doesn't want you to finish the show."

And then he told me that the first lady had announced that "removal proceedings" had been launched against me. I looked at him blankly. "She's trying to deport you," he said. "She says you're a 'convicted felon from a suspicious country.'"

It took me a moment to process that.

"Cal wants me to quit?" I asked finally. "He agrees with her?"

Hughes shrugged. "I don't know that this is a political statement, really. I was told that he said it was the 'last straw.' I think he just wants his show back."

My lip quivered.

Hughes looked at his feet. "You'd really have to ask Cal, I guess." We both glanced at Cal's office. He was still weeping. Hughes sighed. "But I don't know that you'd get a satisfying answer."

I nodded, stood up, smoothed my skirt with as much dignity as I could, and left the set.

There were no cakes or farewell gatherings, no office good-luck cards. I was leaving with no notice, for one thing. And in shame, for another. I packed up my personal belongings in a large box, nodded to Hughes and a producer across the room. I helped myself awkwardly through the door, nearly dropping everything until I was saved by a passing janitor who held the door for me. (A new immigrant to the country, he did not speak English and did not appear to recognize me.) I pulled myself up with dignity and thanked him. "When the time is right," I said, "become a citizen." He nodded at me in a friendly way, but I don't think he understood what I said.

I looked over my shoulder and saw Baxter watching me.

He was standing by his radar tracking equipment holding a bunch of sloppy-looking files. He hesitated and then offered his hand up in a perfunctory wave. I raised my fingers as best I could without dropping my box and waved back.

When I got to the lobby, I saw Hughes looking somber on the bank of televisions, which were always on and always tuned to GUP.

"This is tough," he said. He sat up a bit and straightened his tie. "But Addison has decided to leave. There's been some news from the first lady's office and . . ."

I didn't really hear the rest. I just studied his face the whole time, wondering what had gone wrong. Obviously, we were not meant to marry. We had been wrong, silly at best. But how had we gone from those companionable dinners to this? Me in the lobby carrying the dustings of my career, him worrying about his tie being straight as he delivers the news that my career is over and, oh by the way, I might be deported to a war-torn, famine-ridden desert nation where the language of business is a language I don't speak, where the dominant culture is one I don't understand, where my ethnicity is not considered glamorous or exotic but a huge liability, and where my gender makes all the other points basically insignificant, because the only hope for a woman is that she will marry well and I am far too old and far too strange and, in the eyes of my new countrymen if not the eyes of Nevada, far too *already married* for that.

I pushed my way through the revolving door, walked two blocks, and then realized that the terms of my work release forbade me from doing anything other than proceeding directly to my cell. Not that I had anywhere else to go anyway. I looked at the contents of my box—several of my favorite teacups, framed journalism awards, the wedding photo, and a camera with the undeveloped film from the Derby.

The prison officials would never let me bring this box in. I stopped at a corner and looked down at the box, then up at the street signs, and then at my watch. Even if I were bold enough to try to sneak off for a few minutes, where would I take these things? To my old hotel room? To Hughes's apartment? To a bus-station locker? Do they have those in this day and age? I remembered what Hughes told me the first lady had said about a "suspicious country" and almost laughed. Why not make this worse, I thought, by violating the terms of my work release to go stash something in a bus-station locker?

I got to a corner, stood there among strangers waiting for the light to change. None of them looked at me. I thought, *How can this be? I'm as famous at this moment as I can possibly be and I'm crying on the corner and no one notices me.*

Suddenly there was a loud blast of thunder. I jumped and the sky opened up the way I thought it did only in movies, where the weather goes from sunshine to a downpour in one clap of the clouds. I looked down and the wedding photo was already bubbling with moisture.

I heaved the box into a trash bin, wiped my eyes, and headed toward my cell.

The strangers standing around me? The ones who did not seem to notice my despair? Apparently they were more observant than I realized. I learned later that every single item in that box, including the rain-pocked wedding photo, was listed on eBay within the week. They all made a killing. The award from the East Coast Association of Irish American Television Personalities sold for two thousand dollars. It was described as an "ironic keepsake of a ruined career."

# Chapter 33

That was almost six months ago. I guess I've written everything that Cassie needs. She should be here any minute. And she'll no doubt be pleased.

While I wait for her, I suppose I might as well continue the story, tell you about my time here in prison. In the past six months, I have been on a typical inmate journey. I did sit-ups for hours a day. I read all the great holy books and most of the Harry Potter series. I finished in last place in the fourth floor's wastepaper basketball championship for four straight months. I doodled Baxter's initials in the dust on my window over and over again. I taught myself Mandarin, thinking with pride that if I ever reprised my *Alias* role I would do so much better this time. (I had played a triple agent with a badly executed Chinese accent for three particularly incomprehensible episodes.)

Cassie had smirked when I told her about the Mandarin and suggested that learning Arabic would have been more prudent. I had glared at her.

I also slept a fair amount, which did amazing things for my mood, I must confess. I did not realize how sleep-deprived I had been, but after a few months of sleeping eight and a half hours a day, I started to feel like my old self again. My skin kind of shimmers now. I guess that's why they call it beauty rest.

My mother sends me a box of snack foods each week: jerky, dried figs, a flat, salty corn bread. My fellow inmates were excited the first few times I got a box, thinking a celebrity like me would have great things to trade, but one slice of the flat, salty corn bread and they pretty much gave up on that idea. They weren't trading their Snickers for that. And that was a good thing.

My parents, in fact, stopped by early this morning. Visiting hours had not yet officially started, but the guards were kind enough to let my family come in and speak privately to me before my trip to the courthouse.

There in the visiting room, my mother and father cried with me. My mother said simply that she had failed me, but my father had more specific regrets. He regretted, for example, sending me to school and allowing me to dress in Western clothing. He said that none of this would have happened if I had remained illiterate and married my cousin when I turned thirteen as he had wanted me to do. Or if I had worn a veil.

I nodded solemnly at that. The truth is, after all, the truth. None of this would have happened.

I said, "It's okay, Dad." I said, "Perhaps this is my destiny." I said, "I will go to our homeland and maybe I will do something great there."

My father was staring at me. He finally said, "You do not know that place. There is nothing good to do there."

And it struck me at that moment that my father was looking at his homeland from the beaten-down perspective of someone who has lived with disappointment and adversity his whole life. But I was, despite the place of my birth, a child of America. And I thought, with equal measures of naïveté and arrogance, that a little Yankee ingenuity would surely set that country right.

Looking at my father, I realized something else about him.

Something that should have been obvious long ago. He is *not* the son of a Supreme Court justice. He is *not* a product of our nation's best schools. When he hears the word *football,* he still imagines the game I know as soccer. He loves the opportunities that America has given him, but he doesn't think an American can do anything to solve the problems of his homeland. In all these ways, he is less than the American I have aspired to be.

But in one important way, he is more American than I am, than it appears I will ever be. When I was watching *Mary Tyler Moore* and *Hollywood Squares,* while I was cruising with my Nebraska friends and talking about *Star Wars,* he was doing something else. Sitting at the kitchen table, late at night, he was doing something that I never thought necessary, somehow. He was studying to take the test that allows you to become a US citizen. Sometimes, when I was feeling tender toward him, I would sit down and grill him. Educated in Nebraska's best rural schools, I knew all the answers—or most of them, at least—the three branches of government, the mechanics of the electoral college. I still know these things, but it doesn't matter. Unlike my father, I never took the test.

He took it twice, passing the second time. I had just turned eighteen. At the time, I thought nothing of that. But Cassie explained to me recently that if my father had passed the test the first time, when I was still a minor, I would have, as the child of an American citizen, been automatically naturalized. In the eyes of the law, however, I was an adult when he passed. So my citizenship problems were my own.

Cassie challenged me when she gave me this writing assignment to explain why I had "never bothered" to become a US citizen, never did what my father did when I was eighteen and what my mother did a few years later. Anything I say now, obviously, is going to look stupid. Because it *was* stupid. It was the stupidest thing I ever didn't do. Why didn't I take the test? I think, for me, going through the naturalization process would have, if only for those few months, involved admitting that I was not already a US citizen. It was a form of denial, I guess. Or maybe, it was just a form of "screwed-up priorities." Looking back, I had a lot of those.

So often my parents embarrassed me with their Old Country ways, their ridiculous ideas about dating, their funny foods, and their lack of concern about "appearing American." They would not follow Miss Liberty's advice at all. I always hated that.

But I can hate it all I want and that does not change the basic truth that as a point of fact and as a technicality of law, they are American. I am not.

Now they are on their way to the courthouse and I am waiting for Cassie, who will ride with me in the prison van and walk with me into the courtroom.

Wait—I think I hear her now. She's laughing with the guards, talking about their Thanksgiving plans. They're exchanging cranberry sauce recipes. (There's a lot of sugar involved in that stuff. I had no idea.)

I guess they'll be finished soon, so I'm going to stop writing. Cassie says that even if I'm deported, they'll probably make me serve out my sentence first. So I'll "probably" be back here tonight, and I can finish this document by explaining what happened in the courtroom today.

# Chapter 34

$\mathcal{Y}$esterday did not go exactly like expected. Even Jeffrey Toobin was shocked. I watched his account this morning on Cassie's home television. The judge allowed me to stay with her last night and have Thanksgiving dinner with her today. It was an unexpected kindness. Jeffrey Toobin said that was sort of shocking, too.

I had thought that Cassie seemed uncharacteristically chipper Wednesday morning as she breezed in chatting up the guard about cranberry sauces and creamed corn recipes. The guard—the *Celebrity Gourmet* reader—said she was going to have fish for Thanksgiving dinner, supposedly a tradition in the family of one of the *Charmed* stars.

(Like they even eat.)

Cassie was talking about how tempting that was, because fish cooks so quickly and everything. And they were giggling about how to "sell" the idea to their families.

I thought it was a bit obnoxious, really. I mean, fine, eat whatever you want for Thanksgiving. It's no business of mine. But there I was in my somber suit and they were yukking it up about twisting and perverting American traditions, when I very likely wasn't going to have any American traditions to pervert once the day was over. Certainly not any American traditions involving food.

It made me steaming mad. Cassie took one look at me and could tell I was not my usual upbeat self.

"Oh, get over yourself," she said.

There was a long awkward silence, which I finally broke by asking if were true that Peter Jennings was Canadian. I thought being an immigration attorney, maybe she would know.

"Of course," she said. "He didn't become a citizen until he was in his sixties."

I nodded. Neither of us spoke again until we arrived at the courthouse.

We settled into the courtroom. I was surprised that there were other people sitting in the desks up front. Cassie whispered that there were a couple of short hearings before me. They were sobering. Three people were deported in an hour. A Cambodian woman, whose mother had carried her as an infant out of the killing fields, was sent back for some shoplifting convictions when she was nineteen. She had, by all accounts, lived as a law-abiding, tax paying legal resident for ten years after that. She married an American doctor and thought all was well. But when she applied for US citizenship, her record was discovered. Shoplifting, while neither violent nor a felony, counts as a crime of moral turpitude. Her hearing lasted less than thirty minutes. Her husband and her children wept when the judge gave his order.

A Sudanese refugee with a DUI was next. Then there was a Mexican girl, just eighteen, who had not known, until stopped by immigration authorities while trying to reenter the country on a high school trip to Niagara Falls, Canada, that her parents were illegal immigrants. The entire family had entered the country illegally seventeen years ago. "I don't even speak Spanish," she kept saying. "I don't eat Mexican food."

I nodded throughout her testimony, which seemed moving and compelling to me. But I glanced at the judge and he just looked bored. He banged his gavel and it was over.

"Next up," the bailiff called, "Addison McGhee."

The ICE attorney got right down to business. He called a variety of unlikely experts who testified, quickly and efficiently, that I displayed all the characteristics of a "troubled immigrant," that I was a "loose cannon," and that the famine in my father's homeland isn't nearly as bad as people think. "Usually," the expert said, glibly, "it's only the very young or the very old who die from malnutrition. Not middle-aged women in the prime of life like Addison McGhee."

A murmur went through the crowd. "Middle-aged?"

When it was Cassie's turn, though, she surprised the media and, most importantly, me by telling the judge she was adding someone to the witness list and calling him right away. "Who?" I whispered, but she waved me off dismissively.

"The defense calls Hughes Sinclair," she said. And Hughes seemed to float into the room on the crowd's gasps.

"I object," said the ICE attorney. "The events of the crime against Mr. Sinclair have already been decided. Ms. McGhee has pled guilty. He has no stake in these proceedings."

"Oh please," Cassie said. "You just called a famine expert!"

All this commotion was swirling, but I sat riveted in my chair, staring at Hughes, who had settled into the witness stand with his usual grace and good carriage. He looked somber and more tired than usual.

My attorney said that "Mr. Sinclair" had arrived in her office the previous evening and revealed to her previously unknown details about our marriage and our life together that she thought were pertinent to the court.

"Isn't that right, Mr. Sinclair?" she asked.

And he said it was.

There was some stage-setting nonsense in which Hughes was asked about his honorable parents and his long-standing reputation for integrity and honesty and so forth. And there was some mumbo jumbo about how we met and how long we had known each other and all of that.

And then my attorney said: "Why did you marry Addison McGhee, Mr. Sinclair?"

I leaned forward across the table and I found myself thinking, for just a moment, that even if I got deported, it would be worth it if I heard the true answer to this question.

Hughes looked down at his hands. He inhaled deeply, exhaled slowly, looked at the ceiling, then the floor, then at the attorney, then me.

"Mr. Sinclair?" the judge prompted.

"Yes," Hughes said. "This is just a little embarrassing to admit. Our marriage was a sham," he went on. The ICE attorney put his hand over his mouth in mock astonishment, but put his hand back down when the judge glared at him.

"Addison didn't know it, though," Hughes continued. "I think she honestly loved me."

I nearly fell on the floor with astonishment. And then I was mortified. And then relieved to know the truth. And then horrified that my naive yearnings were being exposed and then relieved that maybe this would, somehow, make a difference.

"I was always fond of her, I don't mean to imply that I wasn't," Hughes said. "She's a lot of fun, Addison is."

He looked at me then, smiled shyly. It was the boyish kind of maneuver that had always warmed my heart—my easily fooled, embarrassingly naive, stupid little heart. "She's good-looking," Hughes continued. "Anyone can see that. And she's . . ." His voice trailed off and he whistled. "Let's just say we had some good times."

I blushed and did not look at my parents.

"But?" my attorney said.

"I love Addison," Hughes said. "But I didn't love her *that* way. Never did. I just thought it would be good for our careers." He paused and then emphasized that. "*Both* of our careers," he said.

*Yeah,* I thought, *it's been fantastic for mine.*

Hughes continued: "You know, Britney Spears, Lisa Marie Presley? Renée Zellweger? Marrying someone without warning is a time-honored Hollywood stunt."

My attorney nodded in a sad, knowing way. "But you didn't share this thinking with Addison?" she said.

Hughes shook his head. "No. A woman like Addison? She'd never go for something like that. She takes these things seriously. She's genuine. Down-to-earth. She still wears CoverGirl, you know. A big star like her? She could buy anything, but she sticks with the company that taught her about concealer as a teen."

I gasped. I didn't even remember telling Hughes that. Plus, I didn't really want it to get out that I used concealer. The whole point of concealer is that no one knows you're wearing it!

"That's the way she is," Hughes continued. "She's got brand loyalty."

He paused for a moment, then added: "And great-looking skin, of course.

"She's old-fashioned. Salt of the earth. The real deal. You should have seen how excited she was to get towels monogrammed with her new initials."

He had been fidgeting with his hands at chest level, but he dropped them into his lap. "I felt terrible."

"And was it your plan from the beginning to end the marriage in a matter of days?"

"Well, weeks. Maybe months. We were having quite a good time, so I wasn't in a big rush. Hell, there was a moment or two when I thought we'd last at least as long as Brad and Jen did. But that would be sort of the 'worst case' scenario."

He flexed his fingers in the air to signify quotation marks around "worst case."

He continued, "Of course, I had no way of knowing that the clerk would make an error and annul our marriage along with the others. So I didn't plan that part. But when it worked out that way, I was positively thrilled. When Addison told me, I was so astonished and exhilarated I was afraid she'd think I was drunk. It was just so clean! Much better than if I'd had to break it off. And the gay angle? It was perfect."

"Why do you say that?" Cassie asked.

"Well." Hughes paused again, looked at the crowd nervously. "Some of you may not know this, but there's a lot of speculation that I'm gay."

The ICE attorney did another of his mock gasps of surprise, but this time the judge met his eyes and smirked, rather than glaring.

"I've never discouraged it," he said. "The gay community is a powerful driver of pop culture, can't hurt your career at all, these days."

"So you were worried that your marriage to Ms. McGhee would damage that?"

"Well, of course," said Hughes. "Of course."

Long pause.

"So when I was able to link the ending of my very brief marriage to the gay rights movement—well, it was just inspired. The people on the Internet thought I had planned it as a way to take a stand without actually outing myself.

"It was serendipity," he said, in a line that would be much mocked by the late-night comedians later.

"But not for Ms. McGhee," my attorney said.

"Well, no," Hughes said. "Not for her. Honestly, I was sort

of relieved when she threw that gadget at me. I deserved that. If she had gone to trial on that charge, I would have stood up then and there and told everyone that it was all my fault. I was the one who had done wrong."

"But?" my attorney said.

"But she pled guilty before I even got a chance to talk to her," Hughes said. "And I thought, Well, okay, let bygones be bygones. And then you know, they put Mia Hamm on the show. I've always had a crush on Mia Hamm."

Several women, and not a few men, glared at him. He cleared his throat. "I'm ashamed to say I allowed myself to put this out of my mind, as long as she was just off serving her prison time. But this week, with the news everywhere, I realized I had to do something. I can't let her get deported without anyone knowing the truth."

My attorney, who had excellent timing, stood silently for a long moment and let the courtroom ponder everything that Hughes had said. While we were all pondering, I looked at Hughes—not knowing if I should feel a rush of fondness for this last-ditch attempt at saving me or hatred at the way he had used me.

He looked at my attorney, then the judge, then turned and caught my eye. He blinked three times before he turned away.

# Chapter 35

The judge said ICE was right and that Hughes's testimony had no bearing on my case, as my criminal trial had already been decided. The question before him, the judge said, was not whether I had a good reason to toss a sharp implement at Hughes Sinclair. No, he said, the question was far simpler than that—though it was two questions, really. Was I a convicted felon? And was I a US citizen? And if the answers were yes and then no, then the matter was pretty much out of his hands. He didn't even know why we had a full hearing. He could have decided this case, he said, in twenty seconds.

He pounded the gavel and declared me deported. And then he said that as a humanitarian gesture, he would allow me to spend the night at Cassie's and have a last Thanksgiving dinner there with my family before being returned to prison to serve out my time. I had nearly a year of my sentence left. That would give me time, he noted, to "get my affairs in order." Then, he said, I would be sent home. I thought of Slater County. And I realized that was not what he meant.

He elaborated a bit on being allowed to go to Cassie's for Thanksgiving dinner and then, almost as an afterthought, said: "Assuming you're willing to have her and her family for Thanksgiving, Ms. Von Maur."

Cassie said that she was. Though she was not exactly quick to say it, I noticed.

We were introduced to Cassie's quiet kids and her rather uptight in-laws and we all attempted to carry ourselves with a bit of holiday cheer, but we mostly just sat around the table awkwardly, chewing the turkey. Cassie's mother-in-law was right. It was overdone.

My brother whispered a complaint about this when Cassie stepped into the kitchen for a butter knife. I shot back that she was my attorney, not my chef. He rolled his eyes and replied: "I don't know about that. She certainly cooked your turkey."

My father put down his fork and said: "*Over*cooked it."

*Well,* I thought. *My family is certainly getting wittier with the repartee.*

I never talked much to my family about my romantic life— perhaps you're not surprised. But there at the Thanksgiving table, I spilled out my reaction to Hughes's testimony. My father looked uncomfortable the whole time, but I suppose he was indulging me because I was about to be leaving.

"Hughes told me," I finished, "that I would always know if he was lying because he would blink three times."

Everyone at the table looked at me, blankly. "He blinked," I said. "Three times!"

I looked at Cassie. "Don't you think he was lying? He didn't really marry me as a publicity stunt! I understand that he changed his mind about us. He realized our marriage was a mistake. Realized that before I did. I see that now. But he wanted to marry me, at least for a few days there. He thought he loved me. He was lying on the stand."

I looked at my mom and said, pleadingly, "Wasn't he?"

My mom put her fork down with great dignity and finished chewing. The turkey was, as I said, tough, so this made for a long and dramatic pause. She chewed and chewed and chewed. She swallowed the turkey, took a drink of water, and then answered me.

"Ada, honey, everyone blinks."

The eldest of Cassie's kids chimed in to say, "Yeah, everyone blinks."

A sheriff's deputy knocked on the door about then and tapped his watch. It was time to go.

I finished chewing my turkey. (Took a while.) Got up, put my hands forward for the cuffs, and walked to the car. I wondered if I would ever see my family again. Then the deputy brought me back here to my prison cell, to wait out the remaining days of my sentence before being deported.

I noticed the women in the cell block had actually turned the channel. They were watching a CNN report about my case. But when they saw me coming, they switched it off and looked at me with shy and guilty expressions. The embezzler waited until a quiet moment and then whispered to me in a knowing way. "Mother Africa," she said. "It will be an adventure."

I said she was probably right. And I think, somehow, that I actually believed it.

It was visiting hours, but visitors never come on Thanksgiving Day. (They come the day before or the day after to assuage their guilt without ruining their dinners.) So we were all surprised when the guard walked in and said someone was here to see me.

"It's the guy with the bow tie again," she said.

# Chapter 36

*I* really thought it would be Baxter this time.

The last bow-tied visitor had been Hughes. But I couldn't imagine that he'd show his face now. And Baxter was overdue for a visit. Wasn't he?

As soon as the door opened, I saw the shiny wig and knew it *was* Hughes. He walked over and sat down as close to me as he could.

*I should turn around and walk out,* I thought. *That's what Cassie told me to do. I'm a smart woman. I shouldn't even need Cassie to tell me that. Or maybe I should call the guards and have him thrown out. You can't use someone else's ID to get into a prison, surely. If I'm going to serve time for our relationship conflicts, perhaps he should as well.*

But I've never once done what I should have with Hughes. I stood there and let him whisper to me. He apologized again and again. His voice broke more than once. I almost pitied him. But whenever I did, I reminded myself that in a few hours, he'd be living it up with Mia, talking on the air about how much they had overeaten on Thanksgiving.

"I just don't understand," I said. "What were you thinking? How could you do that to me? Why did you fool me like that?"

He glanced around the cell, lowered his eyes. He'd been whispering all along, but he lowered his voice even more.

"I'm a sick man," he said.

I looked him up and down. He didn't look sick. Had he said it to make me feel a twinge of pity?

"Are you *dying*?" I asked.

He laughed. "Oh no, nothing like that." He tapped his temple three times. "No, no, I'm sick up here."

There was a long dramatic pause. Then he said: "I've got an online addiction."

I stared at him for a moment. Was that a joke? He gazed back at me seriously and I saw that it wasn't.

"Oh good grief," I said. "There's no such thing." I flipped his chest with my hand. "And *you*? You don't even check your e-mail more than once a day."

He gave me a sad and knowing look. "More like four times an hour. And it's not just e-mail. I get on discussion boards and write about the show for hours at a time. Discuss it ad nauseam."

I gasped a little. Had I talked to him online?

I lowered my voice to a whisper. "Really?"

He was talking so quietly now that I had to lean forward to hear him. "I use more than one name," he said, "so it won't be so obvious that I'm posting all the time. I pretend I'm a housewife from Fargo and fawn all over Hughes Sinclair on the boards."

I gasped again, this time a little louder. *FargoMama?*

Hughes continued: "I spread rumors about my sexual orientation and then log on under another name and argue with myself. Sometimes I just talk about the show's recipes and so forth. It's almost like"—he lowered his voice yet again—"having a split personality. I started doing it to generate buzz, but I guess I got carried away.

"On one discussion board, I swear that for a while I was almost the only one posting. If it hadn't been for some guy named ObjectiveObserver and some weirdo named Weatherjunkie— I'd have been talking to myself."

I put my hand over my mouth. Hughes seemed to take it as a gesture of pity. "I know," he said. "It's so embarrassing.

"You're great," he continued. "So pulled together. So organized. So happy. So normal. I remember that day when you were just casually remarking that you were going to check your e-mail. I looked at you at that moment and I realized that I had a problem. I could never admit to checking my e-mail. My shame was an indication that my usage was out of control."

"Oh good grief," I said again.

"I know," he said, apparently misreading my sentiment.

"What I said on the stand was true," he said. "At least partly. I thought marrying you would be good for my career—for both our careers, really. But there was more to it than that."

His voice broke and his eyes glistened. "I wanted you to cure me, Addison. I thought maybe all I needed was the love of a good woman."

"To solve your *Internet addiction*?" I said, with a note of sarcasm. I will confess that in the various scenarios I had come up with, I had imagined him saying he'd wanted me to cure him of something. Not, however, of an Internet addiction.

"I needed help," he said.

And he never blinked. At least, you know, not more than once or twice. I watched him very closely. But he never blinked three times. I watched his little performance, sad as it was, and I thought it might be something like the truth.

"You know the best part?" he asked.

I shook my head no. I was thinking, *There is a best part?*

"I think it worked," he said. "While we were married, I didn't have as much time to get on the boards. And then after everything that happened, well, I couldn't stand to get on them. Weatherjunkie was always saying something bad about me, and right about then they started promoting the boards better, so other people started posting, too. They were all shouting me down. I really do check my e-mail only a few times a day now."

"Good for you," I replied, in what I thought was a pointed way.

"It has been," he said. "I even took up knitting." He smiled a little. "It's quite trendy, you know. They say even Russell Crowe is doing it."

We sat there in silence for a moment. And then, he just said he was sorry, a sentiment he expressed over and over again in a dozen different ways, sniffling a little through it all. And I think he *was* sorry. Who wouldn't be?

"Is there anything I can do?" he asked.

I started to say: *Just leave me alone.* But then I realized that very soon I would be placed on an airplane and deposited in a strange land. I wasn't even sure what I'd be able to take with me. A change of clothes? A few dollars in cash?

"I don't know how this is going to work," I said. "But I might need a little money when I leave."

"Of course," he said.

"Not much," I said, with feigned good spirits. "Things are very cheap there."

He was nodding his head, waving his hand as if money were nothing. Which to him, it isn't.

"I'll pay you back," I said, offering him a weak smile and a brave joke. "Though it may be in chickens."

He patted me on the shoulder, tried to say I was a hero or something. But he couldn't get the words out for crying.

"It's okay," I said, though I wasn't sure that it was.

I gathered my courage to ask for more. "Hughes," I said. "I know it doesn't really matter now. But for some reason, it's important for me to know if you're gay."

I was scared he was going to press me on why I wanted to know, because I feared that my answer was either silly or transparently needy or both. I just wanted to know if any aspect of our relationship had been real. But Hughes didn't ask.

He looked at me, tenderly. And said he was not.

"You might not believe this," he said. "I'd understand if you didn't. But when I saw that picture of you with the president, before I knew the story behind it, I really was sad and hurt."

Then I asked for a final thing. I asked if he could arrange for me to see Baxter.

He bit his lip, winced, then looked at me evenly. "I'll try," he said. "But that might be a tough one."

I was shocked. Tough? Tough to get Baxter to come see me? Really? Suddenly, it became clear to me.

Baxter had initially come to visit me once a week. He'd bring me one of those little bags of M&M's—you know, the size people give out at Halloween. I could make one of those last until his next visit. And we'd talk about horse racing, or the weather. At least we talked about those a little. We mostly talked about me and my chronic unhappiness—my anger at Cal, my displeasure with the attorney he provided, my resentment of the flexibility expert, even my irritation with Robert Downey Jr., who kept sending me short notes encouraging me to "embrace the pain" so that I could use it as a tool in my acting.

The last couple of times that Baxter came, I remember now, he seemed a little bored with my speeches. The visits became further apart. It had now been weeks.

I realized suddenly that Baxter was sick of me, tired of me and my problems, fed up with my self-involved self-pitying. I was *so* self-involved and *so* self-pitying that I had not even noticed.

I was suddenly overcome with guilt and regret. Regret about everything—Baxter, spending the best years of my life in a hotel room, not being nicer to Whoopi Goldberg. I regretted not listening to my father's tales about my homeland, obviously enough. I regretted never letting Kevin Ford know how I felt. I kicked myself for not trying harder to beat out Lucy Liu for that part in the *Charlie's Angels* movie. Why didn't I go on that date with Steve Burns? I need more disarming boyish cuteness in my life.

I even regretted not entering the Pork Queen competition. Maybe if I had, things would have been different for me somehow. I don't know how it could have made a difference, but maybe it would have. Have you ever felt like that?

I might have stewed like this for days, a good couple of weeks probably. I probably would have stopped pacing altogether. I might even have gained weight. But it wasn't long before a guard came to my cell. She said the guy with the bow tie was back and then she hesitated. "He's looking better," she said. "His hair isn't so shiny."

# Chapter 37

$\mathcal{B}$axter stepped into the doorway and stopped, not taking a step closer to me than strictly necessary.

"Hey, Ada," he said.

"Hey, Baxter," I replied.

We just stood there like that. Baxter was carrying himself in a guarded way, not unfriendly or cold exactly. But distant, careful.

"Hughes said you wanted to see me," he said finally.

I cleared my throat and said, "Yes." Then, "Thank you for coming."

Baxter pulled up a chair, sitting down closer to me than I expected. But then he backed up. His eyes darted around the visiting room but didn't linger on anything. Not even me.

He took off his bow tie, stuffed it in his pocket. Crossed his legs a little awkwardly and ran his hand through his hair.

"Did you want something?" Baxter asked. I cringed, and he seemed to realize how cold that sounded. He tried to soften it, too late. "In particular, I mean."

"Well," I stammered a bit. "I didn't really want any*thing*. I just . . ." I cleared my throat again. "I just wanted to tell you . . ."

What did I want to tell him?

He looked at me, not unkindly, and waited.

"I wanted to tell you how sorry I am, how much I regret everything—I regret . . ." I opened my mouth a couple of times, but the words stopped in my throat. I didn't know exactly what to say. I regret not kissing you sooner? I regret marrying someone else?

I decided to go with the safest. "I regret being such a bore during your visits. You were so kind and I—" My voice broke. "I've been so selfish."

He nodded, smiled a little. "No, no," he said, in the way people do when they mean yes, yes. "You've had a lot going on. You'd naturally be a little preoccupied."

"But it's not just that," I said. "I regret the way I was before, too. I was *always* preoccupied. I was a . . ."

I struggled for the right word, but every one that I thought of made me feel like crying. Finally, I just did cry.

"It's okay, Ada," he said. "I'm sorry, too. I've been a jerk. You're getting deported and I'm thinking I'm going to teach you a lesson by giving you the silent treatment. How stupid is that? You talked a lot about your problems. But, you know, you did have a lot of problems."

I chuckled, even while still crying.

"Besides," he said, "there is something I need to tell you."

It was at that moment that I realized that much of my adult life had been a lie.

Baxter's little confession, right on the heels of Hughes's—it just threw me for a loop. Did I even know what was going on around me, at all?

When Baxter told me he had something to say, I finally found my voice and blurted out, "You're Weatherjunkie."

For one terrible moment, I thought he was going to deny it and think that I was insane. But he just laughed and said that he was, though that hadn't been what he was going to tell me.

"How did you know?" he said.

"I'm ObjectiveObserver," I said. "Hughes told me the other day that he's just about everyone else on the boards. I remembered how the producers were always complaining that we didn't publicize the boards enough. So I thought it would make sense. We were practically the only three people who knew about them, after all."

"ObjectiveObserver," Baxter said, giving me an appraising look. "I always liked ObjectiveObserver."

"But that's not it?" I said. "That's not what you had to tell me?"

I felt something like hope surge in my chest. I can't imagine, looking back, what possible thing he could have said that I could be hoping for. Unless he knew the royal family of my father's homeland or had a country house there . . . What could he possibly say to improve anything at that moment? He used to have a crush on me? I mean, I already knew that. At least, I thought he had.

"Don't you remember me, Ada?" he said.

I looked into his eyes, the ones that always seemed so familiar. And some realization began to dawn on me, but slowly. I couldn't quite make it out yet.

"I only lived in Slater County for a year or two, and you were dating that guy the whole time, but I sort of thought we had a bond."

*Kevin?* I thought. But no, that wasn't right. I looked at him quizzically. There always had been something familiar about him.

"My real name is Ray Ford," he said. "You used to play basketball with my brother."

"Ah," I said. The nice one! Then, "Yes, yes."

# Epilogue

I licked my lips slowly, provocatively. My husband looked at me curiously. "Is something wrong?" he asked.

"I'm just hot," I said.

"You're hot all right," he said, and he cocked his head in that devilish way he cocks it.

I reached down to unbutton the top button of my blouse. As I did so, I imagined my mother, back in the States and still wearing the veil, gasping in horror and disgust. Then I unbuttoned another.

My husband wiped the sweat from his brow. It was an exaggerated gesture. It wasn't really *that* hot. It's not the desert, after all. "It's all that blood you're hauling around," he said, gesturing toward my large belly. And I laughed and said that indeed it probably was. The midwife had warned me that I'd be feeling warmer as the pregnancy wore on.

He had no tie. But I grabbed his shirt and pulled him toward me.

"Don't we need to get this gardening done?" he asked.

"Not right now," I said. "Not at this very moment."

"But Candice will be here next week," he said.

"Next week," I said, "is a week away."

My husband laughed and kissed me.

It's almost funny to think about how much I feared being deported. But here I am now, happily digging in the hard dirt of a different country, joyous in my marriage, grateful for a healthy pregnancy, and secure, for the first time, really, in my career.

I will be forever thankful to the judge, who it turns out was a bit of a fan of mine and who had a copy of my *Vanity Fair* cover framed in his office (supposedly because of a "cameras in the courtroom" article that ran toward the back of the magazine). Just before I was scheduled to be flown to my father's homeland on a military cargo jet, the judge called the attorneys into his office and began to explain to the ICE lawyer—rather emphatically, according to Cassie—that no matter how things played in the short term, in the long term the president, the junior senator from Ohio, the head of Homeland Security, and the prosecutor who handled my original case would all come to regret, in a deep electoral way, any action that ended up with Addison McGhee getting herself killed in the desert while the lying sleazebag she'd had the misfortune to fall in love with was hamming it up, so to speak, with Mia on morning television every day.

The ICE attorney, who had political ambitions of his own, sighed. "I suppose we could send her to her mother's homeland. That whole Turkish system of picking a homeland was haphazard anyway."

The judge snorted. "Her mother's homeland? Like that's an improvement?"

The ICE attorney looked shocked. He hesitated, but then said he supposed any African or Middle Eastern country would be fine. "Americans don't know the difference between Tajikistan and Tanzania," he said, with another sigh. "I'm sure I can fudge it." He glanced at his organizer. "I've got some spots on a plane to Eritrea," he said. "They'll take almost anyone there. We could probably work something out. An entertainment visa, maybe?"

The judge stared at him for a moment and said: "I was thinking, maybe, Europe."

"Europe!" The attorney sputtered his coffee all over the judge's desk and then desperately tried to tidy up with the only available absorbent material, namely his own tie.

The judge shooed him away and added, "Say, maybe, Paris."

"Paris!" the ICE attorney said. "The first lady will never agree to that! Here she is constantly harping on the French about their lax immigration standards and then she's going to ship them a known criminal?"

"I don't give a hoot what the first lady wants," the judge said. "I think France would take her." He smiled. "Maybe some sort of entertainment visa?" The judge stared at the *Vanity Fair* cover, hanging on his wall, and added, "She's certainly entertaining."

The judge and the ICE attorney went back and forth, called each other names, and accused each of perversions both legal and not. Cassie sat silently, stifling a smug smile and waiting for the right moment. Finally, when the tension grew to the point that both men had risen from their chairs and were shaking fists in each other's face, Cassie raised her hand and said: "I would like to suggest a compromise."

The ICE attorney, the judge—they were in their way reasonable men. They did not want to fight. They did not want this to drag into the public arena. They wanted it to be over. And so all they heard really was *compromise*. They had dug in their heels with each other and they had already regretted it, I think. So when Cassie piped up as a third party, they were relieved to have a face-saving way out. They would have agreed to almost anything.

And so when Cassie wearily named her country, slumping her shoulders in a way to suggest that it was a great sacrifice for her client to offer this sort of middle ground, both men agreed instantly.

And that is how Montreal became my city. It is the Paris of North America. That's what I said in one of those "Visit Canada!" commercials I made. (I was required to make those commercials by the terms of my agreement with Canada, but I ended up being sincerely enthusiastic about them.) It's a lovely country, Canada. My street has cobblestones. And Candice Olson is always bouncing around fixing everyone's house. Well, I suppose not everyone's, but she's got a divine design for our family room that's going to show off a great view of our courtyard. (Hence, the frantic gardening.)

Anyway, the prime minister tells me that tourism is up 10 percent since they started airing those commercials in the States. I, single-handedly, have brought thousands of vacationing Americans to Canada.

And I made the cover of *Vanity Fair* again. The month after I emigrated, they featured me wearing nothing but the Canadian flag, jubilant. The headline was: ADA GIRL!

I'm staying very busy. Russell Crowe, who narrowly escaped being barred from the United States himself after tossing a phone, starred with me in a campy comedy called *Tossed Salad*. Oliver and I are talking. Francis sent me a script the other day, but I said: "Francis? I'd much rather work with Sofia."

Baxter was appalled at my reaction. "The man made *The Godfather*," he said. And I said: "Exactly." (I would prefer to make a movie that women liked.)

But it doesn't matter, Sofia and Francis will both have to wait awhile. Baxter and I married a year ago, and our baby is due in three months. After I finished the movie with Russell, I decided to give up acting until after the baby is born. For one thing, I'm writing a book: *Miss Maple Leaf's Guide to Impeccable Assimilation*. For another, it's a full-time job just trying to fend off the hand-me-downs. Katie Holmes, Jennifer Garner, Gwyneth Paltrow, and Julia Roberts are all constantly calling. Britney e-mailed the other day and said she was up to her eyeballs in "plastic Fisher-Price crap." If I could take any of it off her hands, she said, she'd come to my next five movie premieres.

Truth be told, I do not miss the United States that much. I would like to be able to visit Nebraska again someday, and New York—well, of course I miss New York. But Montreal is quite the up-and-coming place. Reese Witherspoon told Letterman that she's going to be buying a home here. And Russell was, I happen to know, doing a bit of a real estate hunt himself while we were making that movie.

Still, I don't want too many celebrities to come. It would ruin the city and my standing in it. They love me here. I am a cause célèbre, which is not quite the same as being a tour de force, but once Sofia and I team up I'm sure I'll be both.

Besides, Montreal merchants really appreciate my efforts to speak Mandarin. (They get all irritated if you speak English, but if you offer up a language they don't actually know, they pity you and use elaborate gestures to get their point across.)

I am learning French and studying to become a Canadian citizen.

My husband thought I should wait until after the baby is here. But I said no, no. I will take the test as soon as possible. It's important. That surprised him, given my history of procrastination on these matters. And he had also been surprised that I wanted to marry so quickly after we started dating. He thought I might want to take things slowly.

But it was because of my history that I wanted to make things official quickly.

If you are of a certain age, you may remember when it was fashionable to say that a marriage is just a piece of paper and that all that matters is what's in your heart. But I have come to see that pieces of paper—marriage records and citizenship documents—those are, in their own way, as important as what is in your heart—or your gut.

Baxter, meanwhile, is doing weather on CBC's morning program. He loves it. Canada has a *lot* of weather. (I'm ready for it with my own James Smith & Son umbrella, a gift from Hughes. It delighted me, but I did not send him a thank-you note. I'm sure Miss Liberty is rolling in her grave.)

Plus, *It's Morning Now* is in a major downward spiral. Mia and Hughes don't get along at all, from what I understand. She thinks he's a pompous blowhard. We were sitting up in bed reading last night when Baxter came across that tidbit in a gossip column. "Mia Hamm thinks Hughes Sinclair is a pompous blowhard," he read aloud.

"Yeah," I said. "But of course!"

I dropped what I was reading—Sofia's latest proposed script for a film biography about me—and flipped on the television. Baxter hates it when I do that. No watching television in bed, he says. But hey, I'm a television girl at heart.

I was surprised to see my old friend, the redhead from *Hollywood Squares*—ol' Fannie Flagg–Charo herself. I didn't catch the question, but whatever it was, she apparently got it right. The contestant agreed, and X got the square. Then she called on the "Former First Couple," and there, before my unbelieving eyes, sat Margaret Clemons-Briarwood and Samson Briarwood, crammed into a single square. His arm draped around her shoulders in a casually affectionate way. They had both lost their reelection bids by spectacularly high margins, I knew that. But I had vaguely assumed they were teaching somewhere, or writing their memoirs or something.

To see such powerful world figures filling up space and time on syndicated television was sobering—in a delightful, giggle-yourself-to-sleep sort of way. I wondered if they had a bum water heater.

I turned to Baxter, who had glanced up from his paper and was staring at the television with his mouth hanging open. "Well, I'll be," he said.

"I know," I replied, using my disinterested voice. "What are they thinking? Have they no standards?"

"Apparently not," he said, still slack-jawed.

I shook the remote at the television in an angry gesture. "I mean, come on. The former first couple never even worked in Hollywood! Where's Kermit and Miss Piggy when you need them?"

Baxter laughed.

I flipped off the TV, and Baxter turned off the light.

# About the Author

*I* have a lot in common with cover girls. First, I am female. Second, I have occasionally been photographed. And third—well, um, uh—I sometimes go many, many hours without eating? Once in a while? At night?

Okay, so I don't have that much in common with cover girls. But I do have a few things in common with my particular cover girl, Addison McGhee. Like Addison, I grew up on corn-filled plains where the landscape meant that you could always see storms coming and where farming felt like a way of life, even if you weren't a farmer. I share her admiration of George Clooney. Also, like Addison, I eventually came to the conclusion that a fine umbrella is a worthwhile investment.

In addition, I ended up making a living in news, though mine was generally a more serious brand of news. I worked in daily newspaper journalism for the better part of 15 years, mostly at the (Louisville, Kentucky) *Courier-Journal,* where I covered sordid crimes, terrible accidents, occasional political scandals, women's issues, parenting trends, and, most memorably, Fabio's perfume promotional tour.

I was better prepared than Addison for a life in news, having had a top-notch journalism education at the University of Missouri—Columbia, which fancies itself one of the best journalism schools in the country. But despite my excellent preparation, I did, like Addison, sometimes struggle to understand the journalism culture, which generally promotes a slightly more cynical and self-important attitude than I could faithfully muster. (This is not a criticism of journalism, which does its best work when cynical and self-important. It's a criticism of me, who often secretly wanted to sneak off to read *People* magazine, or maybe to watch *American Idol*. Or do both. At the same time.)

Still, I did enjoy doing a serious story well. The highlight of my career was in 2001 when I had the opportunity to document an influx of African refugees to Louisville. These were the so-called "Lost Boys of Sudan" and I spent more than a year getting to know these young men and their remarkable stories. They are the inspiration for Addison's parents.

As for me, I now make my living freelance writing in Louisville, where I live with my husband and two sons.

*Beverly Bartlett*

*Beverly Bartlett's*
# Top Five
# Favorite
# Celebrity Scandals

Despite being a hard-edged journalist by training, I'm a little soft when it comes to celebrity scandals. I prefer scandals that are utterly devoid of actual catastrophe and entirely frivolous. In other words, I prefer that no one dies, lives with bite scars on their back, has their marriage ruined, or ends up denying an engagement to Vince Vaughn.

So here are my top five favorite celebrity scandals—scandals that are more likely to make you laugh than cry.

1. Janet Jackson's overexposure at the Super Bowl.

   See, this is THE perfect celebrity scandal. There is a distasteful hint of self-promotion. There is political fallout. There is a new handy phrase that can be applied to ordinary life (wardrobe malfunction). If only Michael could keep his scandals so clean.

2. Does Suri Cruise exist?

   I'll admit this barely counts as a scandal—and it was all over rather quickly. But remember those few delicious days when the entertainment media were inspecting birth certificates and interviewing witnesses in an apparent effort to determine if Katie and Tom's daughter actually exists? It was completely surreal! I read every word.

## 3. A prince urinating in public.

Ah, an oldie but goodie. Prince Ernst August of Hanover, the husband of Princess Caroline of Monaco, was photographed urinating outside the Turkish pavilion at the Expo 2000 fair. Can you imagine a royal scandal that is any purer in its humiliation or any harsher in its humbling? If I had not already suspected as much, this would have been THE incident that told me that royal biographies and royal scandals were ripe for parody. This is what led to my first book, *Princess Izzy and the E Street Shuffle*.

## 4. Paula Abdul's alleged relationship with Corey Clark, a contestant on *American Idol*, the show that Paula "judges."

This is, compared to the others, an actual, bona-fide scandal, because if true it would have arguably constituted an attempted rigging of a hugely popular talent show. But it's hard to take anything involving Paula Abdul or Corey Clark too seriously. And Clay Aiken vouches for Paula Abdul. So we can all sleep peacefully.

## 5. Russell Crowe assaults a hotel desk clerk.

I always suspected he was a jerk, and when he pleaded guilty in November 2005 to a misdemeanor assault charge for throwing a phone at a hotel clerk, it rather confirmed things. (Crowe was angry that he was having trouble making a phone call to Australia. So that explains it. Don't hotel desk clerks control the phone lines to Australia?) Crowe was

lucky to be able to arrange a plea agreement to a misdemeanor; if he'd been convicted of a felony, he might not
have been able to enter the United States even to make
movies. See! You thought the events of this book were far-
fetched!